Not Waving, Drowning

For Rita —
the best book for the
beach!

Not Waving, Drowning

Linda Sands

Ricochet Enterprises, Inc.

Excerpts from the poetry of Stevie Smith appear under the rights of public domain and the fair use rule of copyright law, and are drawn from the following sources:
Me Again, Uncollected Writings of Stevie Smith, © *Jack Barbera & William McBrien 1981*
Stevie Smith's Resistant Antics, Laura Severin ©*1997 University of WI press*
Stevie, A biography of Stevie Smith, © *Jack Barbera & William McBrien 1985*

Printed in the United States of America
First printing, September 2011

LIBRARY OF CONGRESS CATALOGUING-IN-PUBLICATION DATA
Sands, Linda
Not Waving, Drowning / Linda Sands—1st edition

ISBN-13:978-1466409736
ISBN-10:1466409738

Smith, Stevie 1902-1971—Influence Fiction, Poetry 2. Savannah (Georgia)—Fiction
3. Lighthouses—Fiction 4. Women in History—Georgia, New York—Fiction 5. The Waving Girl—
Savannah (GA)—Fiction 6. Man-Woman Relationships—Fiction 7. Historical buildings—Savannah
(GA)
I. Title

DEDICATION

To the best dog ever, Kid Kallahan
For keeping my feet warm on all of those cold, quiet four o'clock mornings, and for never thinking I wouldn't succeed. May you finally catch that squirrel.

ACKNOWLEDGMENTS

To my family, those lovely people I ignored when I had just
one more page to write,
one great idea to jot down before we left the house—
which usually meant we never left the house—thank you for
taking up the slack on my behalf, for understanding,
or at least not blaming me someday in the shrink's office.
I promise, one of these days,
to buy you all the cars of your dreams, or at the very least,
a fuzzy little bunny.

Not Waving But Drowning

Nobody heard him, the dead man, but still he lay moaning:
I was much farther out than you thought and not waving but drowning.
Poor chap, he always loved larking and now he's dead
It must have been too cold for him his heart gave way, they said.
Oh, no no no, it was too cold always (Still the dead one lay moaning)
I was much too far out all my life and not waving but drowning.

—Stevie Smith, 1957
(Born Florence Margaret Smith in 1903, in Hull, Yorkshire)

CHAPTER 1

MAGGIE MORRIS
2011

A phone that rings after midnight never brings good news. Maggie Morris rolled over and reached for the receiver, glad they hadn't yet cancelled the house landline. She never would have heard the polite chirp of her cell phone or even found the tiny thing she'd tossed in her bag the night before.

She put the phone to her ear. "Hello?"

"Mrs. Morris? Mrs. David Morris?

It never was a good sign when they called you Mrs.

By the time Maggie hung up the phone, two local Philly cops were on her porch, as if she needed further confirmation that her husband was dead.

That wasn't what they said, of course. No one was allowed to draw conclusions. After all, mistakes had been made before—wrong doors had been knocked on, boats had returned, people had swum to shore—but Maggie felt the void of David, a fissure in her wall.

They said *missing*. They said there were *some indications*. They said she would need to go to Savannah. They pushed papers at her and phone numbers and offered assurances they didn't have, while Maggie nodded, then closed the door behind them.

She wiped her eyes and began collecting the things she'd need, until she found herself standing in her office sobbing and she realized she had no idea what she needed.

She stuffed the papers in her bag, then pawed through the junk drawer in the kitchen for a working pen while she called a cab. When the drawer stuck halfway, Maggie reached in and pushed things around until she found the culprit, a ratty old book. She tossed it in her travel bag, rolled her suitcase to the door and stepped outside, closing the door to her predictable life.

In the back of the cab, Maggie repeated her mantra. *Rely on yourself. Rely on yourself.* It was her mother's voice in her ear—a voice that whispered to her on the first day of kindergarten, on the day of the fifth grade spelling bee, each time the love of young Maggie's life dumped her. Rely. On. Yourself.

It was from a poem her mother used to recite. The next line came to Maggie.

Oh, but I find this pill so bitter said the poor man. As he took it from the shelf.

Something about the phrase fortified her.

❧ ❧

Maggie had grown up in a house full of words, of books and papers, of literary discussions more lively than any TV program. As the only child of Stan Morris, bookseller and Roberta McGill, literary critic, there was never a dull moment, as long as you liked to read. And Maggie did. Before she understood how cruel life could be. Before she was forced to face reality.

In the back of the cab, Maggie thought of her mother, Roberta, a woman she had always thought to be invincible, immortal—like a goddess or a fairy tale queen. Some people acted outwardly strong, but Maggie was convinced if she had sliced into her mother's skin she would have hit brick.

Her mother told her of the McGill women, how their Irish blood made them tenacious, bold and stubborn. They were forward-thinkers—women who were never to be taken lightly. Maggie figured if you asked any of her ex-boyfriends, they'd say there was an equal amount of distrust, jealousy and uncertainty in the shallow end of her Irish gene pool. According to Roberta, most men were sorely unprepared for McGill women, but that was no reason to discount all of them.

Maggie loved her parents, but had infinitely more respect for her mother and hated that her love for her rarely-there father smelled like pity and reminded her of the way she loved all kittens, until they became fat, smelly cats.

It didn't help that the McGill female history was much more interesting than anything the Morris men had ever done. From an orphaned great-grandmother forced to hide her true identity for years to keep her job as a New York journalist, to an abandoned grandmother raised by British strangers who became a preeminent poet, to her bastard mother, Roberta, Philadelphia's own literary critic, a strong woman with an incurable disease who could make or break an author's career with a single column. It was a daunting lineage.

You didn't succeed as these women had by falling apart when your cake fell or your baby died or your husband lost his job, again and again. No. You relied on yourself and you got things done.

Maggie closed her eyes and tried to call up the image of her mother, but all she saw was what the woman had become in the end, a shape under a sheet, a single pale, limp hand outstretched.

Crying, O sweet Death come to me. Come to me for company, Sweet Death it is only you I can Constrain for company.

"Hey!" The cab driver rapped his knuckles on the Plexiglas divider. "You okay, lady?"

Maggie opened her eyes. "What? Yes, I'm fine."

But she knew from the look he gave her that she'd been talking out loud again and she wasn't fine at all.

CHAPTER 2

BOBBY DENTON
JULY 1894

It was going to be fine, she thought, as the train left Alabama and lurched toward The Sunshine State, rumbling down the track then picking up speed going into the turn. Passenger cars whipped around the bend, jostling side to side as the scrape of metal on metal left sparks in their wake. Whether hurried or uneducated, the engineer took the next turn with even greater speed. Passengers clutched at bags, hats and coats, anything that threatened to tumble.

In a locked compartment behind a thick, red velvet curtain, naked Bobbie Denton grabbed the rail above her head and squeezed her thighs as the man beneath her laughed. A few minutes later, the train slowed and Bobbie slid from his lap pushing her bangs out of her eyes with one hand, reaching for a silver flask with the other.

"You're something else, baby," the man said, running his fingers down her arm, stopping at the scar. He dropped her wrist, then pulled up his trousers and reached for his smokes.

Bobbie watched him, trying to remember his first name, then figured he wouldn't mind if she forgot. "Trade you," she said, offering the flask and motioning to the cigarette dangling from his lip.

He narrowed his eyes, squinting through the smoke, staring at her breasts as he slowly buttoned his starched shirt.

"Suit yourself," Bobbie said taking another swig. She capped the flask and slipped it into her valise, then began dressing, performing a reverse strip tease for a man who had already seen everything.

Outside the landscape changed from fields and woods to farms and houses.

Bobbie pinned up her hair and adjusted her hat. "How far is it again?"

"What's that?" he asked.

"The ocean," she said.

"Oh. Right outside the door."

Bobbie stood at the window pressing her hands against the glass. She spoke over her shoulder. "And you live like that?"

"Everyday I'm home," he said.

The train brakes squealed as they pulled into the station. The man put on his jacket and hat. He started to leave, then turned to Bobbie and brushed his lips against the nape of her neck.

Bobbie heard the door close behind him. She spread her fingers open on the cool glass and said softly to no one, "Right outside the door."

✖ ✖

She was nine the year her brother died, the year she last saw the ocean. There was never a moment when she said, *This is it. This is when my life changes. This is the end of a predictable life and the beginning of a lie.* She did what all survivors did. She wished it had been her. She relived every moment of that day. She became the words *if only*.

Her parents had been good people. But goodness doesn't always win out over silence and people don't always choose the path of pain when there's another way out.

As Bobbie moved around, passed from family to family, from orphanage to church home, she learned it was easy to pretend to be someone else, becoming the choices of the people she stayed with—quiet little Elizabeth, enthusiastic Margaret, and once, a farm girl with ringlets named Tess. All these little girls blended into "Bobbie" when she was old enough to choose for herself, old enough to break the latch on the barn door, steal the money in the corncrib and make her way north.

She had to work hard to remember her old life, having told so many lies since the first time she'd run away that she'd begun to believe them—that she was an abused child, that she was afraid for her life, that she had to pretend to be a boy so no one would come after her.

She didn't even know her true age. Bobbie told people she was from the Midwest, a town in the middle of nowhere, a town where everyone knew everything about everyone else, except her, a town that had fields and corn and flat dry land. There was no water, never any water in her imaginary towns. There was no little girl named Sarah. No girl with a scar on her left wrist and a dead brother.

No matter how far Bobbie ran or into whose arms she fell, she always felt the pull, the tug back to her old life, to the parts she'd thought had drowned that day.

✖ ✖

She stepped off the train into the Alabama heat. Instantly, Bobbie Denton remembered all the reasons she'd left the South, and all the reasons she missed it.

Harry Riggs, her editor, could not have known what he was sending Bobbie into. If she'd asked, he might have admitted that he thought she needed a break from the city, that this was his way of showing he cared, because more

13

than being her boss, Harry was her friend. "Take a few extra days while you're down there, you know, to rest," he said.

Bobbie snorted. "Rest? In Alabama—in the summer?" She leaned over his desk, snagged one of cigarettes and lit it. "Do you know what's it's like down there this time of the year? Imagine sitting in the steam room of that fancy men's club you belong to, except you're wearing a wool suit with a bowtie tied too tight, slapping mosquitoes the size of hummingbirds while someone serves you fried catfish and 'possum pie.

"Doesn't sound so bad," Harry said.

Bobbie stubbed out the cigarette on the bottom of her shoe. "They make shitty Martinis."

"Point taken," Harry said. "So get in, get the story and get your ass back home."

It took Bobbie less than three hours after she stepped off the train in Mobile, Alabama to write the story. Harry might not like her spin on it, but what else was she going to say? The Chiricahua Apaches had been held captive for eight years in Mount Vernon, Alabama. Government officials apparently felt justified in their decision to relocate a whole tribe from their homeland, forcing them to adapt to standards they had never known, raising their children in the white man's world—one in which they were neither understood nor welcome—while secretly burying their dead in unmarked graves devoid of ceremony.

In a few months the surviving Apache would be transferred back to Indian Territory in Fort Sill, Oklahoma. Eight years and hundreds of deaths too late. In an ironic move, the Alabama barracks would be turned into housing for the insane, the federal government perpetuating the pattern of exchanging one sort of lunacy for another.

Bobbie barely heard the interpreter as they walked among the Indian village—stained, patched canvas tents pitched outside the barracks. She spoke their language already. She felt their loneliness, their worthlessness. She recognized the faces of men who drank away their days and gambled away their nights because they have already lost everything that meant anything. They have lost their heart.

CHAPTER 3

MAGGIE MORRIS
AUGUST 2011

Maggie stepped off the plane onto the tarmac and felt Savannah slap her in the face. She had never liked the South, and now that it had killed her husband, she liked it even less.

"Ma'am? Can I help you?"

Maggie looked at the boy with the cow eyes. He was either very dumb or very sweet. He might be both, holding out his skinny arm to take her heavy bag. She readjusted her grip, snugged her purse closer. "No thank you. I'm fine," she said, remembering the trip to Egypt with David last year, how she'd lost her passport, their camera, and all their cash because she thought the nice boy outside the Hotel D'Allonia was a bellman.

Maggie watched the boy scurry off, glancing back as if he thought she was going to follow him and reject him again.

She hadn't traveled alone since her teenaged hitchhiking trek across the US, a trip that had started as a dare, a nod to her newly acquired nonconformist attitude, just one more façade she'd tried on after her mother died.

After three days on the road, Maggie woke up crying in a cockroach-infested motel in some flat, windy state wondering what the hell she was doing. Too stubborn to go home and unable to admit she'd been wrong, she stuck it out and found an alter-ego, a girl who liked partying in strange bars and camping in the Rockies.

She bought a camera with her father's credit card. She learned about light and shutter speed. She began to see the world in two square inches, lit from behind on a cloudy day. She found her heart.

Years later when she met David, she showed him this side of her—the make believe adventuresome girl, the girl that was born of necessity. He loved that part of her. Most people did. David called it *her fire*. "You can conquer the world when you turn on that fire. Our kids will be just like you."

But it had never come to that—the kids part. They had tried since the beginning, but parenthood wasn't happening—wouldn't happen. That still hurt. David was gone and there wasn't a little David to wrap her arms around, no little girl with David's blue-grey eyes. Nobody.

Maggie pinched her thigh. She'd done so well all day, this was not the time to lose it. She'd found strength in her anger that morning, focusing on it as she waited in the security line, stripping off belt and shoes and jewelry, crucifying herself for the guard with the wand. She fed her anger an overpriced, crappy latte at the coffee counter, and didn't disappoint it when she squeezed into the broken coach seat next to the talkative obese woman whose sweat glands were on overdrive. By the time the plane landed in Savannah, Maggie was able to list fifteen things that bugged her about David. Fifteen things she would not miss. Anger was so much more productive than sadness or self-pity.

Sigh no more ladies nor gentlemen at all, whatever fate attend or woe befall; sigh no more, shed no bitter tear, another hundred years you won't be here.

The police had explained there was no way to know for certain what had happened on the boat. There were assumptions. Blood and remnants found on the scene had determined the victim was David P. Morris of Philadelphia. Maggie couldn't bring herself to ask what remnants, because did it really matter? As the cop said, the facts were conclusive. The victim was gone. The evidence was gone. The boat burned and sunk.

When she asked her neighbor, a young excitable guy named Harlen, to keep an eye on the house while she was gone, he said he was sorry to hear what had happened. He—not knowing when enough was enough kept talking—telling Maggie about a TV show where they performed a computer simulation of a boating wreck. They were able to reproduce the light winds and calm seas of the morning of the accident, add in a broken gas line and let nature run its course, as propane leaked into the forward cabin.

Armed with this information, police were able to determine the projectile distance for debris, the probability of fatality and when all the variables were entered, the simulator concluded the negative outcome for anyone aboard. Their simulation became a video of evidence.

But, like Steve Irwin's widow, Maggie knew that was one video she'd never want to see, because even if there had been an artist's touch like a bold sea gull squawking at a computer-generated David, it wasn't like Saturday morning cartoons where the coyote kept dying in impossible situations only to get back up after each commercial break.

She queued up at the baggage carousel and flipped open her phone, tapping speed dial 2.

"What do you think he did?"

"What? Maggie," Lisa said. "What do I think who did? David?"

"Yeah. How long do you think it took him to give up?" Maggie asked.

"Oh honey."

"I mean it, Lisa. You know—knew him. He never finished anything, gave up halfway through all the house projects, couldn't even finish a game of—"

"Why are you doing this to yourself? Listen. I'm taking the next flight. Do me a favor, get to the B&B and wait for me. Just wait for me. Okay?"

Maggie said something that sounded like yes, like okay, then slapped the phone shut and stepped up to the moving carousel. She imagined herself

16

drowning, thrown from a boat by a blast. She'd swim to shore. She'd grab onto flotsam, or was it jetsam? And climb up, like that girl on Titanic. She'd yell and whistle and call until someone heard her. She'd make paddles out of scraps of her shirt and a piece of hull. She would never just die. She wouldn't. But David? He was soft. She could see him treading water then giving up, saying it was too hard, too much. What was the use, anyway?

He had always been a fatalist. He probably did what he always did with Maggie. He gave up when the going got rough. Like that patch early on in their marriage, when their differences caused a gap. When she lost the baby. When he didn't want to go to counseling but she did.

Things were never the same after that. He disappeared. He shut down, like a sore loser whose stack of chips was dwindling. They grew farther apart and actually fought more after the counseling sessions. Maggie wished she'd never insisted on going. She wished she had just taken up gardening, been able to lose herself in something that didn't hurt as much, that didn't remind her she was incomplete. She knew she'd had an atypical upbringing with no mom and a dad that was always traveling. She figured she was probably missing the parent gene, and something else important. Something that pushed her husband away. She couldn't remember the last time they had dinner together. She used to blame her work for sucking her dry—the meetings with clients, the marketing and paperwork, the business side of art. But in the end, her camera as mistress was more reliable company than her salesman husband.

"I could have done better," she whispered, offering her confession to the backs of busy travelers, to the scuffed floor of a strange airport.

She hauled her bag off the carousel and wheeled it out into the sunshine. Stepping up to the first cab, she tapped on the half-open window.

"Can you take me to The Flannery House Bed and Breakfast?"

The driver smiled. "Yes, Ma'am."

Maggie smelled the man's lunch. It was spread out on the seat bedside him, a crust of bread, a half-eaten apple, chicken bones in a plastic container. Her stomach grumbled.

"My wife makes me take my lunch," he said gathering the remains, slapping the lid on the container then shoving it all into a bag on the floor. He slid out of the car and came around to Maggie, wiping his lips on a cloth napkin then tucking it into his back pocket. He took her bag and slung it effortlessly into the trunk then opened her door, motioning her inside as if she were a celebrity or a queen.

The South raised good men. Men women wanted to pack lunches for. Men women wanted to grow old with.

CHAPTER 4

FLORENCE "FLORA" MARTUS
JUNE 26, 1940

I am an old woman, given to rants and daydreams. I earned the right in my troubled youth to act this way. People give me leave, allowing me space to act out my foolishness. In all truth, they encourage me, thinking I should be a foolish old woman, a demented old bitty, a sad, lonely and deplorable creature, so sometimes to assuage them, I am. And it disappoints me when I take joy in their discomfort.

What would George think of me today, in this funeral home, crying over his dead body? What would he tell me to do? And why can no one else say those words for him and fill up my emptiness, unclutter my heart?

"Miss Martus?"

A young girl—but they are all young now—touches my arm. She hands me a tissue.

"Is there anything I can get for you?"

I want to say, Yes, I'd like another forty years with that man. You can turn back the clock and make me a young girl running barefoot on the beach. You can give me back my life.

The girl stares at me, and I blink back to this place, this stainless steel and white tile room where my dead brother lays, the paper in my hand, crumpled, torn.

"I'm sorry," I say, motioning to the paper, but meaning more—so much more.

"Not to worry, Miss Martus," she says, with her business manners. She has learned to soothe the grieving and accommodate the old. "We have more."

I say, "Call me Flora. George did."

The girl, no, the young woman, she is the competent one here. I have become the child, the one who needs to be reminded to eat, to wash, to feed the dogs. I'm not alone, not really. People stop by, and my nephew and niece, they're always hovering.

"Can I have a moment, before . . ." My voice trails off.

There are words that I can't say. It makes me a little sick to think of what needs to happen. I am not surprised by death, maybe a little disappointed, and yes, a little leery of my own. I always thought I'd feel as though I was missing

18

out on something if I died early. But what is early? What is enough life? And who are we to say ours was worse or better than anyone else's?

I grew up in a time when one's age was measured in wars. Children died from disease and illness, malnutrition, unsanitary conditions, undereducated doctors and unavailability of medicine. We were poor and overworked, subjected to typhoid, cholera, the yellow fever, a flu pandemic. People try to tell me I'm strong and healthy, that seventy isn't too old. But I remember that it wasn't so long ago that folks were darn pleased to make it to the ripe old age of thirty-five. Thank you, Jesus.

And then there were the natural disasters. Fires, floods, hurricanes, tornados, typhoons, tsunamis. It's a wonder any of us made it. Especially here in Savannah, where we've had it all. Folks come here from big cities up north. They come from dying farms in the Midwest. They come from England. They bring their stories of misfortune. Maybe it's not that Savannah has it so bad. It's that I have never been to those other places.

This is all I know.

The girl. She's doing that thing again. The staring-then-looking-away thing. I can tell she wants to ask me something. I hate this moment. The part where you're supposed to offer your opinion, your elderly wisdom, or maybe the answer to an question she's been asking and you just now realize you're supposed to offer an answer, even though the question might have been, "Do you need to use the restroom?"

Frankly I hope she'll ask me that one soon, because I drank two cups of tea and my bladder isn't what it used to be. But she isn't saying anything. Just staring with those big brown eyes—big, brown cow eyes.

～ ～

We had a cow on Cockspur Island. An army captain gave it to my father. The army took most of the supplies and ammunition from Fort Pulaski, but left behind goats, chickens, a fortress full of bad memories and a house for my family—an officer's quarters outside the walls on the north side of the island. Ma said life was easy then, plenty of food and no war. The families that chose to stay were put in charge of rebuilding the fort, repairing what was possible.

By the time I was born, Father wasn't only the fort caretaker, but keeper of the Cockspur Light. It was a job he never would have chosen, but oddly suited him. It was a job my brother George coveted.

George had become the other man in the house when Ma's favorite and eldest son Charles died. It wasn't anyone's fault. In one month, forty people died in Savannah from yellow fever. Quarantine stations were full to capacity and funerals became a daily activity. People were afraid. No one knew the source of the virus. There was no cure. Hoards fled cities and towns by carriage, hack, buggy, street dray and boat in an attempt to outrun death.

We stayed. Father believed our simple, stalwart life on the island would protect us and when Charles got sick, Ma blamed him. She knelt by her son's bed and offered prayers to a very busy God. She tried to soothe Charles' fever with herbs and wet rags. She asked him to eat, to drink, to stay with her. But when the black vomit came, so did the death carriage drawn by dark horses, driven by weary men with handkerchiefs tied across their noses.

Ma fought them. She bit and scratched, crying out for salvation, for help that wasn't there, for a life that was already gone. She ran after the carriage down the oyster shell road, choking on the flying sand and dirt, her cries unanswered, drowned out by crashing hooves.

Ma changed after Charles died. She became the kind of woman people left behind.

My oldest sister Annie, married and moved away at sixteen. Rosanne, the impatient sister I shared a bedroom with since birth, followed in Annie's footsteps, disappearing from her chores one night leaving a pitchfork in the haystack and one long, hacked off braid on the barn floor.

It might have been romantic, if it was men who'd loved her then left, but these were her children, her own flesh and blood and they felt no ties, no responsibility. Ma was no longer whole. She was easy to leave—if you weren't eight years old and afraid.

My sister Mary and brother George were old enough to understand. They had chores and responsibilities, while I was left alone, wandering the island. I spent hours on the edge of my world, in the marshy land where the reeds parted and the ducks swam. A noisy mallard flapped her wings, rounding up her ducklings as father duck strutted proudly on the shore looking for food. When the family of seven waddled past I snatched the last duckling, snapping its beak shut as the others continued on, their number reduced to six.

"See how that feels," I whispered grabbing the head of the duckling and starting to twist, but when its heart beat against my palm, and I felt its heat under the yellow down, I stopped and opened my hands. It looked up at me and blinked.

"I'm sorry, George." My voice is wobbly, small and unsure. I pat cold, loose cheeks, shake strange wide shoulders, but he won't wake up. Someone screams.

Cow Eyes is back. "It's all right, Miss Flora. Come on now." She tugs at me, whispering, "You're in the wrong room. That's not your brother."

Her hand on my arm taps, grazes. Is she repulsed by the slackness of skin, the bony skeleton I've become? But she doesn't know me. No one really knows me.

I don't even know me. All I know is that I'm not in my bed dreaming of my childhood. I'm in Clark's Funeral Home. My brother is dead in the next room and I've wandered into a stranger's wake.

CHAPTER 5

MAGGIE
2011

At the hotel, the cops broke the caution tape and let Maggie in. "He was tidy," one of them said. "When we searched the room, nothing appeared out of place."

Life at home in Philadelphia had always been orderly, with David living as though he could pick up and go in an instant, leaving no trace, nothing to suggest he'd ever really been a part of her—of them.

The cops said they'd be waiting outside, "Unless you need some help carrying anything?"

Maggie waved them off, waited for the door to close then reached into her bag and pulled out her current favorite camera, a Hasselblad H1 with a digital back. Its familiar feel soothed her as she raised the camera and rotated, creating a circular photograph, a round David memory. She shot the scene from the window—the wall of another brick building, a slice of grassy park, a street hidden in tree branches.

Why would David choose this room, this hotel? There were so many nicer places to stay. Beautiful little B&B's. Grand hotels on the historic register. New riverfront hotels with luxury suites. This room was nothing like any of the places David would have chosen for them.

To appease her mounting paranoia, she went back to the facts. According to Detective Brandt, the dock master showed the rental boat logged out at 9:45 am and when questioned, the man was able to recall only one detail of Mr. Morris: "He seemed real nice."

❧ ❧

Maggie thought maybe she'd use that as David's eulogy. David Morris was a real nice guy, and tidy, too.

She sat on the edge of the bed, ran her hand over the cheap coverlet. So it was going to be like that. David was gone and all she had was his wallet, a dog-eared paperback detective novel and some clothes he'd never wear again.

She'd known something was wrong days ago, but made excuses as everyone does when the choices are undesirable. What was she going to tell people? That she was worried because David hadn't called her and David always called?

Lisa used to tease her about their phone relationship, saying they would never have survived life without cell phones and computers, that they had a virtual marriage, a technological relationship.

Maggie never admitted to her friend how sometimes she imagined the man on the other end of the phone wasn't David at all and allowed herself to say things she never would have said to her husband. She confessed secrets, admitted phobias, told stupid jokes and whispered sexy nothings—all things she would have felt too self-conscious about to say face to face, not because David was David, but because Maggie was Maggie. Being this alter ego, she could give David more, like the time she bought a long, blond wig to wear to a party.

"Take it off," he'd said. "It makes me feel weird, like I'm cheating on my wife."

"Don't think of me as another woman. I'm still Maggie, just another version of me. Like the me you might have known if we'd met earlier."

As if she could change the way he thought. As if she could change her past.

Maggie had turned down three proposals before accepting David's and still, like most women her age, wondered what might have been if she'd chosen differently. Last year she'd confessed to Lisa that she still had dreams about her high school boyfriend.

Lisa knew Maggie better than anyone else. They'd been best friends since second grade.

"Everyone wonders about the one that got away, Mags. You're no different." Then Lisa said, "I see his mother every month at the salon, do you want me to get his number?"

"No," Maggie said. "Don't you dare. If he ever wanted to know what I was up to, he could Google me. I'm not that hard to find."

"But what if he doesn't know you're a Morris now? What if he's still looking for Maggie McGill-Stone?"

She had a point, and later when David was asleep, Maggie went into the office, opened her laptop and typed in the same name she'd scribbled in the back of her English composition book twenty years ago: Randall Hale.

By the end of the week she'd run web searches on every man she'd ever kissed. She found a man named Tom Gerund who had risen to a very high level in foreign diplomacy and was an internationally recognized painter and archer living in St. Petersburg, the same place the Tom she'd slept with one night in Rochester had said he'd like to live. This became truth for her, just as all the other lovers became the best of their names encountered on the World Wide Web. Forget the same named losers who were jailed or sued or bankrupt.

The longer she was married, the less she thought about the men before, the what if became never was. Something dulled inside as her idea of what love should be, changed.

Marriage, I think for women is the best of opiates. It kills the thoughts that think about the thoughts.

Again with the poetry. Maggie felt the stanza pulled from her.

It is the best of opiates.

Her mother might have disagreed. In the end, all Roberta wanted was the drugs, not people, certainly not her husband. She begged Maggie to help her, to set her free, to let her go to a place where she was whole, a place where nothing hurt, where she would never be cold or angry or frightened again.

Fifteen-year-old Maggie had only meant to help.

CHAPTER 6

BOBBIE
1894

She hadn't meant to go to Tarrabelle.

If Bobbie had been in a court of law she would have sworn on it. It just happened. Maybe a compass in her head was guiding her to Florida the whole time, pushing her onto the wrong train, one she almost missed, hopping on at the last minute, contents of the flask sloshing in her belly as she ran. Maybe it had all been pre-written for her at the moment of her birth by the hands of angels. She was supposed to go to Tarrabelle. She was destined to return home.

Bobbie checked her image in the glass, tamped down her hair and pinched her cheeks. People here wouldn't know her—not now. She was nothing like the girl they'd taken out of here eight years ago—slashed and bandaged, skin and bones. Everyone who might have known her as little Sarah Johnston was long gone.

Just get in and get out, she told herself stepping down from the railroad's horse drawn bus. Close this door and get on with it. As if she could be casual about arriving in Tarrabelle. No one could. It wasn't on the way to anywhere. You had to make a point to find it. It had to want you to come.

The small fishing village on the Gulf Coast was, like Bobbie, a shell of its former self. Once tidy and pruned, the yards of the small village houses were overcome with weeds. Long arms of a spiky ivy-like growth wove in and out of peeling picket fence slats. Some of the shops backing to the docks were boarded up and abandoned. Others had names she didn't recognize.

It's best this way, she told herself. No one should live in the past. Things get broken when you're nine and never heal right. But how do you know? You think everyone is like you. You think everyone hurts. You think you understand. And when you stand at the edge of the water and close your eyes you feel healed.

She was there before she knew that's what she needed. Shin deep in the surf, face raised to the sky, breathing salt, sand and sea as tiny shells battered her ankles and spiny skeletons of dead fish tangled in weeds washed out with the tide.

When the sun went down and the air cooled, Bobbie slipped her shoes back on and made her way into town. She followed the sound of people, the clanging of pots being scraped in an alley, lids slapped on refuse bins. She pulled open the door to a small café, a cowbell clanged against the glass. The place used to be a pharmacy, she remembered, glancing at the pictures on the wall. She slid into a booth and gave the waitress her order. "I'll have the soup please and a glass of sweet tea."

She ate quickly, not wanting to hear the conversation the man behind her was having with his son. She didn't mean to cry out the way she had and she certainly meant no disrespect running out of there without paying the bill. It was the strength of the memory, the way it had hit her—that was the word—slapped her like her mother's hand against her cheek on the day her brother had drowned.

That was how she remembered it, and maybe the truth was nothing like that, because everyone had a different version if you asked them. The people of the town blamed her mother, her father blamed God Almighty, but little Sarah–the girl Bobbie used to be, she only blamed herself, as if she could have known better, as if she might have saved him.

A story like that didn't go away. It was a tragedy, a retold lesson of the boy from Tarrabelle who drowned, about his missing sister and their dead parents, the couple who had clung to each other until the bitter end, jumping from the branch of the oak in the meadow, the noose on her neck doubled around the branch, ending in a loop of rope around his neck. The mother who had needed sixteen stones in her pocket, a counter weight to her husband's limp body.

Someone had taken a photograph and sold it to the city papers, a distant image of two darkly clothed bodies hanging beneath a tall tree. People supposed they had jumped at the same time, stepping off into the air together holding hands.

If you squinted hard enough at the blurry photograph you could imagine they were walking down a foggy path, the distant clouds under their feet a soft road that led somewhere wonderful.

CHAPTER 7

MAGGIE
2011

The police had been more than helpful to Maggie, protecting and serving topped with Southern hospitality. They'd gone above and beyond the call of duty, bringing her multiple glasses of sweet tea, driving her to David's hotel room, then taking her on a scenic ride to her B&B. Their charm was infectious and the sweet tea wouldn't be half bad if only they'd add a little vodka.

In front of The Flannery House Bed & Breakfast, Detective Brandt handed Maggie a brown bag. "Thought you might want this."

Maggie peeked in the bag, fully expecting a jug of sweet tea. It was a shoe, one of David's topsiders wrinkled and twisted from its time in the water.

The cop avoided her eye, instead motioned to the B&B with his hat in his hand. "It's a nice place. You'll like it."

Maggie nodded, then looked up at the building, barely registering the crackle of the cop's radio, his rapid departure sans siren. Regency-Italianate, late 1860's. Someone along the way had added trim work and expanded the porch. It was like something from a commercial, a well-devised prop for a perfect life. Baskets of colorful geraniums and nasturtiums dangled over wide rails that begged feet to prop themselves on its sturdy surface. A sweating pitcher of iced tea waited to be poured. A cat rolled and purred on the wicker swing and the rocking chairs with their floral covers seemed positively too Southern for words. All that was missing was an old lady and a basket of peaches. Maggie heard children laughing in a nearby yard. A car sped by, a snatch of country music in its wake. She climbed the steps, closed her eyes for a moment, letting the world go dark.

A thrill coursed through her veins, followed by guilt at feeling pleasure when she should be devastated. David never understood her love of architecture. Maggie was happiest when surrounded by mirrored skyscrapers, eco-minded solar structures, ancient pyramids, medieval castles and pagodas. David preferred wide expanses of water and nothingness. Once even, Iceland in winter.

She stepped inside the mansion, was about to call out, "Hello," when sounds from the kitchen drew her attention. The door swung open and she was staring right at a cheery blonde in a red floral dress. The woman said,

"Hey," in that Southern way that means hello and how are you and isn't this a great day all in three letters. "Welcome to The Flannery House."

Before the door closed Maggie saw a burly gray-haired man standing at the stove stirring something in a copper pot, steam rising around him.

"I have a reservation," she said to the rapidly approaching woman hoping she was neither a hugger nor a close talker. "For Maggie Morris. And I'll need to add my friend."

"Don't tell me." The woman stopped short, pressed her fingers to her temples like old ladies did when the migraine was coming on. She squeezed up her eyes, then popped her baby blues open, grinned and said in a honeyed voice, "Lisa, ri-ight?"

Mother of God. Welcome to the South. "Right. So she called?"

"Yes, she did, said to tell you she'd be here by supper. Would you like to sit on the porch while I bring your things to your room? Such a pretty day and all."

Maggie stared past the woman out the window. "I guess it is." She was tired. So tired. Her gaze went soft. She saw beach, sand and emerald waters instead of iron bars, bricks and an alley. She smelled salt and sea, heard gulls and crashing waves. She felt David's hand in hers, his arm around her. She leaned into him and murmured, "Sweetheart. I've missed you." She wondered why David was shaking her, why he felt so small.

"Miss Maggie? Are you all right? Hey! I need some help out here!"

Maggie lay on a couch in the sitting room, her feet elevated on a pillow. The blonde fanned her with a Welcome to Savannah pamphlet, each flick of her wrist sending an apple-cinnamon scented waft of air her way. Maggie couldn't decide if she was sick or hungry.

"There you are. Welcome back," the woman said.

Maggie wondered where she'd been. She pulled herself upright, swung her feet to the floor. "What happened?"

"I think the heat might have got to you. You passed out. Good thing Charles was here to catch you."

"I'm sorry," Maggie said.

"No need to be sorry."

But the way the woman looked at Maggie said something else. There was pity on her face, and discomfort. Maggie had made her responsible for yet another thing. She glanced at her gold nametag, *Sadie*, and imagined her going home and telling of the crazy broad who passed out in the foyer of the Flannery House, how those Yankees are weak sons of bitches and how she had to stand over the woman until she woke up, when she could have been making sweet tea, or balancing the books or busting the balls of the chef. But that wasn't at all what was reflected in this woman's eyes. She was too nice to do any of those things and that made Maggie feel even worse.

Maggie started to stand, the world spun a bit, then settled—a bit skewed on its axis, but whole. "I'd like to go to my room, please."

"Sure, honey," Sadie said. "Top of the stairs. First door to the right. You okay, now?"

Maggie nodded and waved, using the banister to steady herself. She climbed a few steps then turned back to ask, "What is that I smell?"

Sadie smiled. "Why, that could be Mamma's fried apple tarts or Charles' pecan pie. I don't know for sure, but you couldn't go wrong with either one. Why don't I bring you a plate?"

The room was elegant yet simple. Tall ceilings, pale yellow walls, cream trim and wide crown molding framed the period furnishings. Maggie took in the intricate mantelpiece, the delicate lace curtains and the cotton matelassé.

The bed called to her, but not as strongly as the claw foot tub in the all white bath. She started the water then stripped, kicking her clothes into a corner, something David would never have approved of. She caught a glimpse of herself in the mirror. A little extra around the middle, a little saggy up top and her roots could definitely use a touch up. But as it was, not bad for forty-five. Another five years and she'd get that boob job. Hell, now that she was single it hardly mattered, or did it matter more? She grabbed the hotel robe, struggled into it and cinched it tight.

Maggie poured herself a glass of complimentary wine, took a healthy swallow then refilled it and brought it into the bathroom, grabbing her tote bag along the way. She checked the water, added some bath salts then pawed through the tote until she found the book she'd tossed in there earlier. It was a thin beat-up paperback, curled and yellowed at the edges, and missing its cover. She recognized it immediately.

"Shit." Maggie raised her eyes heavenward. "You really do have a sense of humor," she said as the tears came.

The book of poems had belonged to her mother. Maggie stole it from her bedside table the morning her mother died and later lied to her father about it, the beginning of a long list of things she would lie to her father about in the coming years.

She opened to a middle page and read, *"Away melancholy, away with it, let it go."*

There was a knock on the door.

"Come in," Maggie said wiping her eyes.

Sadie entered carrying a silver tray with three plates and a glass of sweet tea. She didn't say a word, just left the tray on the table by the window, nodded and left.

Maggie went back to the poem.

The ant is busy he carrieth his eat, all things hurry to be eaten or eat. Away melancholy.

"Perfect," she said. "Just perfect." She set the book down and inspected the tray. There was a slice of pecan pie, two small tartlets, a hunk of thick brown bread with cheese and grapes and some sort of custard. Maggie dipped her finger into the dish. Banana. She licked her finger and went back for more. She had only planned to sample a little of each plate, but after the first bite, found herself ravenous.

"Screw it." She tipped the bowl into her mouth, swallowed the custard, then stacked the tartlets and slice of pie on the grape plate which fit perfectly on the tub's reading rack, next to the book and bottle of wine.

When Lisa finally arrived, the wine was gone and Maggie was asleep in the tub, hand dangling the book over the edge, a smudge of pecan pie on her cheek, a bit of apple tartlet floating in the cooling water.

CHAPTER 8

BOBBIE
1894

"Boy! Wake up."

Bobbie swatted at the rough hands that grabbed her shoulders. She blinked into the bright light. Instant headache. She squinted, taking in the conductor. "Ow. Leave me be."

"Oh, no," he said. "There ain't no leaving you be. I won't have stowaways on my train."

"Stowaway?" Bobbie sat up, pushed the cap back on her head and let the jacket fall from her shoulders. "No, I have a ticket." She held one hand on her head to stop the world from spinning as she felt around for her valise, for anything. "I had a ticket," she murmured.

The conductor stepped back. "Aw, geez. You're not even a boy. Look, miss. I don't want no trouble. Just take your things and get off my train."

"Where are we?" Bobbie asked, getting to her feet, brushing off her clothes.

The man sighed, took off his conductor hat then replaced it squarely on his head. "We're in Savannah, Miss. Welcome to Savannah."

Bobbie was back in the familiar. She knew no one and had nothing, except the crumpled newspaper she'd snagged from a trash bin at the train station. It was a small daily, a few happy headlines, no hard news, though what did she expect? This was Savannah. She re-read the front page article about the architect, checked the address of the offices then folded the paper and stuffed it in her back pocket.

After a few wrong turns, she cut through an alley that smelled like cat piss and cabbage— something that would have made her stomach lurch even if she wasn't hungover. She came out on a street of boarded-up shops. A weathered sign for The Savannah Daily Dispatch hung over the door of a hole in the wall at the end of the dilapidated block, the building itself more rubble than structure. This was obviously an area of town still waiting reconstruction from the big fire five years ago, as noted on page six.

Tucking tendrils of hair into her cap Bobbie pushed open the door to the newspaper office. It was nothing like The Sun in New York. Grinding and chunking noises from a printing press came from beyond a swinging door in the rear of the room. Two small desks cluttered and abandoned faced the street. A broad-backed man stacked newsprint. It was too quiet for a newsroom. About to leave, Bobbie saw something useful—a telegraph.

Lowering her voice an octave, she said, "Excuse me? I'd like to send a telegram to my editor in New York." Whether it was the word editor or the phrase, *in New York*, the paper stacker whipped around oblivious to the sliding stack of newsprint behind him.

"You might want to…" Bobbie gestured to the stack.

The man took a step back catching the sliding pile with his knee and thigh. He braced himself and smiled, a twinge of red creeping up his neck to his ears. Without moving he called over his shoulder, "Boone! You got a customer."

A tiny man with a mop of black hair appeared through the swinging door. He scurried across the room, hopped into the telegraph operator's chair, donned a navy cap with the letters USPS crookedly embroidered across the front then smoothed his shirt front and turned toward Bobbie. He beckoned her with a flick of his wrist. He might have been waving to paradegoers.

"All right then," he said, licking the stub of a pencil, sharpening it on the edge of the wooden desk. "Who? Where? What?"

"Harry Riggs, The New York Sun, New York City," Bobbie said.

He scratched the words on a pad of paper. "Right. You got eleven more words."

Bobbie glanced at his short legs dangling a foot off the ground.

He cleared his throat drawing her eyes back to his face.

She said, "In Savannah. Found assignment. Small problem. Send money."

"That's eight." He tapped the pencil against the pad.

Bobbie looked around then leaned in, lowering her voice, "DeSoto Hotel. Bobbie."

He raised a brow. "Bobby?"

"B-o-b-b-i-e," she said pulling her hat down over her ears.

The operator spun his stool around and tapped out the message. Mr. Broadback had repaired his paper stack and was now loading crates of something heavy into the back room from a side entry. The scent that wafted in through the open door was part fish, part fresh bread. Bobbie's stomach growled.

"No charge. Consider that a professional courtesy," the operator said, spinning around, his short arms opened magnanimously.

"Oh. Yes. Thank you. The Sun thanks you," Bobbie said as she turned and walked toward the door, stopping at the exit. "When you get a reply…"

"We'll send a messenger. To—" He made a show of glancing at the pad. "The DeSoto. He grinned. "Bobbie."

CHAPTER 9

FLORA
1940

"Come on now," Cow Eyes says. She leads me to the door, past the crying family, past the shocked widow, past the woman my age who tsk-tsks then averts her eyes.

"So sorry," Cow Eyes tells them. "I should have been watching her." As if I am a child who was caught pulling the cat's tail.

In the hall, I open my clenched fist to see a lock of the dead stranger's hair. I push it into my mouth, tuck it between my lower teeth and gum. It feels right there, like a mouse or a secret.

In her office, Cow Eyes paces. "Your nephew said he'd be here as soon as he could. I'd stay with you, but I have matters to attend to, other people to see, arrangements to make."

I know there's nothing she needs to do. Young people always use the busy, got to go, I'm already late for something more important excuse when it comes to spending time with old people. We just aren't quick enough for them, not something they can be bothered with. This is 1940, after all. The world is growing at an amazing pace. Who wants to shuffle through it?

I say in a strong voice, a loud voice, "How did he die?"

"Who?" Cow Eyes stops pacing.

"The man in the—" I remind her.

"Oh. Him? I—I don't know. I suppose I should though, shouldn't I?"

She sinks into the chair behind the desk and stares off past me, past this room and the question and into a field of many, many different answers, a place I'm not going.

It isn't important how the man died. He was old, that much was obvious. It might have been his time, like for George, A quiet little passing in the night. But maybe it was something else—not a horrible disfiguring accident, I'd seen the man after all, but what if it was a sudden, painful and unexplained death, one which would haunt the family forever and ever. What if it was that? Then, shouldn't everyone know? That's not the sort of thing one keeps secret or is it? If you understood that your life could change people in that way, would you live it any differently?

Would you make every day matter more?

CHAPTER 10

MAGGIE
2011

"You did not!" Maggie cried stepping into her sandals and chasing after Lisa.

"Bet me," Lisa sang, halfway down the staircase.

In front of the B&B, Maggie caught up to her friend. "Girl, you'd better be kidding about the pictures."

Lisa laughed. "You never know." She dangled a tiny digital camera. "Just going to have to wait and see, Magpie. You were so cute in that tub."

Maggie took a half-hearted swipe at the camera, then stepped back, crossed her arms and shrugged. "Whatever."

As the cab pulled up Maggie reached for the handle, but Lisa leaned against the door, grabbing her friend's arm. "Mags?"

Maggie shook her head, tugged the door harder.

Lisa let go. "Hey, I didn't," she said quietly. "Okay? Maybe I wanted to but I didn't."

Maggie said nothing, just slid in, leaned forward and gave the driver a slip of paper with the name of the funeral home. "Do you know the place?" she asked.

The driver, an older gentleman with a sunburned pate read the paper then twisted around, looking hard at the girls. He smiled then clucked his tongue against the roof of his mouth. "Well, bless your heart."

Yes, bless it. Please. Can you do that for me? Bless my heart and all the other parts of me too while you're at it, because that's what Maggie Morris needs. A good fat Southern blessing on her ass.

As the cab pulled away and Lisa buckled in, Maggie said, staring straight ahead, "I would have, if it had been you."

Lisa said, "What?"

"If the roles had been reversed. I would have absolutely taken the shot. Blown it up poster-sized, even." Maggie grinned. *"Happiness is like England."*

"You bitch! And here I was feeling guilty, with you going through all—all this." She flailed her arms at the universe, at the cab interior, at the space and time continuum. "Me, trying to make jokes and—wait. What? Happiness is *like* England? You feeling okay, Mags?"

33

Maggie reached into her tote bag, pulled out the ragged book of poems and tossed it to Lisa. "Page fifty-four."

"What is this?"

Maggie shrugged.

Lisa opened the book to the page and read, *"Happiness is silent, or speaks equivocally for friends, Grief is explicit and her song never ends, Happiness is like England, and will not state a case, Grief, like Guilt rushes in and talks apace."*

Lisa closed the book, turned it over in her hands. "Stevie Smith? I never heard of her."

"Don't feel bad. Lots of people didn't. She was my grandmother," Maggie said.

Lisa hit her friend with the book. "Yeah, right."

"She was," Maggie said, staring out the window. "Born Florence Margaret Denton Winter, the daughter of my great grandmother, Bobbie Denton, she was adopted by the Smiths of London and got her nickname from a famous jockey at the time."

"Maggie, I had no idea." Lisa held the book more gently and opened to another page. "This book's been through a lot, hasn't it?"

"You could say that," Maggie said.

Lisa flipped more pages. "I didn't even know you liked poetry."

How could Maggie tell Lisa that she didn't know that she did either. She'd closed the door when her mother died and left that part of her heart behind — at least she thought she had.

Maggie felt tears welling up, then heard Lisa sniffling beside her. What the hell did she have to cry about? Her life was perfect.

Mitchell and Clark Funeral Home was a white plantation style house on a street of other plantation style houses, but this one had a circular drive, a gravel parking lot in back and a hearse pulling in.

"You sure you want to do this?" Lisa asked.

"It's supposed to be cathartic," Maggie said. "I read it in *O Magazine*."

Lisa nodded. "All right then. Let's go."

They stepped into the foyer and Maggie's stomach began to ache. The piped-in background music, the scented air and the thick cream carpet underfoot. It was all too much.

Why was she doing this again? She wasn't ready to say goodbye to David. She didn't think she'd ever be ready. Not for any of this. Not for making decisions, not for being a widow, not for moving on.

All those fights she'd had with him that ended with her wishing he'd crash his car on the way to work or fail to return from a business trip just seemed so pitiful now. Those feelings were gone. It seemed like her memory could only find good things. It could only latch onto the romantic moments, the tenderness he'd shown when they dated. The distant pieces of David that she hadn't seen in years and would never see again.

Mr. Mitchell or Clark, Maggie figured they were interchangeable, walked out to the foyer to greet them. "Mrs. Morris?"

"Yes. This is my friend, Lisa."

"Samuel Clark," he said as they shook hands all around, his grip surprisingly firm and smooth. Maggie didn't know what she expected. This was business to him. This was his job, as seemingly ordinary as a grocery store cashier sliding a gallon of milk over a bar code reader. The image of a body with a barcoded forehead flashed—almost making her smile.

Lisa touched her arm. "You okay?"

Maggie nodded, falling in place beside Lisa to follow Clark to his office.

After her mother died, she'd sworn off wakes and funerals, refusing to buy even a goldfish knowing it would die and she'd have to deal with it. Now she was standing in a place where the dead were stored, where coffins were loaded and unloaded, where bodies were made beautiful and lifelike only to be dropped in a six-foot hole and buried forever.

For her, the whole wake, viewing, funeral, procession, burial, reception thing was unnecessary ceremony. They were dead. What did it matter how their coffin was lined or what kind of food was served afterward? It was a waste of money, a waste of an inheritance, if there was one. Maggie believed in glorifying someone's life, not their death.

She and David had talked about it once, reluctantly. They agreed on cremations with no fancy send off. In Maggie's will, she asked that her ashes be scattered from the cliff in Mendocino where they had shared their first kiss.

David had admitted, "I can't say *what* you should do with my ashes. When the time comes, you'll know. I trust you."

Sometimes when they'd argue she'd say, "I'm going to flush your ashes down a public restroom toilet." And once, "I'm going to feed your ashes to a sow," but that had only made them laugh.

⚯ ⚯

Maybe it made perfect sense then that Maggie was here now, with no body and the desire for a ceremony. With no real proof that her husband was dead, only her heart telling her it was over. She needed closure. She had to move on.

Mr. Clark spoke as he walked, guiding them down tastefully decorated halls. "Here at Mitchell and Clark, we believe that everyone should depart with dignity. It is our desire that each wish be met." He opened his office door, ushered them inside and asked, "Was there something special Mr. Morris wanted?"

Yes, Maggie thought. *He wanted to be alive. Can you grant that wish, Mr. Clark?* Instead she said, "As I explained on the phone, this is a bit different from your *normal* . . . I mean, we—"

"I understand," he said nodding. "Believe me, Mrs. Morris. Nothing is normal."

35

In the awkward pause that followed, Clark proved himself not half as adept at segue as small talk when he said, "You're from Philadelphia, is that right?"

Maggie stared at him, incredulous.

Lisa poked her.

"Yes."

"But your husband," Clark said, "He was from Savannah?"

"No," Maggie said, "He was from Philly too."

She heard the question Clark didn't ask and said, "David loved this place, came here every year to stay on the water. He—we planned on retiring down here one day."

Lisa added, "It's a wonderful place."

Maggie wanted to poke her.

When she and David first met, he had just returned from a vacation on Cumberland Island. He told her of his love for the Georgia coast, explained that he'd spent a lot of time there growing up and never got it out of his system. They traveled a great deal as a couple, but never to the south. It had become a joke between them. "Just pick the dates you'll be in Savannah and I know I'll get a job anyplace else," she used to tell him.

And she always was. Maggie's architectural photography took her many places, but usually they were cold, steel, metropolitan places. She had begun to see David's trips as his private thing. She had her darkroom, her friends, her long walks to nowhere. David had Georgia and a well-worn copy of *Gone With The Wind*.

Clark was saying, "...like our city then?"

Maggie attempted a smile. "It seems very nice, though I haven't seen much of it."

Clark returned the smile, his teeth too straight, too white. "We'll have to do something about that, won't we?"

Lisa leaned forward, blouse gaping. "I just love all the squares y'all have."

Did she just say y'all? Oh my God, Lisa was flirting with the mortician. Maggie checked her watch, making sure Clark saw her, and when she looked up, his demeanor changed.

He shuffled a few papers, tapped the stack on the desk, then clicked his pen and said, "So what will we be providing for Mr. Morris?"

"As I said before, there won't be a service as there's... well, no body, but David always wanted to be cremated, have his ashes scattered. You may think I'm foolish," Maggie said, earning her a slow blink from Clark. "But I wondered if you could cremate *these* things. I would pay the same fee. Whatever you would normally charge."

Maggie emptied the plastic shopping bag on Clark's polished maple desk. A floral printed shirt, a battered brown leather wallet and driver's license, the single shoe and a photograph of a handsome man who looked like Tom Selleck fifteen years ago minus the moustache.

Clark eyed the carnage, the remains of David P. Morris of Philadelphia splayed across his desk. He seemed disappointed it wasn't something more exciting, more incriminating. He rolled his chair back and stood.

"Of course," he said. "Let's go down to the display room where you can choose a receptacle."

"Receptacle?" Lisa said.

The word sounded suspiciously like *trashcan* to Maggie. She glanced at Lisa who was grinning madly. Maggie mouthed, "Stop it." Which made her friend mouth back "receptacle," making Maggie disguise her giggle in a cough.

Lisa was able to find humor in everything. Unfortunately, nervous laughter was her forte.

She had wet her pants laughing when Maggie fell out of a tree at thirteen and broke her leg. Lisa was remembered back home as the girl who giggled through the somber wake for their classmate who died in a car crash. She still thought it was funny. "His parents buried him with his purple glass bong. They played Grateful Dead songs with a slide show of his kindergarten years. Come on."

Maggie was afraid to look at her friend. She'd probably have some goofy grin on her face, something that would make Maggie lose it. She concentrated instead on Clark, his straight-backed walk, his stiff neck, his perfect hair. He pushed open a door and led them down another corridor, leaving the plush welcoming area and entering a place where nothing was funny. Maggie glanced at Lisa whose grin had disappeared. She grabbed her hand and squeezed, glad for the return grip.

There was a different smell in the room, unlike the hospital where she'd visited her dying mother, unlike the fusty odor of care facilities–it was the ultra clean non-ness of finality, the end. If a question mark came with a smell it would be this.

Maggie felt panic rise. Once while traveling through Venice, she'd gotten light headed, short of breath. David had calmed her, been able to bring her back to her senses. She lied to him, told him it was something she ate, that it might be a seafood allergy. She said she'd be fine, unable to tell him that for an instant she'd known what it would be like to die. The worst part had been feeling left out, feeling like she didn't matter. Things would happen without her and maybe, just maybe, no one would know that she was gone. That frightened her most. She could die and it wouldn't matter–to anyone. She hated the idea of the end of her, of the end of a life that she hadn't yet begun to live. Then there was the added bonus of not knowing what happened afterward. Would she be a piece of dead meat in the ground? Nothing? Would she be an angel floating around helping others, being good, doing good? It was all too tortuous.

She never told David the truth. She feigned her allergy, gave up eating shrimp and thinking about things for which she had no answer.

Tenuous and precarious were my guardians...my husband was perfidious . . . my name is finis, finis, finis, I am finis . . .

CHAPTER 11

BOBBIE
1894

She was accomplished in a few sordid skills from time spent on the streets after she'd run away from her third family. The first pudgy man dangling a pocket watch was easy, the lady with the unruly dog on the tangled leash unknowingly donated to the Bobbie cause and the third victim—the agitated father of the twin boys— might never admit to losing the folded bills and silk handkerchief, not if his wife was as much of a stickler as Bobbie thought.

Winding her way through the brick buildings of the main streets to the waterfront, past warehouses for cotton and onto the docks, Bobbie ducked behind a wooden cask, slipped off her man's jacket and cap, letting her hair fall loose at the shoulders. She waited until the ferry had tied off and the group was disembarking before she stepped out to blend in with the crowd. A tall man in a hurry was perfect bait. Bobbie bumped into him then threw herself off the dock into the water. She came up sputtering and squeaking, as she imagined a true lady would.

The women on the dock shrieked, "Save her! Do something!"

As they hauled her up, Bobbie put on her best Southern wail, pointed to the tall man and claimed, "It was his fault. Look at me, I'm a disaster. I've even lost my skirt!" The women averted their men's eyes and the doughy wife of the tall man tugged on his sleeve and whispered something in his ear. The man reached in his pocket then handed his wife something while Bobbie tried to look pitiful. It wasn't hard.

"Here," the woman said. "We're terribly sorry. Go into town." She shoved the money at Bobbie. "There's a dress shop where you can get something dry." The woman ran her eyes over Bobbie then added, "Something decent." The woman turned away as the ferry master wrapped a wool blanket over Bobbie's shoulders and aimed her toward town.

Bobbie murmured "Thank you," then limped off determined to come back later and retrieve her jacket, cap and stolen pocket watch.

※　※

Bobbie passed up the first two shops. Too busy, too small, too something.

Her instincts led her to The Clothing Emporium with its brick front and nautical window display announcing the arrival of Spring. It looked the kind of place that would sell everything a proper Savannahian could need and some things they could only imagine they needed. She paused, one hand on the door, thinking she might be able to look back at this later and find the whole thing funny; the dive into the water, the woman throwing money at her, the wet walk through town wrapped in a borrowed blanket, but at this moment, she was cold, tired, hungry and in need of clothes, food and a drink.

The girl behind the counter looked up as Bobbie entered. She slid from her stool, stashed the book she'd been reading and came around the counter revealing her girth.

"Whatever happened to you? Gracious!"

Before Bobbie could reply, the girl took her by the arm and tugged her toward the rear of the store. "You'll catch sick unless we get you out of these wet clothes."

She snatched a towel off the shelf and handed it to Bobbie, pushing open the door to a small storeroom with her elbow. The room was small and warm and with shelves filled with boxes, bags and cans. The girl lit a lantern, trimming the wick low.

"There," she said clapping her hands, as if the party could now commence.

Bobbie stood still.

"Go on. Strip," the girl said, reaching for the blanket.

Bobbie held tight to the ends until it became a tug of war.

"Don't be shy. We're both girls, even though you're wearing trousers." The girl laughed.

Bobbie let go of her end of the blanket, making the girl stumble.

"Hold it up," Bobbie said. "Please."

"Fine," she said and held up the blanket between them creating a makeshift changing screen as Bobbie began peeling off her wet clothes, layer by layer.

The girl babbled a stream of nothings, from her breakfast choice to the book she was reading to the latest fashions she'd read about in the newspaper. Bobbie was tempted to tell her not to believe everything she read, but liked the girl's voice, the rhythm in her words, the way she made the simplest thing seem wonderful.

She listened closer when the girl mentioned the new construction at the wharf and the architect from Boston, the same one who had built the DeSoto Hotel. The girl's arms drooped lower and lower as she spoke, until the blanket was merely chest high. Chest high to the girl, waist high to Bobbie.

"Is this your place, then?" Bobbie asked, as she tugged off her wet stockings.

"No," the girl said. "I'm Lorelei. It's my aunt's. But she's having her monthly and never can get out of bed the first day."

"Seems like a real nice store, Lorelei," Bobbie said.

"Thank you. We had to start over after the fire. It was my idea to add the women's accessories."

Bobbie mumbled something about accessories, as she gathered her wet clothes.

"Just set them there." Lorelei gestured with her chin to a broken chair behind Bobbie.

Bobbie felt the girl's eyes on her as she turned away and wished she'd kept the towel on. She draped the clothes over the chair then turned around and waited for Lorelei to meet her eyes. She took her time. Finally, she said, as if the appraisal had been all about sizing, "I believe I have something that'll fit you. How do you feel about cornflower blue?"

"Is that a color?" Bobbie asked.

Lorelei laughed, tossing the blanket to Bobbie. "Yes, ma'am. It's a color." She closed the storeroom door behind her as she left and Bobbie took a look at the stock on the shelves. Once a thief, always a thief.

She left an hour later, dryer and warmer inside and out, thanks to Lorelei's hidden bottle of corn mash.

"Now, you sure you know where you're going?" Lorelei asked, unlocking the front door for Bobbie.

"I think so," Bobbie said. She repeated Lorelei's directions.

"That's right. You'll be fine, Miss Bobbie. Just fine," Lorelei said.

"Thank you. For everything." Bobbie looked down at her new dress and the calfskin shoes. She touched her hair, feeling the ornamental pins she'd let Lorelei put in. It must have been the booze. She took a tentative step, unable to hit full stride with the dress gathered around her knees.

"How the hell do I walk in this thing?"

Lorelei giggled. "Go slow now and be sure to get yourself something to eat down there."

Bobbie started out again, chin held high and readjusting the package in her arms. Lorelei had dressed her as a woman, *a fine Southern woman*, but also reluctantly sold her trousers, a shirt and work shoes—traveling clothes.

Lorelei waved as her new friend crossed the street taking baby steps. She locked the door then flipped the sign in the window to read, Closed. She walked slowly to the storeroom humming to herself and dragging her fingertips over the neat stacks of garments.

There was still a puddle on the floor from Bobbie's wet clothes, a few damp footprints and breadcrumbs from the loaf of bread they'd shared. Lorelei touched her lips remembering the softness of Bobbie's. She picked up the bottle of corn mash and drank the last of it, belching into her hand.

The round slippery buttons on her dress gave her fingers a hard time. Lorelei sang a church hymn high and sweet as she stripped.

Standing naked and drunk in her aunt's storeroom in the back of a fancy clothing store in the middle of one of the South's finest cities, Lorelei Hunter began to cry. She lashed her arm out at the perfect, neat rows of candles, the cans of tomatoes and peaches. She cried out as she tipped heavy shelves sending tin and copper pots and pans tumbling. She threw glass, ripped fabric and tore open bags of flour. Then she dressed herself in Bobbie's clothes. Her camisole. Her shirt. Her undergarments and trousers.

She sat in the broken chair and laced on Bobbie's wet boots. They were too big and the clothes too tight. But they felt perfect. In every way

CHAPTER 12

FLORA
1940

I blink myself back into today. "Oh," I say looking around the room, a small office done in blues and greens. "This is nice." My voice cracks on the nice, rising a bit like I'm a pubescent boy, not a woman well past her prime. Cow Eyes sweeps her eyes to the ceiling again. I don't know what she expects to find there but I need her to look at me. I feel so far away. It's always that way after I catch myself having a "moment."

At home I had George to ground me. *Had.* There's a word that will take some getting used to. What will I have now, besides memories? My nephew tells me I need to be grounded in reality and not be living in some dream world in my head. I ask him who says the world in my head isn't reality?

It's him we're waiting on. My nephew, Tommy. Apparently the man has been detained. I smile, thinking of Tommy. Yes, he would be detained. Of course. He is an important man in Savannah now, a Monsignor in the church. Something I never would have thought the boy had in him, though George would have disagreed. He would have disagreed with anything I said about his favorite nephew.

I never understood the connection. George didn't like any kids, especially ones that followed him around, but there was something about Tommy. It might have been there all along, but I only saw it in the days that followed the speakeasy night.

❦ ❦

Cow Eyes is saying something about my nephew, something that makes him sound all grown up and special, something that makes it sound like someone I never knew.

We all do it, I suppose, lock a person into an image we have of them from their past. Lock them into a mold. When she says, Thomas. I hear Little Tommy. I see the freckle-faced boy with the ball standing in front of the broken window shaking his head and pointing at his little sister.

I see a gangly-armed boy loading a pickup truck with crates of tea, a boy that came home a man after a night out with Uncle George. But, I cannot see a

42

holy man, a man of the cloth, a respected figure in the city of Savannah. No. He's still just my nephew, Tommy. A little boy who outgrew his freckles, but not his secrets.

Tommy and George had a relationship that grew beyond family bonds. I don't know the extent of it or where it came from. But I know Monsignor Thomas Brennan will be missing his uncle as much as I will.

The telephone jangles. Cow Eyes looks at me. I look at the phone, as if to say, It isn't me, which strikes me funny, because how in the world could it be me calling her, I'm right here and I don't even know her number.

"Hello?" Cow Eyes holds the receiver in two hands. I can tell she doesn't use her telephone very much. She keeps looking at it to make sure she has the right end to her ear, the right end to her mouth. I can hear a man's voice through the connection. Somehow I wonder if he is nearby because his voice is so loud, though my nephew has explained how the machine works, I still am amazed at the contraption.

"Yes. That would be fine," Cow Eyes says.

She laughs a soft tittering laugh as the loud man says, ". . . *fish* . . . something something . . . *good luck charm.*" When she hangs up, she's blushing and can't stop prancing and fluttering.

"Was that your beau?" I say.

She turns more red in the face, if that's possible. Cow Eyes, the human tomato. Is she embarrassed for herself, or for me? I know I'm being rude. It's one of the few perks of the elderly. You are expected to be loud and rude and to have forgotten your manners.

"I wouldn't call him my beau," Cow Eyes says. She sits down behind her desk. "My mother certainly wouldn't call him my beau." She laughs a nervous laugh. "He's a *friend.*"

"A friend," I say. "And does this friend have a name?"

"Alain."

Seeing my raised brow she adds, "He's French."

"Not from Savannah, then?"

"Oh no," she says. "He visits often though. His father's company does business here and—I'm sorry, I'm sure you don't want to hear about my life. Can I bring you something? Some more tea, maybe?"

Cow Eyes looks at the clock, at the telephone, at the door.

She is very wrong about me not wanting to hear about her life. I say, "Why wouldn't your mother call him your beau? Has she met him?"

"Of course she's met him," she says. "They just got off on the wrong foot."

She jumps up again, this time with papers for a file cabinet. It's tiring to watch her waste her energy on nonsense action. The child stands up and sits down more than a Catholic at high mass. What is her hurry? Doesn't she know you can't outrun time? If people knew what lay ahead they might not be in such a hurry to get there. They might remain young forever. They might never leave an island.

I ask, "Could you take me to lunch?"

On the drive over to Johnny Harris's Restaurant, Cow Eyes chatters about the weather and the heat and the traffic. She never looks at me, doesn't say anything about the conversation we were having or why she was so willing to leave. I can't imagine her choosing to spend the afternoon with an old woman, but when the choice is between the dead and the living, most times the living win out.

"This is my father's car," she says gripping the steering wheel, eyes on the road.

"It's very nice."

"It's a Ford."

The automobile gives me no pleasure. I would rather be in a boat on the water. I would rather be walking. But Savannah is too big for that now, too long from end to end for anyone to stroll. I want to tell her about the days we'd walk everywhere, about the days when things moved slower, when no one had their hand on your life and you could do as you pleased. I think she needs a bit of that, my Cow Eyes.

George would have liked a drive today. He would have enjoyed the wind in his face, as we pass the slower autos on the road. He would have been pleased to be headed to a lazy barbeque lunch when everyone else is working. He was never one for conformity.

Cow Eyes turns onto Victory Drive.

I'm thinking of the way she looked on the telephone earlier when I say, "Your mother doesn't have to like him, if you love him."

"What?"

She jerks the automobile's steering wheel to the left as she turns to look at me. The auto jostles and clunks over the bumpy road, careens through a pothole that bounces me off my seat headfirst into the doorframe. Touching my hair I feel something warm and sticky.

"Oh, Sweet Jesus."

Cow Eyes pulls the auto off the road and reaches for me all at once, concern in her large eyes, so brown. She's like George. My George.

CHAPTER 13

MAGGIE
2011

In the room with Clark and Lisa, Maggie chose a hand-thrown ceramic Raku urn, but declined the complimentary matching pendant. She signed the papers, paid in cash and told Clark to call her.

As they were leaving Lisa asked, "Should we have a memorial?"

"No," Maggie said. "David didn't want that. I know what he would want though. Where do you think is the best place to get a good martini with a view of the water?"

"Thank you, again," Lisa said as the waiter brought two more drinks.

Maggie giggled. They were on round three and Lisa had been thanking and paying and ordering and Maggie was fine with that. It was enough to sit in the warm sun with the smell of ocean, the breeze in her hair, just to be numb and still. Part of her wanted to photograph the scene, but the part of her brain required for such functions was semi-paralyzed. She stared at her hand on the table. Her fingers were pale and thin, her wedding ring felt loose. It was too big, too gold, too heavy.

The sun on her back loosened the muscles, draining the anxiety. "I could sit here forever."

Lisa laughed. "At least until you have to pee."

"No, I would still sit here."

They both laughed.

The waiter came by and asked, "Everything all right, ladies? Are you ready to order now?"

"No. Wait. Do you have any pie?" Maggie said.

"Pie? Mags, you serious? Damn. Pie does sound good. Or chocolate." Lisa grabbed the waiter's sleeve. "Bring us chocolate. You know what? Bring us one of everything on the dessert menu."

The waiter raised his brow.

"Yes, please," Maggie said. "And two more of these." She swiped her hand across the table, tipping over her Martini.

Lisa said, "Don't worry, we're not driving," which Maggie found extremely funny.

45

An hour later, Martinis morphed into White Russians, when Maggie insisted on milk with her pie. The table looked like a bomb had gone off in a bakery with multiple plates of half-finished desserts, smears of chocolate fondue, beheaded strawberries and at least six implements. Maggie couldn't use the custard spoon for the crème brulee or share the pecan pie fork with the chocolate cake, and knives were deemed necessary for the pralines and truffles.

"I don't care," Lisa said. "I'm undoing the top button on these slacks. Mags, you may have to roll me out of here."

Maggie began to hum "Roll out the barrel," as she licked her fork then dipped it back in the fondue crock. Fork still in her mouth, she reached for her purse, dumped it into her lap and pawed through the contents.

Lisa giggled. "What are you looking for?"

Maggie spoke around the fork. "That taxi guy's number. I think this place is getting ready to close." She slapped a warehouse membership card on the table, said, "I got this," as she flipped open her phone.

"Mags," Lisa said. "Hey!"

"What?" Maggie removed the fork from her mouth.

"You've got the phone upside down," Lisa said. "Here, give it to me."

Maggie tossed Lisa the phone then reloaded her purse, examining each item. In her artistic eye they held a secret, a special reason why she had chosen to carry them. Her favorite lipstick, the small brush she bought from the blind guy at the Amsterdam train station, the lizard skin wallet—a birthday gift from David, along with his picture in the plastic tag on her keychain. She squeezed the tag between her palms and started to cry.

Lisa clapped the phone shut as Maggie stood and began to recite, *"Yes he is this and much more This is but a portion A sea-drop in a bucket Taken from the ocean So the voices spake Softly above my head and a voice in my heart cried: Follow Where he has led And a devil's voice cried: Happy Happy the dead."*

"Mags?" Lisa waved off the approaching waiter and pulled on her friend's sleeve. "Come on, sit down."

"He's dead," Maggie wailed flopping into her chair. "That shit. He died and left me! How could he do that?"

The next morning Lisa downplayed the scene for Maggie. "Don't worry about it. I told everyone you had a rare form of Tourettes that made you blurt poetry. Besides, you didn't puke until we were out of the dining room, and even then it wasn't so bad. You got most of it in the potted plants. Hey, it's not like we'll ever go back there again."

Maggie draped her arm over her eyes. There were black holes in her night, and though she wasn't sure she wanted to fill them in, she did want to know how she acquired the chocolate stain on her bra and why furry animals were nesting in her mouth.

"It's okay," she said. "I won't mind being alone the rest of my life. I have boxes of memories. I had more with David than most people could wish for in a lifetime."

"Stop it," Lisa said. "You sound like one of those corny romance novels. What do you mean, *boxes of memories*? If you're talking about all those old pictures you never put in albums, well, that's only part of a relationship. You had a life before him and you'll have one after him."

"Yeah, right," Maggie moaned. "Just kill me now." She rolled over and pulled the sheets over her head.

Lisa sat on the edge of the bed and rubbed her friend's back. "Not today. You're going to be fine. But you might want to take these."

Maggie pulled down the sheet and opened one suspicious eye.

Lisa dropped some pills in her hand and pointed to the glass on the bedside table. "Trust me."

Maggie propped herself up just enough to pop the pills and chase them down with the drink. "What the hell?" she sputtered. "Was that vodka?"

Lisa grinned. "Hair of the dog."

❧ ❧

Sixteen hours of sleep does wonders for the soul and a hungover body–for those recovering and the people around them. By the time Maggie was upright again, the world was on a whole new day and Lisa had figured out the rest of her friend's life.

Apparently there was some unspoken arrangement between them. At least that was the impression Maggie was getting. She also got the impression that Lisa thought she was incompetent and maybe even an imbecile, as Lisa had laid out a complete matching outfit for Maggie on the chaise next to a booklet she'd probably filched from the crematory: "Moving On, Now That They're Gone."

"Shit." Maggie pitched the booklet in the trash, threw on yesterday's pants and a wrinkled t-shirt and wondered how to avoid Lisa, afraid she'd produce a lifestyle flow chart for new widows or offer to set Maggie up on one of those online dating forums.

❧ ❧

Lisa had helped her sister get "back on her feet" last year after a messy divorce. The sister was still dealing with a creepy stalker and a venereal disease. Maggie wanted nothing to do with Lisa's cures, though she knew her friend meant well.

When Maggie went down to the sitting room. Lisa was smiling into the phone, looking out the window. She whispered a tender "I love you" into her cell phone, and when she saw Maggie, she rolled her eyes then hung up quickly.

"That Todd," Lisa said. "Such a pain in the ass."

Maggie knew Todd was a great guy, a wonderful dad. The kind of husband most women would cherish.

"Lisa, I think you should go home. I can handle it from here," Maggie said.

"Are you sure? I'm happy to stay. There's still so much to do, and you don't want to fly home alone, do you?"

"Actually," Maggie said. "I changed my flight."

"What do you mean?" Lisa asked.

"I'm not going back—at least not for a while," Maggie said. "I need some time here. Time to see and feel what David felt. I want to understand what drew him here, to this place. Maybe you can't understand."

"No. I get it." Lisa stood and hugged Maggie. "Go ahead, do what you need to do. Listen, I'm here for you. No matter what."

Maggie wrapped her arms around her friend and squeezed. "Well good, because there's something else. I got a message earlier from a local attorney who says he heard about David and needs to meet with me."

"A lawyer in Savannah? Why would—"

Maggie's cell phone rang. She pulled it from her bag, flipped it open. "Hello? Yes. That's fine. I'll see you then. Thank you."

"Who was that?" Lisa asked.

"The attorney," Maggie said. "You seem awfully calm. Doesn't this strike you as a little—"

"Odd?" Maggie said.

❦ ❦

Yeah. Odd," Lisa replied.

"David used to travel a lot for work. Maybe he had a lawyer down here for real estate, or investments, I don't know. Anyway, I'll find out soon enough."

Maggie caught the look Lisa threw her. "Yes, I'll call you as soon as I know anything. Now, get your things together and get on home to Philly. I may need you to water my ficus."

They said good-bye then waved for as long as they could see each other. Maggie stood on the sidewalk after the car had disappeared, stirring only when a gust of wind from a passing bus blew gutter dirt onto her white blouse. She picked a leaf off her lip. "Welcome to Savannah."

CHAPTER 14

BOBBIE
1894

Savannah's cobblestone streets, ridged sidewalks and trolley cars eighteen inches off the ground all posed problems for a woman in a hobble skirt, but were doubly problematic for an inebriated New Yorker more accustomed to wide-legged pants and spread knees.

As she made her way to the DeSoto Hotel, Bobbie's feelings about both her womanhood and the city were tested. The looks from gentlemen on the street had been complimentary, though the women on their arms may have felt otherwise—reference the glare and swat—a feeling Bobbie could relate to as she began to see Savannah in the same way, a pretty woman with a dirty face.

She had memorized every line from the newspaper article about the hotel, but Bobbie was ill-prepared for the sight. Built from stone, brick and terra cotta, the DeSoto was quite impressive, and for half a million dollars, it ought to be. There were verandas on every floor, lounges, restaurants, themed suites, a glass-walled solarium, even an in-ground swimming pool large enough to float a small boat.

Bobbie allowed the doorman to escort her inside. She tried to blend in, forcing herself to move forward, not gawk and certainly not turn in slow circles taking everything in while sighing.

From what she could see, women at the DeSoto did not sit, they posed, as if someone had cut them from a magazine, propped them up, then left. Bobbie half-expected to walk behind one perfect specimen and find wires and wood framing.

At the check-in counter, a gentleman in a felt hat and black suit too heavy and dark for the warm day, argued with the young, flustered desk clerk. He said, "I was supposed to have a suite. Could you please look again?" His voice was a slap. It was the voice of a man who thought Southerners were less wise because they were kind and proper and took time with their words. Bobbie had seen this behavior before, how some people found it difficult to adapt to strange circumstances. They expected to go far from home but never leave it. They expected others to be just like them—regardless of where they were. They would never understand a reporter's job, or Bobbie's wanderlust. They lost out on life because they boxed in possibility, asked it to conform to their small expectations.

The Northerner tried again with the desk clerk, this time waving his arms, as if his motions could magically solve his problem. Another clerk, just as Southern, but older and more assertive appeared from the back room and motioned to Bobbie.

He said, "Welcome to The DeSoto, Miss. Do you have a reservation?"

She glanced at the Northerner at the other end then shook her head.

"I'm sorry," he said. "But we're full up and—"

Bobbie touched her high collar, fingers fluttering. She trailed her hand from collarbone to belly to rest on her hip, then reached the other hand across the counter offering it. Sweetening her voice to a blend of maple and corn syrup, the sound of the ladies of the South, her words dribbled out. "I. Am a *special* friend. Of Mr. Preston's." She winked at the clerk.

If the man had been an apple, he would have fallen from the tree, his ripening completed in an instant, equal parts of dawning light and completion. As it was, he drew his hand back quickly and rustled in a drawer beneath the counter. He slid an envelope to Bobbie and whispered, "Your suite is on the third floor, overlooking the gardens. I hope this will be acceptable." He cleared his throat and straightened up. "If there is *anything* we can do to make your stay more comfortable, please do not hesitate to ask."

Bobbie poured on the charm. "I'd love to have a meal and some wine sent up. When you get a chance, of course."

"Of course. Right away," he said.

Bobbie waved the envelope then walked away. The clerk and most of the people in the lobby stared as the Northerner griped, "Did he just give her a suite? How did *she* get a suite when I didn't?" He glanced around looking for support, getting none he shouted at Bobbie's back. "Who do you think you are, anyway?"

His words echoed in the vast space. Bobbie kept walking. "That's a great question."

Her suite was decorated in a Safari theme. In the living area there was a zebra print rug, various African masks and what looked like a real lion's head on the wall. In the bedroom, cheetah print pillows and a fur coverlet adorned the bed. White pith helmets formed the shades on the bedside tables.

Bobbie had never been to Africa but read of it often enough to imagine it frighteningly exciting, quite unlike the room.

She sat on the edge of the bed and removed the new shoes, rubbed her sore feet, then changed into the new trousers and shirt and wandered back into the living area. A stocked bar looking part tiki hut-part village camp, called her name. She poured herself a short whiskey and made a toast. "To the high life."

The suite was too large for one person, especially someone who lived in a small apartment in New York. There were too many choices: where to sit, which window to gaze out, which view to enjoy? She finished her drink, poured another and eyed the space.

"I think that will work just fine," she said to the lion's head. "Thank you for the suggestion." She shoved the heavy writing desk onto the zebra rug then dragged it over to the window, pulling back the drapes and letting the light wash over the dark wood. She pulled up a chair, found paper and pencil in the drawer and began to write, the gardens of The DeSoto before her and a story in her head.

The room service meal had been better than expected, the article was written and safely stowed away. All Bobbie had to do was stay put and wait, there was sure to be word from New York by morning. But when dusk took over the city and the gas lamps went on in the gardens, and the voices coming from the guests on the patio below rose in the manner of the happy, uninhibited and well-lubricated, Bobbie left the hotel from a service door, and made her way through Savannah, following two drunken men to the harbor.

When one of them stopped to urinate on a pile of bricks, Bobbie slipped past them. She scanned the stacks of crates past the ferry landing, then slipped in when she saw the oak casks. She reached behind the fourth one. Nothing. She felt around again, moved to the next cask and repeated her efforts. Still nothing. "Shit."

A voice came from above. "You won't find it there."

It wasn't God.

Bobbie made out the shape of a man, the moon at his back. He was hunched over and rocking, perched on the highest pallet. She squared her shoulders and stood her ground, gritting her teeth.

He pulled her cap from his head. "This what you looking for?" He dangled it from his finger. "You got a small head, *boy*."

Bobbie caught the cap and with it a whiff of the man. It wasn't altogether unpleasant.

"Care to drop something else?" she asked, lowering her voice an octave.

"Like this?" He swung the gold pocket watch by its long broken chain.

Bobbie held out her cap in both hands, a safety net for her stolen treasure.

"That would make it easy, wouldn't it?" he said. "What fun would that be?"

Bobbie danced beneath him, following the watch, catching glints of gold in the moonlight.

He said, "You look like someone who appreciates fun, don't you, darlin'?"

She stopped and stared. "I'm not your *darling* and I'd thank you to return my things before I go to the police."

He laughed, a soft, gentle laugh—that wasn't altogether unpleasant.

It was too dark to see his face, too dark to tell if he was smiling, if he was serious, though Bobbie felt something in his voice that was familiar, something she had pegged—something she knew of herself.

Before he could call her bluff, she said, "What do you say we go some place and talk about it? Some place that might have whiskey."

The pocket watch swirled in a slow circle overhead. "I'd say that's a fine idea." He stood, tucking the watch into his pants pocket and began climbing down the pallets, jumping the last three feet to the ground. He wore Bobbie's jacket over his own.

"My coat?" she asked.

He took his time drawing his long arms from the sleeves, slapping dust from the surface then shaking it out before handing it over. He was slimmer without the second layer, taller than she'd thought, though from her angle on the ground it hadn't been the easiest way to judge height.

He wore dark pants, thick-soled boots and a fingerless glove on his left hand. He stepped closer and stuck out his right hand. "Sam Winter." He gripped her fingers harder than he needed to for longer than was necessary, finally saying, "Well, you don't look like Benjamin K. Reading."

"Who?" Bobbie tried to extract her hand from his grip. He pulled her to him. Moonlight illuminated his blue eyes and straight white teeth lending a purplish tint to his full lips. Bobbie smelled wood smoke and tobacco, wet stones and cut grass. She wanted to bury her nose in his neck and inhale, grab handfuls of his sandy hair. She wanted to press her lips against his.

"Oh, no," he said. "You most certainly are *not* Mr. Benjamin K. Reading. Which would make a person wonder why *you* have the man's pocket watch and why you are so adamant about getting it back."

Bobbie pulled away. "Let go," she said. "Please."

Sam cupped her hand in both of his, lifted it to his lips and kissed it tenderly, then let go, sending Bobbie sprawling backward into a cask.

He waited for her to get up then said, "How about that drink?"

CHAPTER 15

MAGGIE
2011

Sadie was happy to extend her visit at The Flannery House, but Maggie knew she couldn't stay long at those prices. She and David had done well for themselves, but she was a one-income family now–more like a no-income family, as she didn't have anything lined up, and for the first time ever–wasn't even carrying her cameras and gear. A feeling that simultaneously frightened and pleased her, like losing something you never needed.

She started up the steps to the B&B when she heard someone shout.

Halfway down the block, on the street corner, a woman in a blue skirt was waving her arms, yelling to a boy on the other side of the road.

People had gathered on both sides of the street, but still the cars kept coming as if someone had opened a floodgate. As Maggie approached she heard the woman say, "Stay there, Cam! Don't move. Mommy's coming."

The boy didn't look like he was going anywhere. There was something not quite right in the way he stood, the way he cocked his head, his arms hanging limp. Twice the woman stepped into the road, but cars honked and cut her off. A mother pushing a stroller quickly assessed the situation and yelled across to a man approaching the boy, "Grab his hand!"

"No!" The woman called. "He doesn't like being touched. Please, don't." Then softer, "Oh God, please."

Finally there was a break in the cars–enough that when the woman did run out, they stopped, though one guy flipped her off and the other in his speeding rental car interrupted his phone call long enough to yell, "Get out of the road, whack job!"

Maggie watched the woman with her son. It was an exercise in restraint. Her arms reached for the boy, then drew back as he shied from her touch. She blew kisses at him, wiped tears from her eyes.

What did it take to not touch? To withhold from the physical? When she was single, Maggie had been with her share of men, mostly it was sexual companionship, sometimes work-related. She gave them her time but never her heart. She never spoke of emotions or attachments or dreams. She supposed she used those men, as much as she'd let them use her. She'd thought it would be different with David—that the day they said I do, a wall would come down, her heart would open. But her life wasn't a Hallmark card. She became a pretender, and after a while it was hard to miss what you'd never had, and this became enough.

The light changed, traffic stopped. Maggie crossed the street to where the woman and her boy stood. "Is he okay?" she asked.

The woman looked up. "Yes. Thank God. I don't know what happened. He was right beside me, but I looked away and..."

"It's all right now, though," Maggie said, offering a smile. The woman nodded then straightened up, gathering herself. She waggled a finger at her boy, attempting sternness. "Son, you have to stay with Mommy."

"Fountain," he said.

The mother with the stroller checked her watch. "Why aren't you a smart boy? He's right. It's on a timer, you'd better hurry."

"Can I, Momma?" he asked.

"Okay," the woman answered softly.

The boy ran three steps then froze and looked back at his mother. Her eyes drifted past her son to the park beyond. Maggie wondered what horrible things she imagined were waiting out there. Things she would not be able to protect him from.

Bad things happen all the time.

Perhaps we shall go for a walk in the park And then it will be time to play until dark Not quite when the shadows fall it is time to go home It is always time to do something . . . childhood and interruption come swiftly on.

Maggie walked the long way around the park, enjoying the trees and plants. It was very different from what she knew in Philadelphia. These oak trees with their tangled limbs and gangly branches were something from a science fiction film, a creature that might come to life when the spell was broken. They would rise up, draped in their capes of Spanish moss and rule the world. Maggie stifled a laugh. She wasn't much for sci-fi, or plants, flowers and trees. Most times she looked past the greenery to the smooth glass and steel buildings, to the mottled fronts of historic brownstones and iron-barred row houses.

Savannah was something else, touching a part of her she never knew existed. It left a taste in her mouth that was sweet, warm and homey, like Charles' desserts at the B&B. Maggie swallowed. She walked faster, trying to keep her mind off food—at least for a little while.

She read the bronze markers and imagined Forsyth Park in its heyday a hundred years ago. Couples would have strolled the paths, ladies in their Sunday finest and men suited out in straw fedoras and stiff leather shoes, regardless of the heat. The fountain would have drawn them, a respite from the Georgia sun. The parks of Savannah had been designed as gathering spots for families, a place where children could run and play all the simple games children used to play.

The last time Maggie had been to a public park in Philadelphia, she'd been cutting through to get to her car. She'd hurried past overflowing trash bins, scrabbling pigeons and bums sleeping on benches. The families she saw were lost tourists clutching maps and scolding children who walked too slow, their eyes glued to tiny video screens of game consoles.

The fountains she knew were contemporary pieces of art that spewed complicated water patterns timed to music, most set in concrete outside malls, so kids could run through them in the heat of summer.

She wished again that she'd been born in another era, another place, though this time the wish wasn't for France in the 1700's, but Savannah in the late 1800's. She smiled to think of herself in a tightly corseted dress with a bustle, her breasts served up on a wide silk shelf. She looked down, ruining the image. "Well, a ledge, then," she mumbled.

Maggie came to another turn, took that and meandered toward the center of the park. She heard splashing water before she saw it. Reminiscent of the grand fountain at Paris's Place de la Concorde, this magnificent piece was clearly the focal point of the park. Leaning on the iron fence, she put her face toward the spray and felt the temperature drop ten degrees.

A robed female figure stood at the top of the cast iron fountain. Water sprayed from a rod in the statue's hand then bubbled over the lip of the basin, which looked like layers of flat leaves. It cascaded into the larger basin below where it exited through small holes around the edge. Grasses, cattails, a wading bird, hanging pendants, ornamental urns, tritons with shell horns, and spouting swans completed the structure. It was clean, white, beautiful. She wondered how they kept kids from swimming in it, graffiti artists from leaving their tag and visitors from throwing their trash. She looked around. No one. Why, she could just leap this short fence and—what? Dance around the half-man half-serpent figurines in her jeans and t-shirt? Better yet, strip it all off like something she'd see in a real French fountain, in a place where people were more accepting of nudity.

As if she'd conjured him up, a shirtless jogger approached, did a quick run around the fountain, then headed off in the opposite direction. Maggie enjoyed the view, coming and going, then realized her appetite for lunch was back.

She left the park and walked street after street until her feet ached, until she smelled food.

In the oversized booth of the café, Maggie was overwhelmed. Too much space, too many choices, too many decisions to be made, too much to think about. She'd never felt so helpless. But she'd never been widowed before, either.

For always everything is arranged punctually, I am guarded entirely from the tension of anxiety. Walk tea supper bath bed I am a very happy child really . . .

"Bring me what you would eat," she told the waitress.

When the bill came, she pushed aside the plate of gnawed rib bones, buttery biscuit crumbs and the few greens she didn't finish and asked the waitress, "Is there a place nearby where I can find some sandals and shorts?"

"You could walk down to the waterfront. It's not far." She drew a map on a napkin. "There you are, sugar. Y'all come back."

Maggie stepped into the first souvenir shop she saw and bought a backpack, a map of Savannah, four pairs of shorts, three pairs of flip-flops and six tees and tanks. At the register she tried on a pair of mirrored sunglasses and added them to the pile when the guy behind the counter gave her a thumbs up.

"What's this?" she asked, fingering a keychain statue of a girl and a dog.

"That's our Waving Girl." He said in a soft Indian accent. "You don't know her? She's famous. Waved at every ship that passed her island for forty-four years—"

"Day and night," said his co-worker cleaning the shelves behind him. She wore a smiley face t-shirt that read, *I see happy people.* "As the story goes, Florence Martus, The Waving Girl, had a sailor beau who promised to marry her when he returned. Poor Flora was out on that big white porch waving a cloth by day and a lantern at night. All for love." The girl waved her dust cloth for emphasis.

Maggie struggled against a sneeze. "Did he ever come back?"

The girl dropped her arm and shook her head. The Indian guy shrugged and started ringing up her things.

Maggie pulled the tag off the keychain then clipped it to the backpack. "I'll take this, too."

On the street, she checked the map. The Waving Girl Statue should be easy to find, a big bronze statue on the waterfront. Maggie crossed River Street, kicked off her flipflops and walked barefoot through the grass to the embankment of the river. According to the map, the statue should be right around here. All she saw was a hedge of evergreens and more grass. She parted a tall cypress shrub and stepped through feeling a bit like the kids of The Secret Garden.

There she was. A bronze girl waving a wide cloth, collie and lantern at her feet. Maggie read the inscription, *"Her immortality stems from her friendly greeting to passing ships, a welcome to strangers entering the port and a farewell to wave them safely onward."*

"Forty-four years," said a voice from the other side of the memorial.

"Excuse me?" Maggie said.

The voice said, "Over here."

Maggie stepped around the statue. A broad backed young man was on his hands and knees with a can of cleaner and a red-stained rag. Apparently the youth of Savannah did know about graffiti.

He said without looking up, "She waved for forty-four years."

"So I've heard," Maggie said watching him rub at the remaining mark on the statue base.

"Kind of a long time," he said as he finished wiping and sat back. He looked at Maggie. "Don't you think?"

He had the bluest eyes, perfectly offset by his tan face and white teeth, like an advertisement for outdoor living. There was something familiar about him, in the way you see someone on TV so much you swear you know them. Maybe it was just the perfect smile, the broad chest, his muscular arms. Maggie looked away, feeling the heat rise in her neck.

He said, "They thought she was crazy. Folks in Savannah, back then."

"Was she?" Maggie asked, feeling a bit crazy herself. Her heart beating too fast, her mouth suddenly dry. She walked around the statue and looked up into Florence Martus' face.

"I don't think so," he said. "I think she was in love."

The way the guy said it gave Maggie pause. He sounded so old. She took a closer look. He was young, maybe late twenties, couldn't be over thirty. And yet, he sounded wiser, more interesting than most young men she knew. She wondered where he lived, what his name was, how his lips would feel on hers. She blushed. What was wrong with her?

The guy wouldn't have noticed. He was too busy grinning at The Waving Girl statue, resting a hand on her dog's bronze head. Maggie almost expected the girl to look down and wink.

She took a step back, feeling like she was imposing on a private moment. Before she let the bushes close behind her, she took one last peek. The guy was staring out toward the water. He wasn't smiling anymore.

Later at the B&B, sitting across the table from Chef Charles and licking fried chicken grease from her fingers while eyeing his fresh pralines, she couldn't stop thinking of the stranger at the statue. She felt like a high school girl with a crush. There was no reason to believe it was anything more than a chance meeting, anything more than a curious attraction, but for Maggie, to feel something like that again was magical. Even if it was fake, even if it was something imagined, she liked the way it made her feel alive.

She realized not once during her walk had she thought about framing a shot, not once had she subconsciously grabbed for a non-existent camera, or checked the light. A part of her that she had thought so important, so crucial to her existence had lay dormant all day. And she was still here.

She reached for another praline, closing her eyes as the caramelized sugar melted on her tongue.

CHAPTER 16

FLORA
1940

Sometimes, when I'm walking past a bakery or seated with my back to a restaurant's kitchen, I'll catch the scent of cinnamon and melting butter and I'll be instantly transported to the house on Cockspur Island. I'll be thirteen again, awkward, unsure. Actually, it's not so different from being seventy-two.

I was sitting on the porch steps looking out over the water, listening to Ma and Mary singing in the kitchen as they baked. Father was in the barn. George was rowing back from the lighthouse. I could see him, but knew that I'd have a better view if I climbed the oak tree.

There was a fork in the trunk about seven feet from the top that fit me perfectly. I had just settled in when I saw George start rowing double time, hurtling the small boat through the surf. A second later, I knew why. Dark clouds spread across the horizon. The sea roiled and churned.

George ran up the hill toward the house. I was about to yell to him when a skinny townie in store-bought breeches came running down the oyster shell road, his wet hair plastered to his skull, red patches on his cheeks. I shimmied down until I could see ground then jumped out of the tree, landing just in front of him.

"Hey!" he said.

"Hey yourself, Jimmy. What are you doing down here?"

Jimmy Wilson was a namby-pamby sort who flinches at snakes and hard work. The kind of boy I'd have figured to be in his dry storm cellar with a book, a candle and his mother.

"I came to warn you about the storm. You can come to our place, Flora, if you want."

I saw his lips moving, but the words were ripped from his mouth by the wind, swept to sea. Behind him, George barreled up the slope toward us, bull-like.

Jimmy stepped back as twenty-year-old George, with his whiskered chin and his grown man muscles, said in his man voice, "Get out of here, Jimmy.

Go home to your cellar and stay there."

Then my brother glanced over his shoulder, like the storm was behind him with a bony beckoning finger. "It's gonna be bad," he said. "Real bad."

I didn't like the way he stood there, rain running off his face, eyes too big, Adam's apple bumping in his throat. When George pointed toward the road, Jimmy ran.

I let my brother pull me toward the barn, half carrying, half dragging me when my short legs couldn't keep up. The rain pelted us like gunshot as the wind tried to steal our feet.

We found Father in a stall in the back of the barn. A sick goat lay in the straw. Father was sharpening a knife on a leather strap.

George said, "Hurricane."

Outside, there was a pause in the weather, as if God Himself held His breath and no one knew if He would exhale in a sigh or a bellow. Then the air turned cold and the wind returned more fierce, slamming the shutters, pitching the barn into darkness, then changing its course and whipping them open, off their hinges and away in a cruel game of peek-a-boo.

Father yelled into the noise, "George, open the pens—all of them. Flora, tell your mother we're going to the fort."

Everything slowed. I was frozen, feeling nothing and everything at once. George pushed past me, then was gone. I took a step forward but Father said, "Go on now." His voice might have been an embrace, but his body was a hedge of thorns. He turned back to the goat, stroked his belly then sheathed the sharpened knife and covered the animal with a red flannel shirt.

Outside, the wind had grown teeth that bit my back. The wind had arms with large, salty hands that whipped my skirts, slapped my legs. It pulled my hair, unraveling my neat bun, lifting chunks from the sides of my head making hair wings, as if all I needed to do was lift my chin to fly. But the rain held me down, drenched and heavy.

I fought my way onto the porch, wrestled the front door open. It took three tries to close. The wind was loud, even inside the house. "Ma?" I yelled, running to the kitchen. "Father said—"

"I know, Flora," Ma said. "I can smell it."

Our collie, Junior, pranced and whined, circling then hiding under the table. The room was dim, particles of flour floated like dust mites as we scurried to gather whatever we could carry. Mary stuffed fruit into a sack. I pulled jars and cans off the pantry shelves, looked at the bucket of milk, but left it. Ma grabbed candles and matches, finished latching the shutters. We did what we could, knowing it wouldn't be enough.

Mary screamed when a plate fell and shattered. Ordinarily Ma would have scolded Mary for her carelessness, would have made me clean the mess up, lecturing us on the cost and rarity of the dinnerware, but she only stepped over the debris and handed me another sack of food. "Let's go."

We followed the dog to the door, pushed our way onto the porch just as Father and George arrived. They nailed boards across the windows, and were about to nail the front door shut when Father yelled, "No time, son! Leave her be."

The sky was an odd shade of green. Dark clouds hovered over the water, mixing rain with a salty spray that pickled our skin, burned our eyes. We ran into it, past trees bent in half, swiping at flying branches and clumps of sea grass that appeared fake, weightless—until they connected, hard and sharp.

A shore bird swooped in front of George, wings close enough to touch and when the wind changed course the bird was swept sideways squawking, before he was slammed beak first into a tree.

There was the ripping sound of destruction, the screech of nails as boards were pried from the sides of our house.

We leaned into the wind, felt our feet lift off the earth. For a second, I was free to leap into the sky and skim the land like a butterfly, but there were no butterflies today—only a flying goat. It was the sick ram Father had been tending in the barn, and he wasn't flying so much as sailing.

Ma said, "Oh," in a small voice that could mean anything. She raised her hand, like a command to halt. The red flannel shirt billowed up mast-like around the goat. His little tail became a rudder and his thin bleat became a warning horn for a flying goat ship. George jumped to snatch the goat's leg but ended up with flannel.

Father pushed us harder, yelling, "Quickly!"

We needed to make it to the tip of the island, across the field to Fort Pulaski. I knew what Father was thinking. We should have taken the advice of the old-timers. We should have built a storm cellar, a safe place, like the one under the rag rug at Hannah Noble's. A place like that wasn't just a place to play, it was a place that could save your life.

George entered the clearing first. Running was easier now, something my legs were doing all by themselves. Halfway across the field, a man called to us from the drawbridge. We couldn't hear him, only saw his waving arms, his beard moving up and down. Junior barked as the man's hat was swept into the wind and blew toward us. Dancing on the draft, the cap halted a foot from George, then dropped lifelessly to the ground. The dog growled, hackles raised.

Ma said, "Wait. Listen." She was whispering—and we heard her. The stillness surrounded us like ice. It was a moment of nothing, a slice of space.

Was that it?

Father climbed up an embankment as the rest of us slowly walked toward the fort. I glanced back to see him staring out to sea. I wanted to tell him everything was fine. I wanted to laugh, tell him that hadn't been so bad—until he hurled himself off the grassy ridge and sprinted toward us.

"Run!"

The moment of silence hadn't been the end after all, just the devil messing with us, trapping us under his palm, then lifting a finger so the whole world spun.

I felt it as I pumped my short legs. I felt the thickness in the air, the heft of the storm overhead. All sound was suspended, like a weight dangling by a burning rope. I heard the swish of my skirt, the chuff of my breath, the beating of my heart. I had only one thought: *Get into the fort.*

Never mind that this encampment didn't hold up under a three hour siege from Yankee guns, or that it had been overtaken, ill maintained and abandoned by two separate armies. We were prepared to stake our lives on the strength of those walls. We believed they could withstand the winds of a deadly hurricane. We placed our faith in old brick, worn mortar and etched stone, and prayed to the ghosts of warriors.

The man on the drawbridge was Nate Toohey, a Cockspur Island widower who regularly brought us mail and supplies from Savannah. We sounded like horses crossing that wooden bridge over the moat. Nothing felt as solid or believable to me as that wood under my feet after all the soggy grass and gritty shell roads. The chains groaned and clanged as Nate drew the bridge up and locked it into place.

We passed through the sally port to the open parade ground. Everything inside the fort was untouched. The thick walls had kept the fiercest wind at bay, retaining a sense of normality from manicured shrubs to polished cannons. I tried to imagine the damage from a flying cannon or what twenty-five million loose bricks could do.

Mary sank to the ground hugging the dog, offering prayers into his neck. "Thank you, Lord." And then Mary, being Mary, asked Ma, "Do you think the people in Savannah are safe?"

George and I watched Father. He pulled Mr. Toohey aside and when he saw us staring he held up his hand as if to wave us off or say hello or assure us it wasn't what we thought it was, which made us more anxious.

The next phase came as suddenly and swiftly as someone drawing a curtain from the east to the west. The sound of the wind rose in a banshee wail.

Father grabbed Nate. "Where's the highest indoor point?"

Nate's long teeth nibbled on a calloused groove of lip as he stared past Father. Finally he said, "Follow me."

We ran along the vaulted gallery through the casemates, Nate leading the way. Our shoes smacked the planks, echoing as we passed under massive arches and grand support columns. We stopped short in the southeast corner at the base of a spiral staircase.

Scrunched down as far under the staircase as I could go, it was still too open for me. I wanted a thicker door, a darker, warmer, smaller place—a cave. I squatted on the floor and wrapped my arms around my legs. I tried rocking myself small. Tiny. Invisible. I tried rocking away the sounds of wreckage, the sounds of trees being uprooted, of animals dying, of walls collapsing, the howl and whistle and roar of wind and sea.

When water seeped under the door and lapped against the walls, we moved up onto the stairs, a few steps per person. The dog paced and whined. Ma kept telling us we should sleep, as if anyone wanted to close their eyes. I pretended to, just to please her, and was surprised to awaken with a start.

George stood in ankle deep water at the bottom of the stairs. Mr. Toohey and Junior were gone, everyone else was asleep. I followed George as he inched open the heavy door and squeezed through.

It was so quiet. Not a cricket or a murmur or a rustle to be heard. I whispered, "Hey," to be sure I hadn't gone deaf. George looked at me. I shrugged.

He pointed out over the sodden parade grounds where a long white sailboat was embedded in the grass, part of its call letters, *Calhou*—visible. A cast iron frying pan rested on the grass to its left, a white sheet draped a lavender bush to our right.

Behind us, the door opened. Mary stood behind Ma and Father. Her lips moved in silent prayer as she rolled and unrolled the hem of her skirt. Mary had always been the sensitive one—the believer.

I liked things simple, explainable. I said, "I want to go home."

The storm was over. Everything would return to normal.

But when the drawbridge was lowered and we Martuses stepped outside, every idea I had changed. This was not disaster. This was devastation.

CHAPTER 17

MAGGIE
2011

Maggie knew that putting things off only made them harder to face. She kept telling herself she wouldn't be late for the meeting with the attorney, that she had plenty of time. Enough time to stop and admire the gingerbread-trimmed Victorian on the next block. Enough time for a donut and a latte in the café across the street. Enough time to buy a half-dozen large chocolate chip cookies and stuff them in her pack, welcoming the weight on her back.

On her walk yesterday, she had taken David— the parts of him that remained—the book from his hotel room, the urn of ashes. The stuff had bounced along in the pack as she'd walked down Bull Street, tapping her on the back, reminding her that he was still a part of her. She carried David in place of her camera. He was another kind of weight.

When Maggie began studying photography, she took a class in portraiture. Her professor said it was her job to make everyone look good. But she failed miserably. Her professor complimented her use of light and angles. He said she had vision, but it was mis-directed. Her portraits were empty, devoid of character, devoid of essence. She needed to know love to see love. She needed to feel love to show love. He said he would let her drop the class because what she was missing he couldn't teach.

He suggested a course in architectural photography: a study of human altered landscapes. Maggie signed on and never looked back. Buildings were much less judgmental than people.

It was easier to focus on something she could see than something she knew she had never had in the first place. She tried to explain to David why she was so drawn to architecture. "It's a different form of beauty," she told him. "Something that took lots of people to create. Something that has history in every piece."

"So do people," David said. "Why do you think they say a person's eyes are the window to his soul? Don't you want to capture someone's soul on film?"

"Isn't it odd," Maggie said. "How you just used the architectural term *window?"*

David didn't understand that part of her, maybe no one did. You didn't have to make a building smile and they never needed to be told to stand still. The challenges were controllable. Lighting, shadow, time and angles. It was her unemotional, perfunctory approach that allowed Maggie to remain professionally detached, something she had perfected over the years. Something she was known for.

She'd been in Kobe, Japan in 1995 when the earthquake struck the city, destroying and damaging more than four hundred thousand buildings, killing five thousand people in twenty seconds. Maggie had been one of the few foreign photographers allowed to shoot the demolition. Her steel reserve was read as respect. Her calm demeanor radiated a commanding professionalism.

No one was a witness to her breakdown weeks later, when it all finally caught up to her. David came home from work to find Maggie wedged under her worktable in the darkroom, rocking and mumbling, her hands over her ears, for what she'd seen through her lens had not been as bad as what she'd heard. The sound of destruction was so much worse.

It took a long time, but Maggie could see it now for what it was, a natural disaster made worse by man's choices, his ideas of skyscraping beauty messing with Mother Nature's plan.

Oh grateful colours, bright looks. Men! Seize colours quick, heap them up when you can, But, perhaps it is a false tale that says The landscape of the dead is colourless.

The more she saw of Savannah, the more convinced Maggie was that the architects of this town had shared a glass of sweet tea with Mother Nature and come to an agreement, blending old and new seamlessly into the charm of the gentle old South.

Gardens and squares overflowed with majestic plantings of flowers, hedges and trees. Books told of the disasters this city had endured, but like the growth that comes after the burn on a dying hillside, Savannah kept rising to the occasion, forcing a singular view of beauty onto a harsh landscape, overcoming all obstacles.

CHAPTER 18

BOBBIE
1894

Bobbie believed in serendipity. If something was bound to happen it would. She also believed there were certain ways to increase the impending result. You couldn't win if you didn't play. Meeting Sam was serendipitous. Coming to Savannah? Definitely. Ending up back at the DeSoto? In a strange way—also meant to be.

"You work here?" she asked.

"In the kitchen," he said. "Would you like a tour?"

"Of the hotel?" she asked.

"Of the kitchen," he said.

"Oh. Yes."

Sam laughed. They were in the gardens at the rear of the grand hotel. He'd led Bobbie through the hedgerows to the employee entrance, an unmarked door by a rubbish pile.

"Why do you find me so amusing?" she asked.

"I don't," he said.

"You certainly have been laughing a lot at my expense," Bobbie said. "All the way over here, as a matter of fact."

"It's not you," Sam said. "I mean, not exactly."

The door to the hotel opened suddenly. A man with a bucket of greens stepped out, holding the door with his foot. He upended the bucket and was about to step back inside when Sam called, "Hey! Hold the door."

The man squinted into the dark. "Who's that?" he called.

Sam pulled Bobbie into the light spraying from the open door, saying. "Willy, it's Sam."

The guy relaxed. "Thought that was you," Willy said.

Sam shook his hand, then jerked a thumb toward Bobbie saying she wanted a tour and was Chef around?

"Already left for the night," Willie said. "You're in luck."

❧ ❧

The hotel workers gathered in the kitchen found it amusing that Bobbie, dressed the way she was, telling the stories she told and drinking the way she could was a guest in a suite, at the DeSoto Hotel.

"It's just that you're not the sort of person Mr. Preston built this place for," Willie said. "We got the feeling he was—I don't know, making a place for rich, snooty types."

"At least those are the people we have to cater to most days," added a pudgy chambermaid.

"And the kinds whose soup I spit in," said one of the cooks, eliciting a groan from the group.

Bobbie snuck in a few questions about Preston, learning he rarely took visitors in his room, but she'd always be able to find him on the work site.

When the whiskey ran out and a few heads lay on the table, Bobbie and Sam stumbled up the back stairs to her room on the third floor.

She stripped off her jacket and shoes as soon as the door closed behind them, untucked her shirt and drew it over her head as Sam watched.

He followed her into the bedroom, as Bobbie shed layers, dropping her clothes in a trail to the window. She pulled open the drapes letting the moonlight wash the room in grays and blues and silver, like they were standing in a glass of water. She raised her bare arms to the moonlight scooping it up, rubbing it into her skin. She was glowing when she turned around to face Sam.

"Your turn," she said.

He stepped closer. "There's something you don't know about me."

"There are a lot of things I don't know about you," she said, reaching for him.

"I didn't always work here in the kitchen," he said, unbuttoning his shirt. "I used to be a shop clerk."

"Are you going to try to sell me something, Mr. Winter?" Bobbie cocked her head, picking up where he'd left off on the fourth button.

"Please, Bobbie. I need to . . ." Sam let his arms drop to his side, took a deep breath, wincing.

"It wasn't my fault," he whispered. "It could have happened at any time."

Bobbie pulled his shirt off and began to raise his thin cotton undershirt as Sam said, "It was Hogan's idea to light the display window with gas lanterns."

Bobbie felt the scarred flesh before she saw it. "Go on," she said, softly.

He ducked his head as she bared his chest, his scars. "Good people died that day," he said. "Some that shouldn't have, survived."

Bobbie lay her hand on the ridged flesh of his chest, the wounds held heat like the fire was still inside. She kissed him, drawing him close pressing her cool, smooth body against his tense, rangy torso. He returned her tenderness slowly at first, then melted into her, his lips making their own trail from cheek to ear to neck, breast to stomach.

They fell onto the safari bed, Sam kicking off his shoes, wriggling out of his trousers. Bobbie understanding at once, the benefit of a large bed.

Sam was curled against Bobbie, knees tucked behind hers, his left arm over her waist.

"You don't mind?" he said into her hair.

"Mind?" Bobbie said. "That was fantastic."

"I mean the . . ."

Bobbie rolled over to face him. "What, Sam? Your burns? Am I disappointed that you're not *this* pretty all over?" She lay her hand on his cheek, ran her thumb over his lips. "We all have ugly parts, some are just better hidden than others."

"Some girls—" he started.

"If you haven't noticed by now," Bobbie said, "I am *not* some girls."

Sam smiled, a low laugh escaped, turning into painful coughing.

"Are you okay? Let me get you some water." Bobbie started to get out of the bed, but Sam grabbed her arm, shook his head and pulled her back as the coughs subsided. He cleared his throat, took some shallow breaths and lay back on the pillows, a thin line of sweat on his forehead.

When he spoke his voice was weaker. "It gets like that sometimes. Doc Handley says I have damaged tissue in my lungs. There's nothing they can do. I'm dying from the inside out."

Bobbie pulled the sheet over them, snuggled into him. "Tell me about it. All of it."

CHAPTER 19

FLORA
1940

We're still in the car, I can smell the gasoline. Cow Eyes is stroking my cheek, dabbing at the cut on my head. She says, "Miss Flora?" in the voice you use with a child, a slow, sleepy child.

I hear her but my past is louder, more insistent, so I go there instead, to 1879, when I was eleven.

"George?"

It was quiet in the barn. No rattling machines or scraping pitchforks, no shooshing saws or pounding hammers—nothing that sounded like George—nothing that smelled like him, either. I checked the stalls, stopping at the last one where a black kitten slept in a spike of sun. As I sank into the hay beside her, she rolled onto her back, stretching her legs, exposing her white belly. I watched her chest rise and fall as she dreamed. I wondered what a cat would wish for.

I was lying on my stomach teasing the kitten with a dangling piece of straw when George appeared in the doorway. I looked up, and the cat took the opportunity to strike. Her softly batting paw turned deadly with a clawed swipe that caught the straw and my cheek. Two red lines began to bleed.

"Oh!" I jerked back, pressed my hand to my cheek.

George swooped down for the kitten, but it was too used to danger, bred for flight.

"You'd better run," George called after the escaping cat.

He knelt beside me. "Let me see that." He cupped my chin, tipped it up.

"It hurts."

George wiped my tears, held my head against his chest and rocked me. I could feel his heart talking to mine. His skin was warm from the sun and the work in the meadow. I smelled all the good things he'd been doing, all the places he'd been. I smelled the island on him.

He smoothed my hair, shushed me and whispered, "It's going to be okay. You're all right now." He whispered things that made me believe him, treating me like the lamb with the broken leg he'd rescued from the pasture, like the delicate potato vine he'd carefully snaked through the trellis in the garden. George was hard on the outside. All man. All Martus. But I knew how to reach the soft parts of him, the quiet places. I was his barnacle.

We may have stayed that way for a minute, or an hour. Me with my arms circled around his waist, hiccupping small cries as hay crunched under his knees, as a goat bleated in another stall, as mice raced overhead in the loft. There was a certain womblike innocence in the red barn at the bottom of the hill on an island no one visited. It stood grandly on the homestead of a forgotten family. If a huge tower of light had not been in the bay beyond the reeds, no one might have found us. We were invisible. We were nothing. And at the same time, we were everything to Savannah.

∽ ∽

"Miss Flora?" Cow Eyes repeats, more insistent, shaking me awake.

"I'm fine," I say opening my eyes, waving her off.

"I am so sorry," she says and I can tell this isn't the first time today she's said those words. I wonder how long we've been here, in this automobile, how long we've been away. Cow Eyes pushes a cloth into my hair, pressing into the bump that's forming.

"Are you really all right?" she says.

I touch her hand on my head, pat it then pull it away. "Yes," I tell her and smile a little, then ask, "Could we walk?" as if nothing had happened at all.

I push my hair into place, hope there isn't a red splotch on the side of my head, hope she'll stop looking at me like I'm broken. A young couple stares into the automobile as they drive past us. I shove the bloody handkerchief into my purse.

"It is a beautiful day," I say.

Cow Eyes looks up at the sky then at me, measuring us equally. "Yes," she says. "But, are you sure?"

"I think a walk will do us both good."

Cow Eyes purses her lips. The girl does worry too much.

Finally she says, "All right then."

I let her open the door for me, only because I can't quite figure out the handle, but I refuse her arm and get out of the auto myself. There's no reason to make her think I'm absolutely helpless. My brother is dead, not me.

∽ ∽

Timing. Ma used to say this was the secret of success—not luck, not brains, not connections, but good and proper timing. When you ask for a favor, when you give a gift, when you admit a mistake, when you confess, when you rejoice, when you share, when you gossip, pilfer, or deceive, somewhere God's finger is pushing the hands of the clock.

Today, I think He's holding them still.

Cow Eyes and I walk. Twenty-two steps later she says, "You're right about Alain. We're in love. But my mother forbids me to see him. She says he puts silly ideas into my head."

"Does he?" I say.

"No. Well, perhaps. But they aren't silly," she says. "He makes me believe that anything is possible, that I can have more. Is that wrong?"

"To want more?" I say. "Nonsense. Where would we be if no one wanted more? Still living in caves, I suspect."

Cow Eyes laughs. "Caves. Yes. That's what Mother wants for me. A nice clean cave and four little beasts underfoot."

"What do you want?" I ask.

She speaks to the sky. "I want to be an actress. I want to be the next Jean Harlow." She pulls away, quickens her pace. "I want to live in France. I want to learn to sail. I want to climb a mountain and eat a picnic lunch where no one else has been before me." Cow Eyes laughs and looks back to where she left me. "Listen to me. I'm being ridiculous," she says. "Forgive me."

When I catch up to her, I reach for her hand. She's different now, happier away from that place, though who wouldn't be. For a little while I might be too, happier that is.

We walk this way for a bit, the sun warm on our necks, and I think, there is a way to love. And for everyone it's different, neither right nor wrong, better or worse, you can't categorize a heart. Cow Eyes and her Alain. That feels like love. How can it be wrong when your heart sings, when your eyes open and you see joy?

I squeeze her hand and say, "You should do all that you want. Don't wait. Life won't stop for you to get on. You may have to jump. You can jump, can't you?"

There is a brief hesitation, a bobble in her step, then a reassuring squeeze back, and her small voice seems bigger when she says, "Oh yes, Miss Flora. I can jump."

CHAPTER 20

MAGGIE
2011

When Maggie asked Sadie, stationed behind the B&B desk to call her a cab, the woman refused. "Don't be silly. Charles will take you. I need him to pick up the fish for tonight anyway."

The door to the kitchen inched open.

"Isn't that right, Charles?" Sadie said.

The Flannery House chef poked his head around the doorframe. He looked flustered, and busy.

"No," Maggie said, waving Sadie off. "That's not necessary. I could walk. I have a map, and I need the exercise." She patted her stomach and attempted a smile. "Really, I wouldn't want to hold up your day," she said to Charles. "Besides, I'm sure you have a lot of cooking to do."

"Not really," he said untying his apron and handing it to Sadie. "The kitchen can wait. It would be my pleasure."

Charles pulled up in front of the attorney's office on Bryan Street, a clean brick row house.

He asked, "When should I come back for you?"

"Oh," Maggie said. "No. I—"

"It's all right," Charles said quickly. "I understand."

He waved as he drove off leaving Maggie standing there feeling like a teenager who'd disappointed her father with bad choices and bad grades.

She wouldn't be surprised if Chef Charles was waiting at the curb after her appointment. It wouldn't be because he thought less of Maggie, that she needed help, that she couldn't find her way back if she had to. It would be because he was kind.

Maggie's father had not been a man one would have called kind or sincere or humble. He'd been ill-fitted for fatherhood, too selfish to be a good husband. He took his bread-winning seriously and put it before all else, preferring the road or the office to a home that was in the beginning, messy and noisy, filled with a wife too busy with work to pay attention to him and a child too ensconced in a fantasy world to be able to relate to. Eventually, the only love he produced was stirred into his bourbon; the only attention he could spare was aimed in the direction of the TV.

Maggie thought she'd found a kinder man in David, but when pressed she couldn't mention a single circumstance where her husband had performed an exemplary act of kindness. The "not doing" of something didn't count, did it? As in, he didn't smack the dog when he peed on the Persian rug. Or he didn't beat the shit out of the teenager that smashed the mailbox, tore up the lawn and stole the Omaha steaks delivery, although Maggie knew he really wanted to. David might not have been an extraordinarily kind man, but he wasn't a bad man either.

❦ ❧

Maggie stepped into the attorney's waiting room. It was small and sparse. A woman's perfume lingered in the air. Something exotic, something expensive. Maggie wondered if she stood there long enough she would absorb the scent, the way you smell like someone's cooking when you spend time in their kitchen or reek like charred wood when you stand downwind from a bonfire.

The girl behind the desk looked surprised to see her. "Yes, Ma'am?"

"Good morning," Maggie said. "I have an appointment with Mr. Siegler."

The girl looked past her to the empty room, the closed door.

"I'm Mrs. Morris?" Maggie said.

The girl paused, then made a point of checking her computer screen, running her finger down days that didn't yet exist, before raising lost eyes to Maggie.

Maggie tried again, wishing she knew sign language or the secret password. "Mrs. David Morris. Maggie?"

The girl continued to look confused. She held up a finger then spun around in her efficient office chair, offering Maggie her back while whispering into a tiny headset.

When she turned back around, she offered a tentative smile. "I'm sorry," she said. Of course. Mrs. . . . Morris. Please have a seat. Mr. Siegler will only be a moment."

The girl fiddled with her computer screen, shuffled some papers, snuck another glance at Maggie, looking relieved when the intercom buzzed and Siegler said, "Send her in."

The man behind the desk looked as propped up and fake as the plastic palm in the corner. Someone must have told him that glasses would make him look more distinguished, and it might have worked, had he not chosen round, black plastic frames. Instead the man behind the desk looked like an owl. Maggie expected him to cock his head and ask "Who-who?" while flexing his talons on the edge of his leather chair.

She cracked a smile, and Owl Man smiled back, pushing himself upright and extending a small damp hand. Maggie approached, embarrassed to tower over him.

"Mrs. Morrris-s-s."

Oh dear Jesus. The guy had a lisp, too. No wonder he didn't go into trial law. What had David been thinking? This was not the sort of man anyone took seriously, much less her picky husband. Owl Man wasn't someone David or anyone would have chosen to trust with their life savings, a massive estate, or the division of a household. This man, Maggie would be hard pressed to trust with her dry cleaning.

He said, "Al Siegler. The pleasure is mine."

Maggie nodded then shook the guy's hand, thinking, You got that right, pal.

"Dave spoke highly of you," he said motioning to the seats in front of his desk. "Please."

Maggie dropped into one of the low leather chairs wondering who the hell Dave was.

"I suppose we should get right to it then," he said. "Would you mind verifying a few things for me before we begin?" Owl Man peered over his slipping lenses.

"All right," Maggie said.

Owl Man tipped the manila folder, shielding the contents from Maggie. "What is the address of the home you owned with David Morris?"

"170 Stable Lane," she said.

He thumbed through the papers. "And the year you were married?"

"1995."

Owl Man pursed his lips, furrowed his brow, flipped a few more pages, then slid out a paper clipped packet, closed the folder and set it aside. He nodded. "Very good."

Maggie glanced at the papers in his hands. She tried to read the upside down print, got as far as "My last will and testament," before the attorney slapped his hands on it.

Maggie looked up. "I'm sorry?"

"I was saying," Owl Man sputtered. "Dave wanted you to know the house is paid for. You'll find the deed and any stock certificates in the safe deposit box at your bank in Philadelphia. Here's the information."

He slid a piece of paper across the desk.

"I understand this is a difficult time for you, Mrs. Morris. But once you are home with friends and family—"

"I don't have any," Maggie said. "David is—was—"

"I am sorry for your loss." Owl Man's words fell into the empty space of the room with a dull thud, a handclap in a soundproof space.

Maggie knew the attorney meant well, that those were the words he was taught to use but she wanted to reach across the desk and slap him. She wanted to pull off his round glasses and poke out his owl eyes and squeeze his beak nose until he understood pain until she could stand over the weak and bloody man, as he lay sightless and dying and say to him, "No, I am sorry for your loss."

Owl Man blinked at Maggie. He cleared his throat and adjusted the framed picture of his equally owlish wife on his desk, then pushed the paper at her again, reminding her where she was and why she was there. David.

What if she had misjudged her husband? They say you don't marry your soul mate. You create your soul mate out of the person you marry. What did that mean?

"Why?" she asked.

"Pardon me?" Owl Man squirmed behind his big desk.

"Why did he make his will with you—here in Savannah?"

Owl Man suddenly became interested in his filing stack.

"I am sure I do not know." He said in his soft southern lisp. "People do things for many reasons."

"It just seems odd to me," Maggie said. "That my husband chose an out of state attorney whom he hardly knew to—"

"Oh, no, Mrs. Morris," Owl Man interrupted. "I knew Dave."

"Really?"

"Yes," he said. "We practically grew up together. His family owned the beach house next to ours on Tybee Island. Every summer we'd terrify the coast."

Owl Man grinned, baring wide Chiclet teeth. Maggie smiled weakly, trying to imagine Owl Man terrifying anything.

She vaguely remembered hearing David speaking of family holidays. She admittedly had distanced herself from the stories he told of "the seventies," as Maggie had been a baby and her input on the subject was always met with sighs and disapproving glares, usually accompanied by a quip like, "That may be the way it seemed, but you had to be there."

Maggie hated when David did this—threw their age difference into the mix. She swore sometimes he played all that Woodstock, hippie flower power bullshit on her just so he could have the upper hand. What was ten years in age difference, really? It might seem like a big deal if you were sixteen and he was twenty-six, or a huge deal if you were eleven and he was twenty-one. But when you were twenty-five and thirty-five like Maggie and David were when they met, then age was only a number.

Maggie thought initially that David would have the baggage of an unhappy marriage, that he would be divorced and consumed by kids and a snippy ex-wife like many other older men she'd dated. It was to her great and wonderful surprise, that he was a bachelor, not even one illegitimate child that he knew of, he often joked.

Her girlfriends had been incredulous, saying, "You met him where? At a gas station? Oh my God. I am so buying an SUV!"

Their courtship had been ideal, nothing stood in their way. It was as well orchestrated as a theatrical production. Enter stage right handsome, well-dressed gentleman. Jaguar in background. Gas pumps click and ping. Door to the Jiffy Mart swings shut with a cowbell jingle. Beautiful woman locks keys in rental car, curses softly then reaches for her cell phone.

Gentleman approaches, saying, "Locksmith will charge you an arm and a leg, the cops will be too busy and the rental company won't make it out here before seven. I may be your only hope."

The woman returns his smile and slips the phone back in her pocket.

That was just the beginning.

Maggie had a feeling now that she was stuck in another kind of production. Maybe a David Mamet movie and this was the part where the con is exposed, where the twist becomes apparent to everyone but the duped wife/lover/partner/friend.

Yet how could a man that was shifty Look so purposeful, And when he was looking purposeful Seem beautiful?

David had been the perfect husband, hadn't he? Provider, companion, masseur, lover. He cooked, too. Made the best eggs Maggie ever had. She remembered watching the muscles in David's broad back flex when he stood at the stove in his boxers, pan of eggs in one hand, executing the perfect scoop and flip. She'd never been able to do that.

She rotated her head on her shoulders, zoomed in on Owl Man who was looking increasingly uncomfortable. He stood, offering his hand. "Again, my regrets."

"Yes, well. Thank you," Maggie said shaking his hand, taking the papers then stepping toward the door. She paused and turned back. "Can I ask you a question?"

Owl Man bobbed his head and pushed up his glasses.

Maggie said, "Did you see him? Dave? Often when he was in town?"

"Not that much," he said. "Though, we did run into each other at the marina a few months back. He invited my family onto his boat for drinks." Owl Man leaned back in his chair and grinned. "First time we'd ever been on a boat that size. She's a real beauty. But I'm sure you know that. He said he bought it for his wife, after all."

"Yes. She is a beauty. " Maggie tried to keep the anxiety out of her voice. At the door she turned back, and in a Columbo moment said, "You know, I can never remember the name of the marina."

Owl Man had a phone in one hand, a folder in the other. He barely glanced up before spitting out, "Blue Cove."

Maggie said, "That's right," as if she knew it all along, as if she knew everything, when really she wondered if she knew anything at all.

CHAPTER 21

FLORA
1940

At Johnny Harris's restaurant, the tables have filled up around me and Cow Eyes and I feel, for the first time in days, at ease. There is so much activity that I become invisible, just a fixture, like an antique propped in the corner that someone will forget to dust. I close my eyes and breathe.

Food has a way of bringing back memories. With barbeque, it's more than hickory smoke and heat. It's the sizzle of dripping fat, the spit of popping skin, the scent of the cook's tangy sauce, and all the extras that go with it: cornbread, greens, biscuits, cold sweet tea, the wink of a lover.

I do believe if I was ever one of those men waiting in prison for their execution, I would ask for barbeque as my final meal. I think if Jesus came back, he'd have barbeque at the last supper before he left us again.

If Cow Eyes knew how I felt about a half pig on a bed of coals, she might never have brought me here. I may end up embarrassing myself, eating away my sorrow. There is an intelligent part of my brain that tells me life goes on, and as old as I am and as much as I have seen, I do understand this. I may not accept it, but I do understand. There is no need for the woman to coddle me, but also, I am not quite ready to celebrate my brother's ascent into heaven.

There will be enough talk of that when my nephew the priest gets hold of us all. For now, I want George to be looking down at me from above thinking, *that barbeque sure looks good, Flora.* So this is for you, dear heart.

"Yes," I say when I'm handed the menu. "Yes." Then I close it and hand it back.

In the ladies room, I'm taken in by the décor, the little extras. On the island, George and I had barely gotten used to having an indoor privy before we had to leave. He would have thought me more than crazy had I hung a picture in there like the one on the wall here, with its perfectly painted meadow, its bristling tips of hay glinting in the morning light, the small brown mouse standing alert in the undergrowth. The sky is a cloudless blue, except for a spot in the highest corner. Squinting my eyes I see the red-tailed hawk.

Who chose this painting? Who picked the delicate blue flowers pressed between sheets of glass? Who crocheted the trimmed towels? Who loves lavender as much as I do? Maybe the owner, Mr. Johnny Harris is not at all who we think he is.

Behind me at the window, something catches my eye. The curtain edge dances on the sill, only a portion of the white gauzy cloth as if a snake or a bird is caught in the fabric and wriggling itself free. But as I approach I can see it's just the wind, playing with me again, reminding me of another window, another curtain, another day.

George was in the garden, repairing the fence as Ma had asked. The rabbits were getting the sweetest parts of our harvest and Ma was determined to do something about it, short of feeding them to the owls.

She'd refused to come down for supper two nights running. I'd put up with her odd requests for breakfast foods in the middle of the day, and even hung a pretty lace curtain in her window and set a vase of flowers by her bed, just to cheer her up. Some days she seemed fine, then the smallest thing would set her off and there would be angry outbursts followed by tears. I'd begun brewing a special herb tea to settle her, but there were still days when Ma would be so ornery that I had to get George to deal with her.

I sat on the edge of her bed trying to talk some sense into her. "I can bring you some of the leftovers from last night. I made a ham," I said. "Your favorite, with green beans and potatoes."

"I'm not hungry," she said closing her eyes and waving me away. "Leave me alone."

"You have to eat," I said. "Look at you, you're skin and bones."

"Go away," she said.

"Ma? How are you going to get better if you don't eat?"

"I don't want to get better." She pulled the covers over her head. "Get out!"

"Ma- "

"Get out!" She slapped the covers down and grabbed the vase on the bedside table.

I ducked as it crashed into the wall behind me sending daisies and ivy and water and shards of glass flying. I screamed and went to find George.

He was in the garden adding chicken wire to the bottom of the fence. He took one look at me standing there, nibbling my lip, squeezing up my face, then took off his hat and wiped his arm across his forehead. "What did she do now?" he asked.

"She won't eat," I said. "And she threw a vase at me—broke it too."

"Where is she?"

"In her room where I left her," I said trying to be strong, but my voice broke. "She acts like she hates me."

George reached for me then stopped and looked over my shoulder.

I followed his gaze. The edge of a white lace curtain blew out of an upstairs window, delicately flapping, then as the wind grabbed hold, the whole panel pulled out into the breeze and

flared open, revealing a ragged red slash across the fabric and a bloody hand print. We counted the windows, then ran.

I skittered to a stop outside the bedroom, bumping into George frozen on the transom. He whispered, "Oh Jesus. Sweet Jesus."

The bed was empty and there was a pile of bloody laundry on the floor under the window. No, not laundry. Ma.

I ran to her into the room of blood and glass and sunshine, speed reciting all the prayers I knew and making some up on the spot. Outside a bird sang, its tune too hopeful, too gay.

I knelt beside Ma and pulled her into my lap away from the pool of blood. I cradled my mother as she had done for me many times, smoothed her hair off her forehead and held her sick, sour body close to mine.

George pale and shaking whispered, "Flora." He pointed to Ma's clenched fist, and when I pried her hand open, a triangle of glass dropped to the floor. I ran my finger across the jagged cut on her wrist that was already starting to close.

"We need a doctor," I said, in a borrowed voice.

George stared at me.

"George," I said. I tugged on the curtain, pulling as hard as I could. "George, help me."

He yanked the stained fabric from the rod, held it uselessly in his limp hand. I had to stretch to reach it. I tore it into strips with my teeth, a constant string of promises and prayers muttered under my breath, a combination plea for succor and absolution as I wrapped a bandage around my mother's wrist, as I removed her bloody clothes.

She was even more frail in her thin, pink slip, like a newborn calf. I lay my head on her chest, closed my eyes and listened for a heart beat.

"It's faint," I said. "But it's there."

We lifted her onto the bed then pulled the covers up.

"Fetch Doc Handley," I told George. "Tell him Ma's sick. That's all you tell him."

George looked five years old standing there working his hands into fists then steeples and prayer hands. "But what about—"

"Don't worry," I said. "I'll fix everything. Now go."

He ran down the stairs, and out the back door. A moment later, I heard the motor on the dory start up. I was alone, but not really. I had my mother.

CHAPTER 22

MAGGIE
2011

Maggie lay propped up in the bed at the B&B, her grandmother's book against her bent knees. She thumbed the pages, letting them fall open again and again, until she felt a thickness, like pages stuck together. She opened the book wider. On the pages were a set of short poems: *Like This (1)* and *Like This (2)*.

The first was written from the viewpoint of a young man in an asylum, a poem of loneliness and isolation. The second was written from the viewpoint of a young girl in an asylum claiming there is no love at all, unless it is found in speaking to one another.

Maggie picked at the corner where the pages were stuck together and separated the delicate, yellowed paper. She recognized her mother's handwriting immediately.

Sweet Maggie,

There are times in your life that you will believe you have it all figured out. You will see the world as a smoothly operating machine and know without a doubt, what your place is in it. You won't think about who you will hurt or what you will leave behind, only what you will gain, and where the rolling wheels of the machine will take you. There is never a bad place ahead, no forks in the road, no dead ends. You will not imagine regret, anger or sadness, only desire, happiness and pleasure. You will have accepted that you want more and you deserve it. Everything you have known before has brought you to this place.

Unfortunately, the machine feeds on all emotions, on all lives, on all possibilities. And you can't take and take and take without ever being asked to give. Some people call it karma, some call it religion, some call it fate. Why you were there when he was there. Why you said that and why he laughed. Why it lasted. Or didn't. Why she was born and he wasn't. Why she died and he lived.

Trust me, it isn't that simple. It never was. In the end, you will say no to what you said yes to in the beginning. You will understand that you bought into an absurd and hopeless lie.

This is the truth: If it's too easy, it's wrong. If it never hurts, it wasn't worth it. If you feel lucky to be handed something, be wary. My darling girl, earn your life's rewards and don't ever stand still with your hand out. Run forward or run away, but run, darling. Run.

The date under her mother's signature was the day before she died. The day before she asked her darling daughter to pour all the pills into her hand and leave a glass of water on the bedside table.

In the end, you will say no to what you said yes to in the beginning, or will you?

"Today, Mom?" Maggie threw the book across the room. "Shit."

Maggie mourned her mother twice a year, once on Mother's Day and once on the anniversary of her death, the date exactly thirty years ago.

She'd done what her mother wanted, without even trying, McGill women were good at running away. Even when they were standing still.

Maggie had run from everyone who'd ever loved her. From every boy, every man, even her own father. She could be standing right next to them, holding their hand, saying all the words they needed to hear, but her heart was already over the rise and pulling into the next town. . . . suitcase in hand.

CHAPTER 23

FLORA
1940

I was still in the pretty bathroom at Johnny Harris's, looking out the window, my fingers tracing the delicate embroidery on the curtains. If I squeezed my eyes shut tight enough, the cars outside became boats.

When George returned with Doc Handley and his daughter, Miranda, I watched them from Ma's window. They came up the path from the dock making purposeful strides toward the house. George hurried, carrying the old man's case, and once, offered his arm to Miranda when she stumbled. I watched until I lost them under the eaves and when I heard six feet on the wooden stairs I rushed to the bedside, held Ma's uninjured hand and softly sang the one song I could think of, "Hush little baby, don't you cry . . ."

I tried to not look up as the door opened, afraid my face would say more than my lips. I felt George enter the room, felt his eyes scan the floor, wall, window, bed, looking for any sign of calamity. I wanted to catch his eyes in mine. I wanted him to scoop me out of there, gather me in his arms and run. Instead, I snuck a glance as he set the doctor's valise on the bed. The floor was clean and damp. I'd spread a rug from my room over the spot where Ma fell, and hung mismatched curtains in the window. George nodded, then retreated to the far wall.

Miranda stood in the doorway, as Doc Handley removed his jacket and rolled up his sleeves. He said, "Mrs. Martus? Cecelia?" as he lifted her eyelids.

"How long has she been like this?" he asked.

"Not long," I said. "She goes in and out of it."

Doc pulled a stethoscope from his bag. He slipped his hand into the front of her bed jacket then looked away, using his mind's eye to see what ailed Ma.

I wondered if the doctor could identify what ailed me, if my sin was brazenfaced? If his hand was on my breast, what would my heart reveal?

Doc said, "George told me your mother's been feeling poorly. Is that why we haven't seen her at church?"

"I told Doc that she's been tired and sleeping a lot lately," George said.

"Told him how we thought the boat ride might be too much for her."

I said, "That's right."

Doc Handley looked at me, at George, at a spot on the wall and said, "I see," then went back to listening to his stethoscope.

"But she never misses saying the rosary," I told him. "In fact, Mary and Thomas came out last week and he led the prayers."

While Doc fussed with something in his satchel, Miranda pushed forward, saying too loudly, "Are they going to get married? They look so happy together. It's so romantic, don't you think? I heard they were moving."

The girl kept babbling, as if we were having a picnic instead of nursing the sick. "Someone told me they were going to Charleston. If you don't mind my saying, the Wilson's seem real fond of Mary. Why, when I saw her yesterday, she was wearing the prettiest dress, said it was a gift from Mr. Wilson."

I tried to make my voice soft and even, a tone I usually reserved for the barn cats when they shit in the corncrib. "Miranda. This is not the time or the place to discuss dresses, or my sister. My mother is ill and I would appreciate it very much if you'd shut your durn—"

Ma stirred, moaning.

"There, there. Just rest," Doc said, patting her shoulder. He held Ma's head and offered her medicine, a powder he'd stirred into a cup of water. "This will help you sleep."

Ma sipped slowly, then gulped the liquid and lay back. She pulled her arms from under the covers. When the bed jacket sleeves rose, Doc noticed the crude bandage around her wrist.

George held the doctor's jacket. "Thank you for coming, Doc. We can take it from here."

The doctor hesitated.

George said, "I'd like to have a word with you—outside?"

The man continued to stare at Ma's bandage.

"Sir?" George said, touching Doc's elbow.

"Yes, yes of course." Doc snapped his valise shut, tipped his head at me. "Miss Flora," he said then followed George into the hall.

Miranda watched me smooth the coverlet, tuck Ma in like a child. "Flora," she said. "Do you remember Talia Benning? She just had her third baby. Another boy. And she's *our age*. Can you imagine? Babies, children? Heck, most days I still feel like a child myself. But we're twenty. We're *old*."

I remembered Miranda from our days on Cockspur Island. We used to catch frogs in Baker's pond, climb trees, swim in the shallows. We were twelve years old, in the same class, spending our Saturdays playing soldier with George and the other kids at the fort. It was all fun and innocent until the day I caught my brother kissing Miranda when we were supposed to be playing hide and seek.

CHAPTER 24

MAGGIE
2011

Maggie ended up on the riverfront by The Waving Girl statue. She pulled another cookie from the bag and idly stroked the bronze dog. When her cell phone rang she answered without looking. "Hi Lisa."

"Hi Mags. How's it going?"

"Fine," Maggie said.

"Fine? Oh, good," Lisa snipped. "Glad for that. So, does that mean you're coming home soon?"

"Not sure," Maggie said.

"What does that mean? C'mon—I mean—" There was a rustling on Lisa's end, a muffled curse, then she said, "That's your choice and you know what you're doing." A big pause and more rustling. "Did you see the lawyer?"

"Yeah," Maggie said.

"And?"

"Seems I own the house and some stocks too. I'm a well-off widow."

"Oh Mags. Come home. I ran into Raymond at the Café and he said they are piled up with jobs for you. He says he has a shoot in Paris as soon as you're ready. You know how much you love Paris and hell, I'd even go with you. It would be great, like when we were single—"

"I am single."

"Shit." Lisa sighed. "You know what I mean."

Maggie waited. The silence would be filled whether she said anything or not. That was how friendships were. Sometimes just to hear someone breathing was enough to call it company. And sometimes you didn't say things because your friend already knew what you were thinking.

"I'll let you get back to... whatever it was that you were doing," Lisa said. "Hey. I miss you."

Maggie opened her mouth to say something and when no words came, she pressed the end button and snapped it shut.

"What am I going to tell her?" She asked the dog statue. "That I never even knew him? That he led a double life? It sounds like a bad movie." She adopted a director's voice and said, "Our heroine hires a PI to uncover the truth. Together they find the hidden millions while engaging in a hot and heavy affair. Fade out to final scene: the sun sets on the horizon as tangled bodies fall from a swinging hammock onto the white sands of Paradise Island. Cue music." Maggie laughed until tears formed in the corners of her eyes.

"You have a great laugh."

Maggie whirled around, swiping her wet eyes.

He came the rest of the way through the hedge. "Sorry. Me again."

It was the graffiti cleaner.

He said, "I hope I'm not—intruding?" He looked around and Maggie realized how ridiculous it must seem, some lady sitting under a statue petting a bronze dog, talking to herself and laughing like a crazy person. Great.

"No," she said. "I was just thinking about . . . Anyway, no. You aren't interrupting. But, me, am I in the way?"

He wasn't carrying a bottle of cleaner, didn't have any rags. Maybe he had a cart someplace to keep his cleaning supplies. There must be hundreds of statues to clean—all those squares and parks and memorials—all visited by vandals and hoodlums, messy tourists and pigeons.

"In my way?" he said.

"To clean the statue," she said.

He was looking at her the way a baby looks at a babbling adult. As if the baby was planning his first words and they would be: "You are a complete idiot."

"Oh." Maggie said, flustered. "I'm sorry. It's just that I thought your job was to . . . I had no idea that you weren't—I mean, I don't know what I mean. You seem very nice and . . ."

He let her babble as he stood there in his faded blue jeans, boots and t-shirt, needing only a black cowboy hat to complete the picture of Southern boy handsome. She stopped mid-sentence and reached for her backpack.

"Wait," he said. "You don't have to leave. I was just going to drop these postcards." He left a stack of postcards by the bronze lantern. "You should stay. She likes your company."

"She?" Maggie asked.

"Miss Martus—Flora," he said, tipping his chin toward the bronze girl with the cloth.

"Is that right?" Maggie wondered why she had worried what this guy thought of her. It was apparent he was the one with reality issues.

A large ship passed on the river, yellow and black with a red emblem on the side, men on deck scurrying fore and aft. Maggie knew next to nothing about boating lingo. She knew next to nothing about boats. Her personal experience was limited to a canoe at the family camp and a ferry to Canada. Both times had been less than fulfilling with one trip leaving her wet and cold, the other nauseated.

The guy stepped onto the Waving Girl pedestal and waved his arms at the ship like he was flagging down a train. The ship looked too busy, too far away. But the men on the ship returned his greeting with shouts, whistles and raised arms, all to be outdone by the ship's horn when it let out three mighty head splitting blasts.

Maggie covered her ears as the young man hooted and hollered, pumping his fists in the air.

"Damn. That must have been how Flora felt," he said turning back to Maggie." Did you wave?"

"Uh, no."

"That's all right," he said. "There'll be more ships."

The way he said it, Maggie believed him. Like he was offering her a second chance. A moment to back up and slow down. A do-over.

Maggie felt something she hadn't since her mother died. She felt hope.

"I'm Sonny, by the way," he said.

"Maggie," she said laying a hand flat on her chest. "By the way."

He laughed, crinkling up the corners of his eyes and showing off teeth that would make an orthodontist proud. "So, have you seen it?" He motioned toward the stack of postcards. "Flora's lighthouse?"

"I thought she waved from the porch of her cottage on some island."

"She did. They lived on Elba Island, after the move from Cockspur. But tending the Cockspur Light was their job—their father's first, then George's and sometimes Flora's. Anyway, you should see it when you get a chance."

A girl in a blue mustang convertible pulled up near the grassy area and waved, calling, "Hey, Sonny!"

"I better go," he said, backing away toward the street. "See you later."

"Yeah. See you." Maggie watched him jog to the waiting car and hop over the closed door.

She heard the girl laugh as they drove away and a part of her fell inside.

He jumped into a taxi when he saw me coming, Leaving me alone with a private meaning, He loves me so much my heart is singing.

"Now you're being ridiculous," she mumbled, turning back to the statue and picking up one of the postcards Sonny had left.

"Waving Girl Tours," she read. "Guided tour of the Cockspur Lighthouse and the Martus home on Elba Island. Proceeds benefit the Lighthouse Preservation League. Your donation is appreciated."

There was a number to call to set up the tour and a website for more information. Maggie tucked the card into her backpack, slipped it over her shoulders and headed back to the street.

She remembered seeing a chocolate shop near the souvenir stores, thought she might be able to smell it even.

CHAPTER 25

FLORA
1940

"Miss Flora? Are you all right in there?" A knock at the door, urgent rapping.

"Yes, dear. I'm fine. I'll be right out." I run the water and watch it swirl in the ceramic sink, then pick up my hat and gloves and open the door.

Cow Eyes. She is still my Cow Eyes. I pat her shoulder, and though I have to reach up a little, I manage to feel like the adult in what might have been an awkward situation. People hovering behind her drift off. Perhaps I disappoint them. There is a certain power in having nothing to lose.

I feel their eyes on me. I smile as we take our chairs at the table in Johnny Harris's Restaurant. Cow Eyes is saying something about the weather, then a recipe. My eyes follow an errant ray of sunshine to a wide bank of windows at the rear of the building. As clouds pass, the light fades then returns, making shadows across the floor, across my plate. If I let my gaze go soft, the barbeque short ribs appear to be moving, undulating, like a boat on the water.

We had been coming into Savannah from Elba Island by boat a few times a month, for George to court Miranda and for me to buy books and gaze in the window of Hogan's Dry Goods. When George saw me staring at the mannequin in their window, he told me I should buy a dress like that.

I laughed. "Now what reason would I have to own a dress like that? You don't just buy a dress because you can, George, you buy it to wear. You buy it for an occasion."

"Maybe so," he said, "But if you sit around waiting for the right occasion, by the time you decide you need it, the dress will be long gone."

I could see what George was thinking when he looked at me, that I was different from Miranda—a girl who thought poetry had to rhyme, and that the only good art was expensive and hung on the wall of a gallery. George couldn't speak of goodness and selflessness to a girl who had ten pairs of shoes and changed her clothes for dinner. Not to a girl who didn't know starboard from port and thought the ocean was *too salty*.

86

No, he couldn't speak his mind to his future wife and on some days he could hardly stand to be in the same room with her. He said she was nattering and noisy, like a small caged bird, always flitting, always trying to get somewhere, always pecking.

But he won't back down from his promise. Doc told him it was the right thing to do. For Ma, for him. For me.

Miranda had set her heart on a late Spring wedding, something I was sure she'd read in a book somewhere when she mentioned *seasonal blooms*.

I felt sorry for her, just a little, the fact that she'd lost her mother to some sort of disease even a doctor father couldn't fix. But this same reason also had me envying Miss Miranda, and I immediately crossed myself and said three Hail Mary's for even thinking the thought, much less smiling wistfully.

That night, I went to George's room. I slipped beneath his blanket, curving into his back, stealing his warmth like I used to when we were little and the storms came through. He sighed in his sleep, then a moment later woke and rolled over.

"Flora?" he asked. "What are you—"

"Shh. I need to—talk to you," I said. "I'm worried about Ma. I think she needs help."

He yawned. "Didn't Doc say there would be good days and bad days?"

"Yes, he just didn't say there would be so many bad and so few good."

George looked away.

"Sometimes," Flora whispered. "Sometimes, I wish she was dea—"

"No," he said. "You don't."

But when George looked at me, I could see it in his eyes. He knew I wasn't the timid girl he used to kick under the dinner table. I was a woman, capable of hate.

I said, "I just want things to go back to the way they were, before." I wanted to say—Miranda—instead I said, "Before Ma got sick. If only we could—"

"Flora, it ain't like that. You can't go on saying if all the time. You have to accept what you are given."

"What I am given?" I pushed a finger into his chest. "What does that mean, George? You have been given. You're getting married. You have a job. You have a life. What have I been given? I tend to a mother who doesn't even know who I am most days. I keep her house clean, sew and cook for her—for her and my brother. I have nothing. I'm going nowhere."

I pushed him again, making him look at me. "Don't you see George, there's no more for me." I flung out my arms, the blanket falling away as I said with a mad grin, "This is all I have."

As he stared at me, my grin slid away and tears leaked on the first blink. I wanted to break his heart. The heart he'd promised to Miranda June Handley. George opened his mouth to say something, then closed it and rose from the bed, dropping the covers on his empty side. He pulled on a shirt and walked out of the room.

I watched him leave, knowing exactly how broad his back was beneath the shirt, how hairless his calves, how ticklish his neck and how sad he thought the mockingbird song really was. I knew that the scar from the fall out of the pear tree fifteen years ago looked like a raised letter 'J' on the inside of his left thigh.

I whispered into the empty room, "Don't leave me, George."

The moonfaced woman who'd seated me and Cow Eyes is leaning over our table. Her breath is pungent, as if she's been sampling the garlic that goes into the rib sauce and she smells like she needs a bath.

"How is everything?" she asks.

I let Cow Eyes talk. No one pays me any mind as the chatter in the room has increased in proportion to the number of cocktails served. Folks at Johnny's appear to be more interested in the social hour than the food. These ladies pinned and zipped into their slender outfits have probably never tasted the fatty skin of a spit-broiled pig. They've probably never had sauce under their fingernails so deep it took two days to get out, never stained their grandmother's lace trimmed napkins.

Moonface taps the table, murmurs thanks and turns to leave.

But I stop her. "I'd like something to drink."

Cow Eyes stops chewing. Moonface finds a fake smile somewhere in her repertoire.

"Yes, I believe I'll have a cocktail," I say, as much to her as to myself. Not that I need any convincing. It just sounds more ornery, more old lady if I repeat myself. I'm acting like a precocious child and I don't care at all.

"Join me," I say to Cow Eyes, flouncing my napkin over my lap. "Let's have a drink for George."

The waiter arrives with two glasses of whiskey, ice tinkling, and a short while later removes our plates and brings another round.

I can tell Cow Eyes isn't a drinker. But I give her credit for trying.

"He was almost married once," I tell her.

She raises a brow, but says nothing.

"Her name was Miranda Handley. She was the daughter of the doctor."

George courted Miranda for months after Ma's accident. He called for her in Savannah, then started bringing her to our island. I kept the house running and lit the beacon lamp for him on the nights he didn't make it home. I played nursemaid to Ma, while he took bouquets of flowers from my gardens into town and ate in fancy houses.

"Florence?" Ma called from her bed. "I'm thirsty, dear."

I heard her, but stayed at the window—that same window she had smashed and George had repaired. I watched my brother and Miranda stroll from the porch to the garden.

"Florence?"

"Okay, Ma."

Outside, George kissed Miranda. She curled her skinny hand around George's neck, fingers that might have been curled around my throat.

"And a biscuit," Ma said.

"Biscuit," I whispered. "Yes, Ma'am."

Miranda's tinny laughter taunted me as I ran out of the room, barreled down the stairs, my tears blinding me. I wanted to break something, anything, like the part of me that had been broken. I wanted to go off into the woods like a dying dog, find a deep dank cave and wallow.

I ended up on the porch where our collie, Cornbread was sleeping in a patch of sun. He thumped his tail on the planks, then rose shaking his thick lion mane to join me at the railing. We stood, girl and dog staring out at the sea.

Cornbread barked as a long green ship emerged from the mouth of the river. I pressed myself against the warm wooden rail, jammed it into my hips as I leaned over. I pulled the white cloth from my apron pocket and waved it overhead. I kept waving and waving until my arm turned to lead. Until they sounded their horn. Until someone noticed me.

That night, after supper and dishes and laundry and mending, I closed myself in my room, opened my journal and wrote down the names of the ships that had passed Elba Island that day. I tried to remember the way the men looked, the things they yelled—words of encouragement, prophecies of love, lines of poetry—each one trying to best the other. All drowned out by the sound of the whistle blasts from the Captain.

I ran my hand down the pages capturing the names in my palms, then closed the book and slipped it under the mattress. I blew out the candle and climbed into bed. The sheets were cool on my bare legs, the pillowcase rough and scratchy under my cheek like a half-day beard. I wiggled around, riding the nightdress up to my waist, then sat up and pulled it off, baring myself to the moonlit night. My nipples rose partly from the brush of fabric, partly from the images in my mind and when I scooted down into the featherbed, I felt the familiar itch, the tingle growing from my belly, spreading itself into my groin. I closed my eyes and ran my hands down my flesh. And for a little while I wasn't lonely. I was someone's waving girl.

CHAPTER 26

BOBBIE
1894

Sam rolled toward Bobbie and wrapped his arms around her. "You sure you want to hear the story?" he asked. "Especially today?"

"Why not today?"

"Today is the fifth anniversary of The Great Fire of Savannah," Sam said. "A fire most folks still blame me for."

Bobbie snorted. "How could they blame you for that?"

"They might not say it, but you can see it in their eyes." Sam stroked Bobbie's hair, tucked a lock of it behind her ear. "I can't fault them," he said. "It's not just the lives the fire took, but the city itself. You should have seen Savannah before. We lost more than fifty buildings. In some places that's a whole city."

"But they're rebuilding," Bobbie said.

"It's not the same," Sam sighed, his breath warm on her face. "It's never the same. You can't rebuild a memory."

"Maybe we can make some new ones," Bobbie said, flipping herself to face him then trailing kisses from his cheek to his collarbone.

Later, she whispered, "How did you get out?"

It took Sam so long to answer, she thought he'd fallen asleep, until he said, "To tell you that I have to tell you about the two girls who didn't."

He told Bobbie how he'd lit the window display, how the girls had come in the shop late, alone and in a hurry. One of them was getting married. He found out later it was the doctor's daughter marrying the lighthouse keeper from Cockspur Island. All Sam had known then was that he was behind filling stock. The store was full of crates that shouldn't have been there—like the crack in the window that should have been fixed. A crack in the glass that fed a breeze to lanterns dangling over the Spring display, a flammable combination of straw grass lawn and paper stuffed clothing on wood mannequins.

"The girls were young and pretty," Sam said. "So innocent. We thought we smelled smoke, but we were in the back of the store and didn't see anything. And then the whole front of the store was in flames–part of the roof was hanging down. The girls started screaming. Smoke was everywhere. The crates were falling and the one girl she ran away from us toward the fire. I kept calling to her. It was so hot, with smoke everywhere burning my eyes, my throat.

"You couldn't hear anything but the noise of the fire. Sometimes I can still hear it like rushing water, like the sound when you put a seashell to your ear. I told the girl to stay put while I went for her friend. I had to move slow, too fast I'd feel the hair on my arms singeing off. I found her, crushed under a ceiling beam. I tried to pull her out. I tried."

He held up his partially gloved left hand, his voice a whisper. "I don't know how many burning things I touched. After a while I couldn't feel anything. The other girl wasn't answering me and I was about to give up, just lay down there in the fire, when the back wall of the store fell away. Someone grabbed me, dragged across the street to the square and dropped me on the grass.

"You could hear it. Snapping, creaking, whistling, crackling, roaring. We watched the fire leap rooftop to rooftop. Buildings were falling into themselves and even though everything was going so fast? It wasn't. It was like time had slowed. I could see everything crystal clear. Shopkeepers lining the street with whatever they had managed to save clutched in their arms—a bolt of red silk, boxes of cigars. Two boys duckwalked a heavy gold cash register across the street as windows shattered behind them. Sparks flew from the rooftops. People, hair and clothes were burning. And everywhere, someone was screaming, crying or yelling. But it was like I was far away, like I wasn't part of it at all, like I wasn't supposed to be there."

"Jesus," Bobbie whispered.

Sam said, "Yeah. Where was He?"

CHAPTER 27

FLORA
1940

There are two photographs on the wall near our table: quaint downtown Savannah circa mid-1800's, and a few inches away, the same street in full blaze. A horrible moment captured during the fire of 1889. This wasn't Chicago, but we had our horror stories too.

"You should have seen it after the fire," I say motioning with my glass toward the photographs.

"Did you?" Cow Eyes asks, her eyes a little too wide for curiosity.

I nod.

"Right after?" she asks.

"Yes," I say.

❧ ❧

It was a good day for Ma. I set her up with some recipes in the kitchen while George tinkered with some kind of machine in the barn. Spring was on us. I had to divide my time between gardening and racing Cornbread to the porch to greet ships. My leather journal was beginning to fall apart. I had almost two years of entries, having added evening passages as well as daytime. I made a note to buy another journal on my next trip into Savannah.

George stayed home, leaving twice a day to tend to the lighthouse. It was like old times. We played cards after dinner, said goodnight to Ma and waited for her soft snores before we closed up the house. I checked the lantern by the front door. It was full, with matches nearby.

Upstairs, George paused at his door at the end of the hall. He looked at me for a long time, then said, "Good night. Happy dreams," and stepped inside his room. I heard the knob click back and a moment later, the bolt slid across.

At least he was home.

I must have been in a sound sleep, because when I woke it took me more than the usual few seconds to orient myself. Cornbread wasn't by my bed. I could hear him downstairs, whining and scratching at the front door. I pushed open my window and stuck my head out. It might be Ma. She could have wandered outside, or worse, fallen and hurt herself. Then I smelled smoke.

92

I dressed and ran downstairs to the porch. George was already there. Faint smoke thickened as black filled the sky. Savannah was burning.

I stood on our dock handing things to George in the boat: a rope, a satchel, a basket, a thick wool shirt.

"I'm sure she's fine," I said, my lips forming those simple words as I brushed aside more complicated ones—the kind of words that spawned dark, evil thoughts. I crossed myself and asked God for protection, for hope, for forgiveness.

George wiped his eyes with the back of his dirty hand. I felt a tug on my heart, wondering for the first time if he really loved Miranda Handley.

"Stay here with Ma," he said, pulling in the rope then starting the motor.

He knew me well enough to know I wouldn't and there was no time to argue. I dropped into the dingy and held on as he gunned it.

We stepped off the boat into a ghost town. The few people who walked the streets were like charcoal stick figures drawn on dirty paper. There was an oiliness to the air, the smell of annihilation lingered. The town we'd strolled through last week was barely recognizable as our lovely Savannah. She looked like a war zone. I pulled out my handkerchief and tied it around my face.

George pointed toward Broughton Street and began to walk faster, his shoes tapping a rhythm. Mi-ran-da, Mi-ran-da.

The wind picked up, ash rained down, covering our clothes, sticking to our exposed skin, coating us in white and gray, like proper mourners. As we passed the Square, a charred branch broke off a massive oak and crashed into the fountain. Someone screamed.

Families passed us on the debris-ridden street. They were headed to the port dragging sacks and suitcases behind them. Children with toys in their arms looked with interest at the burned junk in the road, while their teary-eyed mothers sweated under the weight of the extra dresses they wore, dresses that wouldn't fit in the luggage, dresses husbands told them to leave, dresses they had been asked not to buy. The men held their heads high, their crying done. They were ready to face whatever life wanted to throw at them.

George tripped over the broken remains of a baby doll, her plaster face chipped and blackened, a few tufts of burned blond hair remained, one eye was stuck open in a rude wink. He backed away and bumped into an old woman with a soot-smeared face.

"Sorry, ma'am," he said, but the woman didn't reply.

She stumbled off in her single shoe and torn dress calling, "Here, kitty. Here, kitty, kitty."

I grabbed George's arm. We ran.

By the time we reached Chippewa Square, we had followed the path of the fire from Hogan's on Barnard and Broughton Streets to Telfair Square. It had consumed the Odd Fellow's Hall, spared the Telfair Museum of Art, and on Bull Street it took down the steeple of the Independent Presbyterian Church, igniting the wooden fixture and toppling it into the interior burning the structure from the inside out, a testament to the fires of hell.

On Hull Street, The James Blois house was gone—only a chimney remained in a pile of brick rubble. The Handleys lived at the end of the block. There was still hope.

The house looked perfect. Flowers bloomed on the porch in vibrant yellows and purples. The white gingerbread trim bore only a hint of dark smudge. Damp blankets hung from two upstairs windows, talismans that had held the fire at bay, changed the course of destruction.

It was quiet. Too quiet. The cook's sons who were always running in the gardens or swinging in the trees were absent. George opened the gate. We were breathing heavy as we climbed the steps. tears staining stripes down our blackened faces. He reached for the door knocker, lips moving in silent prayer as he rapped.

No one answered. We cleaned up the best we could, brushing off ashes and wiping our faces, then we stepped inside. When the heavy mahogany door closed behind us, there was an instant separation between the horrors out there and this— safety, comfort, wealth.

The elegant room reeked with prestige and privilege, opulence and happiness. It was difficult to believe anything disastrous could happen between these walls.

"Miranda? Doc?" George's voice sounded wrong, like whistling in church.

I followed him into the parlor, ran my fingers across the lid of the piano. I imagined this house during the war, Yankee soldiers entering the mansion, seeing gold, satin and velvet, after months of dirt, forest and trail. They would have smelled delicate flowers curving from crystal vases instead of sweat and gunpowder. They would have been eating hot tea and lemon cake, instead of burned squirrel and moldy venison jerky. Who could blame them for wanting Savannah for themselves?

When I looked around the Handley's living room, with its velvet drapes, brocade chairs, and marble-topped tables, I knew my brother could never be comfortable here. This was as foreign to him as Paris.

We turned at the sound of footsteps in the hall, a large black woman in a white apron and cap passed. George called, "Miss Treasie!"

The maid stopped in the doorway, peered into the room, dabbing her red-rimmed eyes. She started to smile until George said, "Miss Treasie? Where's Miranda?"

The maid dropped her eyes to the floor and backed away stuttering, "Oh, Mister George. Let me find Doc Handley for you, just wait here."

George started to say something else, then must have realized as I did that there was only one reason Treasie would need to get Doc and not Miranda.

"No. God, no." His knees buckled. George fell onto the piano bench, his elbow smashing the keys making a discordant sound that echoed in the empty room.

I wanted to comfort him, to say that I was sorry, but I'd be lying. I was afraid the truth would come out of my mouth, that I would say, "See, this is how I've been feeling. Now your life is as bad as mine." So I didn't say anything. I just sat there beside my mourning brother, with a heart as smoky and troubled as a burned city. And when he reached out his hand, I took it.

CHAPTER 28

MAGGIE
2011

Maggie nodded to the people on the street, the tourists with their cameras and worn copies of *The Garden of Good and Evil*. She'd seen the touring van packed with movie buffs headed to Bonaventure Cemetery.

She paused under the burgundy awning of a riverfront store. Out of the sun, the temperature dropped a few degrees, yet still there was no breeze. Inside the store, Savannah t-shirts were draped over a bentwood rocker, packages of tea and cornbread were positioned near stacks of coffee table books, one in particular caught her eye: *Lighthouses of the East Coast*.

Maggie pulled open the door, felt the cooler air within. The bell jangled against the glass and someone called, "Welcome."

It had been years since she'd been in a bookstore like this. She stopped reading soon after her mother died. It started with her giving up reading love stories, until she figured out they were all love stories. When Maggie and David were dating and he'd wanted to spend a Sunday afternoon curled up by the fire reading the classics, she'd begged off telling him she preferred non-fiction, loved how it made sense to her, felt more real. And besides, it was more educational.

He tried to woo her back to fiction by reading to her in bed. He bought her books on CD for her car, volumes of beautiful poetry every Valentine's Day, but she held her ground, choosing scientists, politicians, theoreticists and technical photography manuals over adventure, thrills and romance. No loved ones died in her books. No one's heart was ever broken. If anything was lost, no one stopped until it was found.

Maggie gave a wide berth to the romance books on the circular racks, with their gorgeous busty women and handsome muscular men, another testament to unreality. She picked up the lighthouse book, able to appreciate the photography, able to see the architectural shots for what they were. Not simply a structure, but a story told in brick and stone and glass. She noted the photo credits and each caption. One had a quote from the architectural artist, John Ruskin, claiming the ". . . superfluity of ornament as beauty and its total absence as simplicity."

The buildings charmed her, the lighthouse towers were hauntingly beautiful, but it was the old black and white portraits in the book that tugged at her. She turned each page slowly, allowing herself to fall into the eyes of the lighthouse keepers, of the families and friends. For the first time, Maggie saw more than shapes and angles, more than lighting and background and proper image development. She saw what was happening outside the frame. She heard the wind on the island, the gulls in the sky, the waves crashing against the rocks and the people shouting. She could smell the salty sea air, taste the brackish water, feel shells crushing underfoot.

Why is the word pretty so underrated?...Cry pretty, pretty, pretty and you'll be able Very soon not even to cry pretty. And so to be delivered entirely from humanity. This is the prettiest of all . . .

She turned to a picture of Florence Martus, Savannah's famous Waving Girl. The statue from the riverfront came to life as a delicate long-haired woman whose skirts billowed behind her as she stood on the porch of her house on the hill waving a large cloth. Something broke inside Maggie.

She saw behind the photograph. She saw the whole story, a secret tale of a young misunderstood girl, a girl who was drowning on dry land.

Maggie turned the pages and read about Flora, as she was called, and her brother George, of the storms they and their family survived, of the people they had rescued. How did this wisp of a woman become a maritime legend?

There were copies of letters from sailors all over the world, calling her their waving girl and thanking her for always being there, for giving them hope. There was a list of the gifts she'd received in the forty-four years she'd greeted ships, from money and silver teapots to llamas and exotic plants.

Maggie picked up another book, one about the women of Savannah. She ran her finger down the index until she found The Waving Girl. There was a photograph of Flora and George on Flora's seventieth birthday, when she'd been honored by the mayor and the city of Savannah with a parade and a grand celebration at Fort Pulaski.

Maggie turned the page and read the accompanying newspaper article from New York. The reporter said she'd met Flora years earlier at the Desoto Hotel and had never forgotten her. Maggie looked closer at the photograph of The Waving Girl, the mayor and the reporter. She'd seen the picture somewhere before.

She turned back to the beginning of the article and read the byline: Bobbie Denton. Her great-grandmother.

CHAPTER 29

BOBBIE
1894

The telegram from the Sun had been slipped under her door before she rose. Bobbie dressed carefully, affecting a casual bicycle rider's glibness with the serious undertones of New York reporter. She wouldn't be wearing the hobble skirt, not on a riverfront construction site.

Harry had wired money and details. Bobbie loved her editor. Sometimes it seemed like he was the only one on her side. Most of the men at the paper openly resented her position. What did it matter that she was a woman? No one could do what she did better—or would want to.

Pausing at the top of the stone steps leading down to River Street, the waterfront was laid out before her; ships pulling in, their decks crowded with men hauling ropes, rolling barrels, moving crates, preparing to load carriages and wagons. On the docks, mothers pushed buggies stuffed equally with babies and produce, the latter purchased from the stalls of an open air market. The sound of commerce rang in the air, mixed with shouts from the construction site below. Savannah was making her comeback and with William G. Preston at the helm, she was destined for beauty. Bobbie had seen the courthouse he'd designed and his award-winning cotton exchange building. She was thinking Greek revival when she approached his current site, a mere hole in the ground with a bunch of men gathered around unfurled blueprints, arguing.

"Hey, watch it!"

Bobbie stopped short sidestepping the hole she'd almost fallen in. She nodded to the guy who'd shouted the warning. "Thanks," she said.

At the sound of her voice, the men looked up. Bobbie glanced at their feet, dismissing all of them but the blocky guy in the brogues.

"William Preston?" She stepped forward extending her hand. "Bobbie Denton from the New York Sun."

He stared at her, taking in the cap and trousers, the sensible shoes, the pad and pencil. "Excuse me, gentlemen. I believe you can carry on without me for a few moments while I have a chat with the lady."

He slid a brick onto the edge of the blueprints he'd been holding flat then stepped forward and took her hand. "Call me Preston. So, you're the Bobbie in my suite."

The men chuckled.

Bobbie dropped her hand quickly. "In one of your suites, yes sir. I do apologize for—"

Preston started walking. "No need," he said as she caught up. "Did wonders for my reputation." He grinned.

Bobbie stopped, anger crossing her face, but when the man kept walking she raced to catch up, saying, "That aside, Mr. Preston, could we talk about your vision for Savannah?"

"We could," he said. "If you'll join me for dinner."

"Dinner?" she asked. "But I thought this was the interview?"

"Consider this the opening act," he said. "Come on, I'd like to show you something."

Bobbie was already thinking about how she'd write a description of the man, the way he motioned when he spoke as if he were on stage and everything he said was incredibly important. More than important, necessary. She matched her stride to Preston's and flipped open her notebook, barely able to keep up with his architectural tour. She didn't know how she'd missed the cobblestone streets, the bricked archways, the terra cotta towers, sculpted finials and decorative cast-iron lintels.

By the time they wound back through the city to the waterfront she had seven pages of notes about everything other than Preston. The man loved Savannah. Even better, he respected the city.

"It's not enough for me to tell you how I see Savannah," he said, pausing on the corner as the trolley passed. "You must see her through your eyes. Someone once said, 'Everyone finds their heart in Savannah, or loses a piece of it.'"

"That's very poetic," Bobbie said.

"Architecture is poetry. My kind of poetry. Have you read what John Ruskin said?"

Bobbie shook her head.

"I'll paraphrase," Preston said. "'In the wild struggle after novelty, the fantastic is mistaken for the graceful, the complicated for the imposing, superfluity of ornament for beauty and its total absence for simplicity.'"

"That's beautiful," Bobbie said.

They walked in silence for a few moments. "But what does that mean?" Bobbie asked.

Preston glanced at her, a twinkle in his blue eyes, then shrugged. "You'll have to think about that."

They parted ways at Bay Street, with Preston returning to his men on the job site and Bobbie taking the long way to the DeSoto. She'd promised to join him for dinner when he told her she'd be the fourth at his table. A friend and his sister would be joining them.

"On the record, right?" she called after him. Preston waved over his head and kept going. Bobbie took that as a yes.

As she strolled through the entrance of the DeSoto she did the thing she hadn't allowed herself the day before. She paused and stared at every architectural element, ceiling to floor, window to doorway trying to see it through Preston's eyes. It gave her a headache. As far as she was concerned buildings like this were all for show, and fancy houses? They were just another place to run away from.

She headed up to her suite, determined to write her column and find some way to mention the architect's poetic nature while avoiding the words fanciful, ornamental or superficial.

In the bedroom, an envelope was propped against the pillow, reminding Bobbie of one she'd left on a pink coverlet in an attic room in Ohio. She picked up the envelope, felt the weight of it then ran her fingers over the words To Bobbie, wondering if bad news was heavier than good. She carried it to the sitting room, propped it up on the bar and poured herself a drink.

Three hours later, she pushed back from the desk, rolled and lit a cigarette then slit open the envelope. His handwriting was neater than she'd expected, lending a false sense of education or care. She could hear Sam's voice in her ear as she read.

"I need to see you again. Tonight. Meet me by the pool. Ten o'clock."

Bobbie smiled. She checked the clock then gathered the pages she needed to send to Harry.

A telegram was waiting for her at the front desk.

"It just came," the clerk said. "Maybe five minutes ago."

Bobbie exchanged her papers for the telegram. "I need to send these to New York. Can you do that?"

"Certainly, Miss Denton."

Bobbie fingered the telegram, glanced around for a quiet place to open it.

"Might I suggest the solarium?" The clerk said, gesturing to a sign on the far wall with an arrow leading to a curved stairway.

She'd never been in a solarium before. It sounded so—scientific, as if she was part of an experiment. In fact, the way the glass walls rose curving into the ceiling overhead she was reminded of transparent garden domes used to protect shoots of delicate flowers and plants.

The room was split in half by a massive freestanding stone fireplace with an impressive mantle. Someone had thought to leave a gap in the stone, a portal to the glass-walled half of the room, so the effect was of a cozy cave on one side and a goldfish bowl on the other.

Bobbie sat on a padded bench by the fireplace and opened the telegram.

Need you back now. Most important. Will explain. Harry.

She thought she was alone in the space until she heard a rustle and a sigh from the glass side of the room. She hesitated before she stepped around the corner, remembering another time she thought she'd been alone.

❧ ❧

It was the winter she'd turned twelve and her new foster father was away again. Her foster mother, Pamela, had sent her to school that morning with sniffles and a warm forehead, saying she'd be fine. By noon, the fever rose until even the teacher could see "Bobbie," who went by Elizabeth at the time, needed to be at home, in bed.

Coming through the front door hours earlier than normal, Bobbie expected to be alone. Pamela volunteered at church and today was altar cleaning day. Bobbie hung her jacket on the coat rack in the hall and started upstairs when she heard laughter.

In the living room, Pamela was serving coffee to a slick-haired man in a checked suit. She wore an unusual amount of make-up and a dress Bobbie had never seen before. The man's tie hung loose around his neck and where his shirt was unbuttoned dark curly hairs sprung out.

Bobbie thought about sneaking back outside and re-entering, this time with a cough and a door slam. Instead she sneezed.

Pamela spun around. Her face registered surprise, anger, disappointment. The man ran a hand through his hair, said something under his breath, then picked up his coffee cup and eyed Bobbie over the rim.

Pamela recovered quickly, replacing the silver pot on the tray then rushing to Bobbie, pushing her toward the hall, sputtering, "Sweetheart. It's early. What are you doing home?"

"I'm sick," Bobbie said. "My teacher told me to go home."

"Sick? Then you should be up in bed. Go on."

The firm hand on Bobbie's back was more demanding than encouraging. As she climbed the stairs she heard the man say, "Looks like playtime is over. I best be on my way."

"Oh Arnold, do you have to go?"

Bobbie hardly recognized her foster mother's voice. It was the kind of voice you used when talking to kittens or cooing at babies, a tiny little girl voice, innocent and cloying.

The next day, Bobbie asked Pamela about the man in the living room.

"He's a book salesman. No one you need to tell your fa—Jim about."

A few days later, Bobbie found the salesman's books shoved in the back of the hall closet. She took two of them with her when she ran away; *How to Grow a Marigold* and *The Ways of a Man in The Wilderness.*

❧ ❧

Wedged between a tall ficus plant and a wide wicker chair, Bobbie peeked around the fireplace. A woman in a dark dress approached the wall of glass.

101

She reached out testing it, as if it might be hot to the touch, then stepped closer, widening her arms and flattening her palms against the smooth surface. Bobbie wondered if it felt like the retained heat of a boulder in August, the kind she'd warmed herself on after a chilly river swim.

She imagined the heat running from the woman's palms to her elbows to her shoulders then down her back and around, until her torso tingled. As if she heard Bobbie's thoughts, the woman leaned into the glass, pressing herself to it like a tree frog on a willow.

Someone entered the room. Bobbie slipped behind the ficus as a tall man appeared in the shadows.

"I've always wanted to do that," he said.

The woman jerked back from the window as the man stepped forward. He carried his hat under his arm, a tall shiny helmet with a feather, the uniform of an officer of the Georgia Hussars. He set it on a side table. "The first time I saw that wall," he said. "I wondered, if it would be hot or merely warm to the touch? I wondered how the glass would feel under my hands, against my skin in the heat of the day? I thought it was silly—but now, observing you standing there? I wish I'd taken that opportunity."

"I've heard it told," the woman said with a smile in her voice, "that memories of things you could have done are something you should set store to, memories of things you have done are something you should tell others."

The expression on the officer's face as he stepped into the dying light mirrored Bobbie's thoughts. It was unusual to find a woman who spoke her mind, odder still to find her alone in The DeSoto's solarium spread-eagled against a glass wall.

"Do I know you?" he asked.

She turned back to the glass wall, stretched out her left arm then flattened the palm on the surface. "I don't know how you could."

The officer put his palm on the glass near hers.

As the sun made its final blaze across the evening sky, a beam of light shone through the glass illuminating their hands. The man's splayed fingers dwarfed the woman's. More than grasping appendages, they were sensors to the world– a way to experience life, clapping in joy, smacking in anger, flailing in distress, warding off evil. They blessed, cursed, cradled, killed, praised and loved.

The woman arched her fingers once then laid her hands flat.

The officer slid his hand over the glass until it touched hers. "Captain Adam Everhart of the Georgia Hussars. At your service, Miss."

She did not look at Everhart but stared at the setting sun. "Flora Martus of Elba Island, at your service."

The sun made its final drop and as the room went dark Everhart stepped away from the glass, Flora's hand in his. He kissed it then placed it gently on his arm escorting her from the solarium.

When she was certain she was alone, Bobbie stepped around the fireplace. Moon and stars had taken over the sun's job of lighting the open room. She approached the glass wall, feeling Flora's presence. The scent of lavender lingered, as if she had left a piece of herself. Bobbie stared at the handprints, two slender palms with long, narrow fingers evenly spaced. She placed her hands on the glass matching finger to finger and leaned in.

CHAPTER 30

MAGGIE
2011

At The Flannery House, a late dinner was being served on the patio. Moonlight and candles, gardenia scented air, it was beautiful. Even the traffic on the street seemed to have lulled for the moment. Maggie poked at the food on her plate, trying to be polite, but for the first time since she'd arrived in Savannah, she had no stomach for food.

She wanted to blame it on the moon, on the tidal pull, on anything but her emotions. That was a weakness. She had chosen to never fall in love because that was what it did to a person, it weakened them. It lessened them. It made them vulnerable. She hated that she could hardly remember David in that soft, caring way, but could not stop thinking of Sonny, a man she hardly knew. It felt so wrong, and yet, part of it? So incredibly right.

She reached for the wine and filled her glass, turning away when the honeymooning couple on the wooden swing kissed. Forget books and movies. It was all right here in front of here. Unavoidable.

She thought about the pictures she had seen in the bookstore, the portraits of the couples living on islands, maintaining lighthouses, saving people. What had she ever done that was slightly important? How did her life matter? What was she supposed to do next?

In the quiet room of the B&B, under the starched sheets and heavy cotton matelassé, Maggie fidgeted with the long nightgown, her legs tangled, the fabric scratchy. Finally she sat up, throwing off the covers and pulling the gown over her head, dropping it to the floor. She snuggled back into the big bed, punching the pillows into shape, trying to not think about how the cool sheets felt on her hot skin, trying to not think about Sonny, about another life, about possibilities she had never thought of, like sailing around the world.

"You are an idiot," she told herself, reaching for her mother's book of poems. She thumbed the edge, letting the pages fall like an oracle. She stuck her finger in at random, opened to the chosen page and read:

I do not ask for anything, I do not speak, I do not question and I do not seek. I used to in the day when I was weak. Now I am strong and lapped in sorrow, as in a coat of magic mail and borrow from Time today, and care not for tomorrow.

Maggie closed the book and propped it against the empty pillow, drawing up the covers as if she were putting a baby to sleep.

In the morning, Maggie felt drained, as if the sobbing, tossing and turning had taken all her strength, depleted some major organs and left her with an overactive brain and an overly sentimental heart.

She looked at herself in the mirror, puffy, bloated, her thin figure filled out in all the wrong places. The recent sweets addiction made an obvious appearance on her hips and thighs.

"Who cares? It's not like anyone is seeing me naked," she said, cinching her robe. "Great. Now I'm talking to myself."

She poured a cup of coffee, took it to the veranda and phoned Lisa.

"What would you think," Maggie said, "If *hypothetically*, you believed your husband had been keeping secrets from you?"

"Hypothetically?" Lisa asked.

"Yes," Maggie said.

"Well, I'd hypothetically kick his ass."

"Yeah, right." Maggie laughed.

"I mean it," Lisa said. "There is one thing I can't stand and that's a secret. Did you know that Melanie said she knew that Jackie was pregnant months before she told the rest of us? I mean, what's the point of that secret? It wasn't like she was still drinking and damn she put on that baby weight fast. Anyone could see, even if she didn't tell the rest of us—"

Maggie sighed. "Remind me to never ask you to keep a secret."

"Oh honey," Lisa said. "I can keep a secret. I just don't like when the secret is kept from me."

"I know what you mean," Maggie said softly.

"What's that?" Lisa asked.

"Nothing. Anyway, about this hypothetical situation, if you knew a little bit of the secret, what would you do? Like, say, Todd had a secret bank account in Switzerland—"

"Todd has a secret bank account in Switzerland?" Lisa's voice raised an octave.

"No," Maggie said. "I'm just saying, what if it was something like that—even if he had a loan with some bank in Kentucky, I don't know."

"Well, honey, if I had that sort of information," Lisa said. "I'd follow it up, and ask him about it when I was good and armed."

Maggie thought she wouldn't be asking David *anything* any time soon.

"Why all these hypothetical questions, Mags?" Lisa asked. "Does this have anything to do with David?"

"No," Maggie said quickly. "I was just reading a book and this girl, she—"

"Crap. Hang on," Lisa said. "I've got another call coming in."

Lisa clicked over to the other line, giving Maggie a few minutes to perfect her lie. But it turned out unnecessary as Lisa clicked back. "Sorry, Hon. Gotta go. That's the school. Jimmy just puked all over some girl in the lunchroom. Apparently he has a problem with school bologna."

"I know how that is," Maggie said.

Lisa laughed. "You go girl and have fun today—hypothetically. Seriously, I'm here if you need me, you know that, right?"

"I know," Maggie said. "Thanks."

CHAPTER 31

BOBBIE
1894

Bobbie stood in the doorway to the restaurant. She had changed into the hobble skirt and pinned her hair back, making a genuine attempt to be a girl — a woman. She took in the room, the centerpieces of fresh flowers on every table, the candelabra and white tablecloths. She was sure she'd spill something.

Her dinner companion was easy to find. William G. Preston was the kind of man who drew attention wherever he went. Bobbie skimmed the tables until she saw Preston and a man head to head in an animated discussion, apparently infused by the contents of now empty cocktail glasses. Bobbie took baby steps across the room, her chin held high imitating the ladies she passed.

"Gentlemen?"

Preston jumped up, almost knocking Bobbie over. "Miss Denton. Allow me."

He scurried around to pull out her chair, holding it as she maneuvered the bustle and herself up to the table. Bobbie had a chance to appraise the other man who'd been slower to rise as Preston fussed and chattered.

He was older than her, maybe by ten years, though it was hard to tell, as he had the weathered, tanned skin of a fisherman or a farmer. She glanced at his hands. They were large and capable, the hands of a working man. He had a droopy mustache that hid most of his lips but she could see he had a generous mouth, and knew before he spoke that his voice would be deep, in the way she found charming.

Preston found his chair, but hovered before he sat. "Miss Denton, this is my friend, George Martus. He's been helping me procure workers for the building."

"Pleased to meet you," Bobbie said.

"And you, Ma'am." Still standing, George offered his hand then went to tip his hat, but realizing he wasn't wearing one he made a series of grand gestures instead, something foreigners do.

Preston poured Bobbie a whiskey. Then another. A waiter appeared with the menu.

"Was there to be a fourth, this evening?" Bobbie asked glancing at the empty seat.

George and Preston looked at each other.

"Oh, yes," Preston said as if he had just remembered. "George's sister is in town. We believe she may have been delayed. Isn't that right, George?"

"Delayed? Right. Most likely delayed." He held his empty glass out to Preston.

Bobbie saw the look that passed between them. She was about to say something, hating when she was being sold a line, but was distracted by the arrival of the officer from the solarium. He crossed the dining room to join two similarly dressed Hussars seated near the window, men who were already well into their meals and wine.

"There's Flora," George said, tipping his chin toward the entry.

Flora Martus was the woman from the solarium. Bobbie tried not to stare.

As she approached, Flora made a point to look not at the officers, only at George.

"I am sorry," she said in a tiny voice that was sweet sincere and commanding, all at once, as the best Southern women have mastered. "I don't know what happened. Have you ever had time get away from you? As if you—thank you Preston," she smiled as he helped her into her chair. George barely raised himself from his seat before settling in again.

"As if you what?" Bobbie asked.

"What?" Flora blinked. "Oh. As if you were so insignificant that your space in time didn't matter. As if no one knew you—"

"—were even there." Bobbie finished the words with her.

Flora laughed. "Exactly."

George shook his head, bumped Preston's arm. "Ain't them two peas in a pod?"

Preston laughed. "Quite." He motioned to the waiter for another round.

Flora introduced herself to Bobbie, placed her order with the waiter and sank back into her chair, as obviously uncomfortable in the bustle getup as Bobbie was. They scratched their cinched waists and tugged at the tight necklines. Bobbie caught Flora glancing over at the Hussars table, but was unsure how to approach the subject. What was she supposed to say? *I was spying on you in the solarium*?

"You're not from around here," Flora said.

"No," Bobbie said.

"And you're traveling alone?"

"I'm a reporter for The New York Sun. I often travel alone. Sometimes it's what you have to do to find the story." Bobbie didn't know why she said that.

Flora caught Bobbie's eye. "Interesting. So did you find one here?"

"Perhaps," Bobbie said finishing her whiskey as she looked across the room at the Hussars table then back to Preston and George who had lapsed into a construction discussion.

Someone in the dining room might have thought the two women knew each other better, that they were friends, maybe even related. There was never a lull in the conversation, or a moment of uncomfortable silence. Bobbie had finally found a woman on her own level. Flora was witty and sharp, well-read and intelligent. She laughed in all the right places and the way she laid her light fingers on Bobbie's arm was a welcome touch. Perhaps too welcome, as she began to return the gesture, and eventually left her hand there as if it was the most natural thing in the world, as if nothing was wrong with holding another woman's hand at a table in the middle of the grandest hotel in the south.

After the meal and a few more rounds of drinks Bobbie asked Preston to talk about his work. She went through the usual paces, but couldn't help feeling the interview had fallen flat. Something was missing. Preston was the mediocre novel on the bedside table that she wanted to shove onto the floor to make room for the newcomer, the page turner, Miss Flora Martus.

When the Hussars left their table everyone noticed. It was hard not to, between the raucous shouts and backslapping, they had been the current that flowed through the room. Now the only noise heard over hushed dinner conversations was the jangling of their swords as they passed Preston's table. They tipped their heads to Flora and Bobbie. "Evenin' Miss. Evenin' Miss."

A moment later Flora excused herself saying she needed some air. As she walked through the dining room, some of the diners nodded, others pointed. The women gave her a wide berth, crossing their legs and smoking their Sweet Caporals, following her with their eyes then rolling them.

Bobbie said, "What was it you said you did for a living, Mr. Martus?"

George laughed. "Nothing. Well, that's not entirely true. I do have to climb some stairs."

Preston said, "George tends the Cockspur Light in the channel, off Elba Island."

"And Flora?" Bobbie asked. "What does she do?"

"She's my sister," George said, setting the glass on the table, ice clinking. "That's what she does."

CHAPTER 32

MAGGIE
2011

Maggie pulled Charles' car into the parking lot of The Blue Cove Marina, at the tip of The Isle of Hope. When she'd asked the chef earlier about the car rental place in Savannah he'd tossed her his keys saying, "Don't lose those and leave me enough gas to get home tonight." He wouldn't take no for an answer and made sure she was clear on directions before she left.

The marina consisted of a small shop, restroom and shower building and a few service areas for refueling and repairs. Most of the activity seemed to happening past the manned gates. There were two short docks peppered with fishing boats, day cruisers and glittery speedboats. At least seven long docks housed larger boats—yachts, houseboats, multi-masted sailboats, mega-yachts, floating mansions. Remembering Owl Man's story, Maggie concentrated on the deep-water boats—twenty on each side, plus the scattered dozen or so moored off the docks. She figured she could pass over the sailboats. David wasn't the sailing type–or was he? This wasn't going to be easy, especially when she had no clue what she was looking for.

The first hour, she sipped coffee and tried to remember all the detective novels she'd read. She imagined herself slamming the gatekeeper up against the wall of his little tin shack, grabbing him by the collar and squeezing until he gave up the goods.

Gave up the goods? Maggie grimaced. "Helluva Private Eye I'd make," she grumbled, reaching for her bag.

The Hasselblad felt like a talisman in her hand, reminding her of better days. Days when she'd been a happily married woman with a job, a loyal husband and a house in the suburbs. She hefted the camera, wondering what would happen if she tied the damn thing to her ankle and jumped off the dock. Instead, she set it on the seat and opened the bakery bag.

When the donuts and coffee were gone, Maggie was ready. She had a plan. Watching the guard and the visitors through the powerful telephoto lens, she'd been able to discern a pattern. After the guard let you through the gate, you were free to wander from dock to dock, and in some cases from boat to boat, as she'd watched some bathing suit clad babes do. Some folks showed an ID badge, some leaned in and said something, others–the deepest tanned, most scruffy individuals—just waved or nodded in the guard's direction.

She had hoped to squeeze in behind a group, or slip past a distracted guard but the flow of boaters had dwindled. It was starting to look like it wasn't going to happen, until a red SUV pulled into the lot.

Six women climbed out, complaining of the heat and the need for another glass of wine. Singing Happy Birthday and calling out toasts, they unloaded coolers, beach bags, and a case of wine.

Maggie pulled her floppy hat down and pushed on the new, mirrored sunglasses. She followed the ladies to the gatehouse, walking close but maintaining her distance with a phone jammed against her ear, two hands fiddling in her bag. Anyone watching would have thought she was part of the group, a straggler, maybe one who didn't like the sun.

While the ladies joked and flirted with the guard, Maggie slipped through the gate and strode down the slatted walk, trying to look like she knew where she was going. She popped the lens cap off the Hasselblad and lifted the viewfinder to her eye, snapping away, getting the names of the boats, focusing her efforts on those that seemed abandoned.

Maggie focused on the bobbing line of boats, big and small, clean and dirty. She saw them in sepia—just a flash—hurricane-damaged pier, boats smashed, masts broken and dangling, some on shore, some half submersed, others broken and chewed like a stick in the jaws of a large dog.

There was something true in sepia. Your eye couldn't be fooled by high colors or special effects. It wasn't a slap like highly contrasted black and whites, but a smudge, a soft reality of good and bad. In sepia, blood was not as disgusting, tears looked the same, poor became beautiful in a gaunt majestic way and despair seemed more honest than glory. She had learned early that she was blessed with an eye that saw the end result, the potential of what would stamp the paper, while other photographers pointed, shot frames beyond measure and hoped.

She was happiest in the darkroom, the acrid scent of chemicals enveloping her as she swished prints from tray to tray, timing each movement. She loved watching images unfold, hanging the wet paper on the line, returning later to find magic printed and curling at the edges.

Out in the world nothing was as controlled, nothing as predictable, nothing as simple.

⚜ ⚜

Maggie walked to the end of a pier. She shot the wooden and inflatable dinghies, the pelican roosting on a buoy. The water sloshed around the pilings, rocking the boats into their bumpers. It was a hypnotic noise accented by the odors of rotting wood, algae and diesel fuel.

I have plunged in a poem of the sea Alight with stars at first and growing milky It ate the pretty blues and greens as I went down . . . There like a piece of flotsam torn about and stained, a pensive corpse came floating to my side . . .

Maggie backed away from the edge and drew her attention back to the boats docked around her. She dismissed most of them for their size or their sails, but one caught her eye. A bird had built its nest in the aft section on a coil of mildewed rope. The tarp stretched across the forward section was sun-bleached and ripped at the seams. Maggie glanced at the inscription, *Rose Shutup N Fish*. Maggie wondered if Rose had decided to shut up Mr. Rose permanently and now no one was going fishing.

She adjusted the range on the telephoto lens and shot the sterns of the money pits anchored out in the cove. From *Reel Love* to *South Pause* to *My Mistress*, they just got bigger and bigger. Maggie didn't see the allure. Standing on the dock was enough motion for her. She started toward the next row of boats, but stopped when she saw Sonny and the girl from the blue Mustang standing on the back of a boat called, *Merrily, merrily* . . . . Music thumped from the party boat. People hung off the railings on all three levels.

She was close enough to hear Sonny say, "I don't know, Susie. I really shouldn't."

"C'mon," the girl teased. "You want it. No one will ever know, I promise." She held a plate and a forkful of something she was trying to feed him.

Another boat approached and tied on, joining the two boats like Siamese yacht twins, doubling the party size. Maggie was sure no one would notice her — until Sonny turned his head and locked eyes.

He hesitated, then called, "Hey!"

Shit. Maggie spun around, tried to look interested in her camera, then whipped out her phone and flipped it open, as if she'd just gotten an important call.

She clapped the receiver to her ear and walked quickly toward the exit. From the corner of her eye she saw the girl grab Sonny's arm.

He yelled again, "Hey! Maggie!"

But Maggie pushed through the gate and kept walking. Halfway to the car, she glanced back, to see the girl throw a protective arm around Sonny guiding him into the boat interior, eyeing Maggie the whole time.

"So much for inconspicuous," Maggie mumbled.

CHAPTER 33

FLORA
1940

Johnny Harris's Restaurant is clearing out. It's time for people to go back to work, back to their lives. They pass our table, a few recognizing me, or maybe just commenting about the old broad drinking whiskey. I don't care.

There are so many ways to tell a story. There's the truth, and there's all those other ways. I think I need to tell Cow Eyes a true story. I think I owe it to George. There's a story I never get to finish, a story that should be told. But not here.

❧ ❧

I let her think it's her idea to come to the water. I'm not sure whose idea it is to take the whiskey bottle. There's a bare spot around the actual decision. There's a bare spot around a few other moments of my day, like a trench dug around a fortress, there's a channel of nothing before my mind leaps to the one big thing I can't forget. George is dead.

My feet are getting wet, but I don't move them. I've wandered away from the place Cow Eyes chose, a safe place high up on the beach. She's fallen asleep there, flat on her back, arms splayed like a snow angel. I believe I should tuck her skirt around her legs, but it's pretty the way the wind draws the blue fabric up then whips it back down, its timing similar to the slap and crash of the breakers against the dilapidated pier to my right. This is a nice place. Cow Eyes was right.

She reminded me a bit of myself, on the way down here to the water. The way she held my elbow and brushed the sand smooth before we collapsed on it. Like I was her mother and she was supposed to take care of me. That's what daughters do, don't they?

That was what I used to do with Ma, especially toward the end.

CHAPTER 34

BOBBIE
1894

In the kitchen with the hotel workers, Bobbie sat on Sam's lap, the laces of her dress loosened, shoes flung under the table. She asked about Flora Martus.

"*Everyone* knows The Waving Girl," they said. "She's famous."

"The Waving Girl?" Bobbie looked at Sam.

He picked up one of the white cloth napkins and fluttered it, like a miniature matador. "She waves to the ships from her porch on the island, uses a lantern at night. Been doing it for about seven years now."

"Why would she do that?" Bobbie asked.

"For love," the chambermaid said, her eyes glazing over.

No words were spoken as glasses were raised.

A moment later, the housekeeper said, "I met John Martus, their father, after the hurricane of 1881 when I went to the fort to help clean up. That was a bad one. Now *there's* a story for you." She pointed to Bobbie.

One of the workers joined in, "It was a shame when the other Martus boy died of the fever. "

"Worse," another added, "when one of the sisters ran off with that salesman."

It was like something from a bad musical as each person added something else about George, the grumpy lighthouse keeper, and Flora his crazy sister who waved at ships. Bobbie fully expected the bellhop to come crashing through the swinging doors and burst into song, the chambermaids stripping their aprons hopping on the table and joining in.

Someone said, "George is the last male Martus, and it looks like this is the end of the line, what with his situation."

The ladies tittered. They might have said more if Sam hadn't changed the subject and brought up llamas.

"I heard it was an alpaca. It's a regular zoo over there with all those exotic gifts from sailors."

The housekeeper tossed a stubby pencil to Bobbie. "You might want to write down something about her saving those two men."

Bobbie caught the pencil. "She saved two men?"

"At least." "Is that right?" Bobbie took the napkin from Sam, leaned in and said, "Start from the beginning."

The sun sneaking through the gap in the curtained window was cruel and blinding. Bobbie rolled over. Sam snored lightly, his face soft, eyes moving beneath the lids. She reached out to touch him, then afraid she'd wake him and ruin the moment, Bobbie pulled her hand back, drew it under the sheet and hugged it to her chest.

Sam grumbled, "A man can't sleep when he's being stared at."

Bobbie kissed him, softly with the hint of something more.

For the first time in a long time, she knew exactly what she needed. She laid her hand on his cheek and said, "Come with me. Come to New York."

CHAPTER 35

FLORA
1940

I settle into the sand next to Cow Eyes and rest my head on her warm dry arm. She doesn't move, doesn't pull away, so I go on with my story.

It was 1909. My older sister Mary was pregnant again and this time the baby didn't want to ease her way into the world. This one, unlike her big brother Tommy, wanted to fight the whole way. I called it the devil baby. But I only said this to George when we were home playing cards or walking the oyster bed island or climbing the stairs to the lighthouse.

Ma was coming to stay with us on Elba Island. Just our mother without her nurse. She had spent the last year living in town with Mary, Thomas and little Tommy, but with the difficult pregnancy and Thomas off on another mission trip Mary asked if we could take Ma for a little while. "Just until Thomas gets back, or the baby comes," Mary said.

"Of course," I told Mary, hating the look she gave me and hating even more the fake smile I returned.

I had a few days to prepare, but was still nervous to have Ma under the same roof again. I stood in her room. The bed was neatly made, embroidered pillows arranged just so. I had tucked lavender sachets in the dresser drawers and there wasn't a glass vase in sight.

My mother Cecelia was seventy-nine years old. She'd never known hunger and her pain had been limited to outliving a child, a husband, herself. She was not a brave woman, hardheaded perhaps, but only when necessary. Though she never spoke of her life before Father, before the army, before all of us kids, Ma hinted that she had secret stories to tell. But whenever she tried to recall specifics from her past, they eluded her, like smoke from a chimney.

That morning, Mary put Ma on the ferry, unaccompanied, a fact that bothered Mary, but not enough to get her to make the trip too. I'm sure the Captain told my sister that he'd keep an eye on Ma, and I'm sure this soothed Mary, a woman who never rode the ferry herself and had no idea of its perilous nature.

116

I could imagine my mother sitting in the ferry's uncomfortable slat chairs. I'd sat there myself and listened to the huffs and groans from the engines, the loud shushing noises. I'd felt the motion of the ship, the slap of waves on the hull, the spit of salt spray.

The Shift family on the boat told us later how Ma had left her seat for a better view at the railing when someone shouted, "Look, it's The Waving Girl!"

At the same time, the skipper angled the boat away from the island to meet an on-coming wave. The sudden maneuver sent chairs and people sliding portside, Cecelia among them.

No one saw Ma fall. No one heard the crack and crunch as she landed on brittle bone. No one noticed Cecelia Martus, staring through legs across the water to Elba Island, to the porch of the house where she'd spent many years of her life, a house where her daughter now stood sentry, waving a white cloth.

Most folks were able to grab a railing or someone's arm and hold themselves upright as the ferry rocked over the swell. Annabelle Shift, a petite woman, a weary new mother, stumbled, but her husband, Ted, arms full of child, managed to catch her. As he pulled her upright, something caught her eye—a package, sliding toward the edge of the ferry, slipping overboard. A package with legs.

Annabelle screamed. Her husband pushed the baby into her arms and rushed to the side where Cecelia dangled, clawed hands clinging to the base of the railing, her tiny black shoes hammering on the windows below. He slid onto his belly and grabbed Cecelia's arms. Another man held Ted's legs and together they pulled her back through the bars and onto the deck. She whispered, "Thank you, Jesus" before passing out.

When George rowed out to meet the ferry, he heard the whole story.

"She'll be all right, won't she?" The Shifts asked, eager and concerned. George told me later that he wanted to say his mother never was all right. Nothing was ever all right, but when he looked at that family, standing on the ferry deck, he thought they were what America was supposed to be, a perfect family—heroic father, loving mother, quiet, well-mannered children. That was the picture in his head: perfection. How could he ruin that?

So he told them what they did was good and right. He thanked them when I knew he wished they'd let her drop. They should have been watching for porpoises or whales and let the shark slip overboard.

As George pulled away from the ferry, Ma raised a feeble hand in thanks. The older Shift child's bonnet was blown off revealing wiry, black hair and a dark complexion. She reached for the hands of her fair-skinned mother and her blond, blue-eyed father.

❧ ❧

There were secrets in every family tree, and sometimes the holes in which you store them are deeper than the roots and certainly more dangerous.

"Maybe it's best that she's laid up," I said.

"Best? For who?" George spit back.

We were in the lighthouse tower. My hair swirled around my face, revealing an eye, a nose, my throat, then my whole face as I caught my hair with one hand.

"*Whom*, George. And for us of course," I said.

"Yes, well, it certainly isn't best for her." George stepped back and crossed his arms, looking flustered. "For God's sake, think of Ma," he said. "Damnit, think of Mary. She's going to have a conniption when she finds out."

"We can't tell Mary," I said. "She has enough on her hands already. Besides, there's nothing she can do. Skipper radioed Doc. He said he'd be out tomorrow, to keep her quiet, let her sleep."

"That's easier said than done, isn't it?" George huffed.

I started down the winding steps. "Not as long as I have laudanum."

The mind is a funny thing. No matter how damaged the body, the mind can convince it anything. I'd watch my mother lying there on the couch in her daydreams and fits, her arms twitching as she fought her demons. I'd see the light in her eyes when George came into the room, hear her mistake each of us for the other, for a stranger in her past, for her dead husband. She yelled for her eldest son, Charles Francis, the boy she continued to fail, once in real life as he died in her arms, then over and over—unable even in her dreams to save him—forced to watch him wither away, more fish than man in the end. She'd weep then, my mother.

One morning, two weeks into her recovery, I found her screaming, writhing and clawing at her bloodied face. I grabbed her hands, pinned them beneath her as I pressed my weight into her chest. Her eyes were wild and bugged. She spat at me like a feral cat. Then a shudder ran through her body and she was still.

"Ma?" I looked into her eyes and saw myself reflected in the glossy pupil. Something behind me. George.

"What happened?" he asked.

I jerked back, releasing my mother. I wiped my hands down the front of my blouse, leaving bloody handprints.

George said, "She's not dead. Is she?"

The old woman blinked her eyes and smiled an evil grin. "John, give your wife a kiss."

I stood there bloody and shaken as my mother kissed the cheek of her son and called him, "Darling."

Two days later, Ma was still confused. George and I played along. He sat on the edge of the divan as our mother stroked his arm—the arm of her dead husband attached to her son. When she fell asleep, George left to light the beacon, taking longer than was necessary.

I tried to stay busy in the kitchen, tried to avoid being alone with her. But when George stayed away the next afternoon, I ran out of excuses. I put together lunch with sweet tea and cakes, a plate of ham and bread, some cheese and a knife to cut it all. I walked softly as I carried the tray, half hoping she wouldn't wake.

As I set the tray on the table in front of her, my hands shook, rattling the cup in its saucer. She snapped her eyes open and grabbed my wrist with her veiny, bird claw hands, her sharp little nails piercing my skin.

"You stay away from him!" she said, in a blast of putrid breath.

"What are you talking about?" I said, trying to pull away.

"You heard me. Think I ain't seen you looking at him? Think I don't know what the two of you do down there in that barn? It's disgusting! I told them so."

"Who?" I studied her face, felt the grip slackening. "You told who?" I demanded.

The old woman clamped her lips shut, released my wrist and reached for her tea, turning the tables again.

"Ma? What are you telling people?"

She smirked, "Wouldn't you like to know?"

"Yes." I said. "I would."

The old crone sipped her tea, then placed the cup on the saucer and smoothed her coverlet, each swipe punctuated by words. "I. Don't. Have. To. Tell. You. Anything."

She glared at me, pointed toward the door, the barn, the years gone past. "That's my husband, and I won't have you bedding him."

"That's not your husband, it's your son, George," I told her. "Father is dead. You're tired, and confused." I reached for the tea tray. "Let me take that and you can rest."

"Sweet talking won't work on me, you harlot!"

She moved fast, swiping her arm across the table upending the teapot, swinging her legs around and snagging the knife from the tea tray.

I jumped back too late as the blade sliced through my skirt, into my thigh. Ma raised the knife and lunged. Her hip gave out, legs crumpling beneath her. She hit the floor hard, sending the knife clattering and skidding across the planks, landing at my feet. She screamed, writhing in pain, and when she turned her eyes on me, it was the face of a woman who hated her daughter completely.

I reached in my pocket for the syringe of laudanum and when that was empty, I opened the box the doctor had left and refilled her medication.

CHAPTER 36

BOBBIE
1903

Harry had insisted on buying them dinner, then drinks and more drinks. Sam took to the editor from his first tasteless joke. Bobbie was beginning to regret her idea nine years ago to bring Sam home to New York. To marry him.

"We'd better get going," she said, poking Sam under the table.

Harry laughed. "Why? Your boss isn't going to mind if you come in late. Trust me on that one." He clinked his glass too hard against Sam's.

Harry was still the same guy. He was still her knight. She should be more grateful, the way he saved her job, the way he championed her.

"Hey," Harry said, "Did I tell you I met some guys who know your Savannah girl?"

Sam stopped nuzzling Bobbie's neck and glanced across the table with hooded eyes. "What Savannah girl?"

"The waving woman, or whatever you call her."

Bobbie said, "It's The Waving Girl. You published her story, remember? Flora Martus?"

"That's the one," Harry said. "These guys were fishermen from the area, said she helped their buddy once, a guy with an old skiff and no sense. Somebody who thought gray clouds, whiskey and boating mixed."

Sam laughed. "Dumb ass."

"As the story goes, she saved him. Rowed right out there in the middle of a storm."

"By herself?" Bobbie asked.

"Sounded that way," Harry said. "Bet the guy was embarrassed to be saved by a woman."

"Be more embarrassing if the idiot had died," Sam said.

They drank to that.

Bobbie woke to the sound of singing and thought she was dreaming. But when she opened her eyes she was in her own room, in bed, alone. There was a smear of dried blood on the back of her hand and a soreness in her lower back, more than a cramp.

She sat up as a slice of the previous night flashed: noisy pub, angry face, barstool, hard, cold floor.

Standing in the living room in front of a dirty window where morning light fought its way through splotching Bobbie's bare arms, she stood listening to the neighbor's sad baritone asking *who's kissing her now*? She leaned on the windowsill, pressed her forehead into the cool glass and closed her eyes.

A groan broke her reverie.

Sam had slept where he fell. One shoe on, one shoe off, he woke on the floor by the sofa. "Shit."

"You can say that again," Bobbie said. She glanced at her husband, then at the dying plants on the sill. She picked up a small tin watering can. Water sloshed in the bottom. With a shaking hand, she poured most of the water into the pots.

Seeing Bobbie at the window like that, someone might have thought she was an old woman, hunched and fragile. Except for the rise of her back under the thin dressing gown she might have been frozen, trapped like a bug in a jar, her movements contained in the spray of light, the fiercest beams cutting through the fabric exposing her slender frame, her swaying breasts and slightly pooched abdomen. Someone might have wondered why she would exert such effort on a tiny plant, one that seemed wasted beyond salvation.

As Bobbie stood, the robe fell away. She made no move to close it. Sam held up an arm, crooked a finger at her and she went to him, watering can clattering to the floor, rolling under the bed, forgotten.

Sam pulled Bobbie down onto the slanting dusty floor. She was warm all over except the tips of her fingers and when she touched these to his temples he said, "I love you."

She said nothing, but her eyes welled as she tucked her head under his chin and covered him with kisses.

Sunlight reflected off Bobbie's hair, a sheen of copper, red and gold against russet. She was pyrite moving down his body, snaking over the surface, popping buttons she would later sew, making promises she had every intention of keeping.

⋙ ⋘

The newspaper room was changing. Bobbie took a sabbatical from the road. She stayed in New York and wrote about local politics, getting information from people in bars, diners, the grocer on the corner. She went to church across town, more for connections than religion. She drank in small rooms in Manhattan sitting on Sam's lap when Sam was around.

When the next round of storms, flooding and fires hit Savannah, new long distance telephone lines allowed most reporters to file first-hand reports. Although the information was timely, it didn't feel right to Bobbie and the difference showed in the flavor of her column, in the words she chose. She could imagine wild winds and the froth of the sea, as anyone could. She knew the ocean wasn't really any different off the coast of New York as off the coast of Georgia, but there was a mood that struck her when she stood in a place and wrote about it. There was an undeniable honesty to those words. She liked to think readers could tell the difference, that they appreciated the difficulties she went through to bring the story home.

Stuck in New York, writing in a library carrel or at a newspaper desk, she was losing her voice, losing her way. The words took longer to come, the pace of the writing slowed and not because the piece was smarter or more thoughtful but because she didn't know where it was going or how to wrap it up. She struggled with which parts to skip over and which parts to make bigger. It didn't help that her belly was growing every day, that she was having a baby she didn't want and couldn't raise, that she hadn't seen Sam in weeks and didn't know if she wanted to.

When Sam opened the apartment door a month later, Bobbie let the scene play out. Wrapped in a blanket from their bed, she recited the lines of every clichéd scorned woman, of every lover left behind, every mother with a lying kid, every soldier's wife, every politican's mistress.

"Where have you been? I've been worried sick. You could be dead or hurt or worse."

"But I'm not, sweetheart," Sam said. "I'm here and I've missed you."

Bobbie hated loving him at times like this. She knew it wouldn't take much to bring her right back into his arms, to brush aside whatever harmful thing he'd done this time. Her capability for forgiveness was God-like. His hold on her, satanic.

Bobbie glared at him knowing the only reason he was home was that money and favors had run out. The good times had ended. Locks had changed. Women had moved on.

Bobbie threw a book at him. "You're a son of a bitch!"

Sam raised his arm, a little late. "Ow!"

Bobbie threw another book. "You're a bastard!"

Sam ducked. "Hold on there, sweetheart," he said, coming toward her, talking her down like a man on the ledge. "Put the book down. Whatever it is, I'm sure we can fix it."

"No. Don't come any closer. Just take your things and go."

She tipped her chin toward a suitcase and a box by the kitchenette. "And don't forget your mail."

Bobbie left the room, slamming the door to their bedroom and sliding the lock home.

Sam picked up the slit envelopes on the desk, one from his doctor with test results, and a pink scented one addressed to *Darling Sam* from his latest fling, an actress named Simone.

"Aw, crap."

CHAPTER 37

MAGGIE
2011

Now that she had borrowed wheels, Maggie took advantage of it. She drove to the beach on Tybee Island and walked the shore, remembering to slather on sunscreen.

She was surprised to see a white band where her watch usually was. She couldn't remember the last time she'd been tan. David preferred her skin pale, freckle-free. They'd spent countless vacations under sunhats and parasols. Well, she had. David had been bareheaded and bare-chested fishing from a pier, snorkeling a reef.

She wondered what else had she missed.

Maggie ordered a fish sandwich, cold beer and fries at a beachside café then drove to an electronics store and bought a laptop, printer, photo paper and ink cartridges.

※ ※

"Thanks," she told Charles handing him his keys. "I filled it up and parked it in the alley."

"Everything okay?" he asked.

"Sure."

"You need help with any of that?" Charles pointed to the computer and printer boxes Maggie had hauled in. "I'd be glad to help," he said. "Had a few years of tech school. Most people think older folks like me don't know a thing about computers, but I email everyday, even put a wireless router in the attic. Every room's ready to search the World Wide Web."

The way he said it made the offer seem irresistible. Maggie smiled at the thought of a honeymooning couple uploading photos to their Facebook page at midnight, checking their online auction bids, watching the weather patterns in Aruba.

Before she could decline, Charles hefted the boxes and led the way to her room. They plugged in wires, ran extension cords, uploaded programs and created passwords. They tested cartridges and adjusted print patterns, chose browsers and logged onto mail programs.

Maggie opened up her email box. "I have 742 messages!"

"Hoo boy," Charles laughed. "You got some catching up to do."

Maggie highlighted the whole column, positioned her finger over the delete button.

"Now, wait a minute," he said. "What if there's something important in there?"

"If it was that important, they wouldn't be emailing me about it."

Charles shrugged.

Maggie took it as Southern for, *Do what you're gonna do, Yankee fool.* She hit *end* instead. "I'll look at them later, just good to know it works."

"Sure it works. I told you I know what I'm doing." Charles plugged in the printer and smiled when the LEDs lit up.

Maggie figured a lot of people bought into the cliché that Southern men were hot-headed and dumb, all because of an accent. A heavyset Southern man like Charles, with his mouth of crooked teeth and can of chaw in his back pocket, might be thought of as one of those less intelligent types. But the way his eyes crinkled when he smiled, made Maggie think he was more like the desserts he baked, crusty on the outside but sweet where it counted. He reminded her of the soft-spoken Georgia boys in those TV specials, the kind where the horse is always saved and the dog finds his way home.

Charles collected the empty boxes then stacked them in the corner of the room and backed out, glancing with affection at the computer setup. "If there's anything else you need."

"Thanks, you've done more than enough," Maggie said, then seeing his face drop added, "But maybe a little nighttime snack—for all our hard work?"

Charles grinned. "I know just the thing."

They sat in the kitchen perched on stools drawn up to the butcher block island, sipping a sweet Viognier that Charles had produced from a hidden cupboard. Maggie turned her glass in the dim light admiring the color of the wine reflected in the hand-blown crystal.

After one sip she felt the warmth running down her throat into her belly. Eyes closed she heard the refrigerator door open, then shut. She breathed in the smells of the kitchen: oranges, brown sugar and barbeque. She opened her eyes when she heard the clink of a plate touching butcher block.

It was a parade of goodness, a platter of temptation: chocolate-dipped strawberries the size of a baby's fist, tiny lemon sun cakes covered with mounds of raspberries and fresh cream, custard cups of crumble-topped peach cobbler.

They ate in silence interrupted only by murmurs of praise from Maggie followed by humble grunts from Charles, who was the first to give, setting down his fork.

He said, "When I was eight, I was sure I would be the best soldier the South had ever seen. My daddy loved to tell me stories of war. He taught me the strategy of battle. He was a fighting man through and through, and his daddy before him."

Charles topped off Maggie's glass, then refilled his own.

"I do believe I disappointed the old rooster when I chose culinary school instead of the army."

"I'm sure he understood. How could anyone deny your talent?" Maggie asked raising another forkful of cobbler.

Charles shook his head. In the dim light of the room, his features were shadowed. The light from the stove behind him formed a halo around his body, disembodying him, reminding Maggie of the first time she'd had nitrous oxide at the dentist and seen Dr. Finn's head and red tie floating over her as he told her to open wide.

Charles said, "My daddy would take me fishing and every time we'd end up out past the fort near the Cockspur Lighthouse. He'd tell me the same damn story, until I could mouth the words right along with the old coot."

"Tell me," Maggie said.

Charles leaned back in his chair and recited, "January, 1861. Georgia troops seize Fort Pulaski from a single ordnance sergeant. Their assignment is to prevent the fort from being garrisoned by Federal forces. With walls twenty-five feet high and seven feet thick, the fort appears impenetrable.

"At that time, most of the batteries are using smoothbore guns and the distance across the water is too far to do any damage to Pulaski. So secure in his command, Colonel Olmstead orders the abandonment of nearby Tybee and joins the forces behind one garrison wall. What our Georgia boys don't know is that while they were relying on the strength of position and structure, Union soldiers had been building batteries up and down the coast of Tybee and installing new and improved artillery guns.

"On April 10, 1862, when Colonel Olmstead refuses to surrender the fort to Union forces, General Gillmore orders bombardment, opening up with a barrage from Jones Island and Bird Island– the six-gun batteries across the river.

"There are three hundred thirty-seven men and twenty-four officers in the Confederate garrison. They put up a good, but short-lived fight, as the Patriot guns of the Union tears through mortar and brick, outdistancing the old artillery and burrowing two feet deep in the fort walls.

"No one's more surprised than Colonel Olmstead when thirty hours into the battle the attack breaches the southwest scarp of the fort and threatens the powder magazine in the northwest corner. With too many lives at stake, Olmstead is forced to surrender."

"What happened to the men?" Maggie asked.

"They were sent to Governor's Island in New York," Charles said. "The fort remained under Federal control as a POW camp until the end of the war, then it housed political prisoners. But my favorite part of the story is what didn't happen." He pointed to a painting on the wall. "See that?"

Sandwiched between a glass-fronted cabinet and a floor to ceiling window was a framed picture of a lighthouse surrounded by water.

Charles said, "That's the Cockspur Light. It was built on an oyster bed in the South Channel—directly in line with the path of the Union artillery.

"During the entire battle, not one hit, not a single nick marred its surface. The enemy fires thirty-six pound shot over *a mile* of water to the fort–and what are we to believe? They all hit true? Not one went astray?" Charles shook his head. "And yet, the lamp, the glass walls, the structure itself was unblemished."

"Amazing," Maggie said.

"Yes, it is."

As the sun rose, breaking the dimness of the kitchen, a ray of light was cast onto the painting. Waves broke white-tipped in the sea around the mighty lighthouse, a beam of yellow from its lamp, illuminated the hull of a gray ship in the sea beyond. Maggie held her breath. She could have sworn the painted water moved.

The walls of the pale tower were heavy, in a heavy mood The great stones stood as if resisting without belief. Oh how sad sighed the wind, how disconsolately, Do not ride alone in the dark wood at night.

Charles glanced at the clock, then scraped his chair back. "Folks will be wanting breakfast in an hour. I'd better get cooking. You know what they say, 'No rest for the wicked.'"

CHAPTER 38

BOBBIE
1917

Bobbie found war to be like living in a foster home. She had to do what they wanted when they wanted and usually it made no sense at all and always, someone got hurt.

She spent hours with the soldiers, telling herself she wasn't like them but eating their food, wearing the same uniform and using the same shitter. She tried not to think about how the enemy saw them the same, how there probably wouldn't be time to say, "Wait, I'm a journalist, not a soldier. You can't shoot me."

She met people she supposed she would like in The Real World, that place she'd left behind where people walked safe streets, bought bread in corner stores and slept in private, comfortable beds each night. She made the distinction of the two places in her mind: The Real World was a place she had left her heart and somewhere, Sam and a greater piece of the two of them in the form of a daughter, a child she'd named Florence and given up for adoption to her British housekeeper, Sadie Smith. A daughter who would never know her father. The Real World was not a place Bobbie wanted to think about. This was The War, a place she was forced to think about daily, a place where nothing ordinary happened.

She couldn't write about everything she saw. Sometimes it took hours before she could put any thoughts on paper, but once she understood the stories she wanted to tell were about the people of the war not the politics, once she got that, the words came with no small sense of relief.

No one wanted to die, but worse yet to die in a war that wasn't yours. In battle, a man became nameless, just another armed person in khaki. Bobbie wanted more than anything else to give the soldiers a chance to tell their stories, to have a piece of them live on. There were too many who wouldn't make it.

She thought reporters were an integral part of the war, that what they wrote mattered. She didn't realize she'd have to lie and that her words would be picked over and censored, like the letters of soldiers.

Everyday Bobbie pushed away memories: fresh baked bread from the corner shop, ironed cotton sheets, hot bubble baths, Sam's neck, the rhythm and rush of the ocean slapping the shore, moon-lit evenings of chocolate and stolen kisses. She wrapped herself in the color gray, dank like a root cellar. She felt warmth, but could not take comfort in it and where she felt cold she reveled in the way it numbed her. There was a part of Bobbie that needed the war, needed to see evil and anger and unhappiness, so that she could feel blessed, lucky, saved. As if the Lord himself had passed over Bobbie and chosen to play Job with someone else.

She played another kind of game everyday. She woke up guessing who would die and if she would be there to see it.

Last week marching through a quiet French village, they detoured through a narrow alley for the shade. They were joking about the meal they would eat when they returned home when a stray shell tore into the walls of stone. Rock and debris pelted them as they fought for the shelter of too few doorways, as they squeezed themselves under narrow sills of windows, as they rolled into balls and prayed. The luckier soldiers were killed instantly, others were pinned writhing and screaming under impossibly heavy mounds of debris. One soldier was impaled on a section of iron railing, his body twitched above them, then hung limp like meat on a stick.

Bobbie spun in circles until Jack, the Private assigned to protect her, tackled her to the ground.

"Stay down!" he said. "It's going to be all right."

He wedged them under a splintered door and put his body over hers.

There was another hit, more screaming, a hail of debris then the sound of retreat. Jack rose, pushing the door off them. They stood, coughing, coated with stone dust, unable to see farther than a few feet. Bobbie sensed others rising around them, but couldn't hear anything over the buzzing in her ears. A soldier crawled past, missing the lower half of his body. Bobbie and Jack turned to look behind them. The alley exits were blocked. They were trapped.

The ground shook, a fissure in the earth widened, its mouth swallowing Jack as the wall behind them fell, crumbling down to fill the hole. Someone grabbed her arm—the medic—pulling her backward. A pile of stone, wood and glass filled the place where seconds earlier Jack and Bobbie had been standing.

"Jack!"

The medic shouted, "He's gone. Leave him!"

He said something else. Bobbie saw his red mouth moving, the urgency in his eyes. She followed his gesticulating arm, the pointing finger and she understood that they were to pull the men from the wreckage, save who they could and get the hell out of there. She froze until he slapped her.

They worked fast, pulling stone and wood from piles, looking for anything human. Bobbie tugged on a khaki uniformed arm, felt resistance and began to uncover more stone to free the soldier. She pulled and came away with the limb, nothing more. After that, she dug deeper before she pulled, hoping each time to find a breathing soldier at the other end.

The crushed limbs covered in stone dust looked the same. She thought about making a pile of right arms and left arms, of legs and of feet. There really weren't enough body parts to make piles, but she allowed herself the moment of exaggeration, a stagnant piece of time where she was a pawn on a chessboard, a character in a hastily drawn comic strip. She wasn't real and she wasn't there and she certainly wasn't holding a bloody shoe with a foot still inside.

Her ears began to clear, the dust settling enough for them to see an exit. A few soldiers had cleared a path, and they were able to walk out with the injured braced between them, tags of the dead jingling in their pockets.

That night in the trench, Bobbie cried for Jack and the others who hadn't made it. She cried and then she wrote. She wrote letters to the wives and girlfriends of the nine men who had been badly injured. She told their loved ones how brave their soldier had been and that he would be home soon. She wrote letters to now broken families and obituaries for the dead. She wrote to a post office box addressed to Sam, lying and telling him she was fine, they were fine. The war was not as bad as he thought. But when she looked around, she saw the truth. War was messy. It was dirty and smelly and bloody. It didn't know how to stop. Every day endings were written, but still the war raged on.

When Bobbie returned to base camp with the wounded, something was different in the tent town.

"Welcome back."

Bobbie stared after the voice. A woman. A nurse. Glancing into the makeshift hospital as they passed, she saw more women in white.

Two soldiers exited the tent with a stretcher. They loaded the body into the back of an ammo truck. Someone had made an attempt in kindness by covering the bodies with a hole-riddled blanket, but Bobbie could see them. They were obvious to every healthy soldier in the camp.

A new enemy had moved in while they were away. The doctors were calling it Spanish Flu. There was no cure and no one understood how it spread. For Bobbie, it was just another battle. Something else destined to end badly.

CHAPTER 39

MAGGIE
2011

When Maggie woke, the sun was high in the sky, the air humid enough to make showering a futile activity.

The printer had been working through the night. A hefty stack of photos lay in the tray and the blinking light indicated more were on the way. Maggie replenished the paper, grabbed the pictures and headed downstairs.

Sadie was coming in from the garden with an empty juice jug and a handful of plates. "Good morning, Miss Maggie."

"Morning. I know I missed breakfast, but is there any chance you might still have some coffee?"

"Of course," Sadie said. "Tell you what, why don't you go sit in the back garden? The fountain is running and the sun won't be over the roof for another hour. I'll bring something out to you."

Maggie smiled. "I'll do that."

She followed the path to the flagstone patio. Thick branches of shiny green leaves and large white gardenia blooms softened the brick walls of the courtyard. There was a burst of color planted around the fountain—a single bubbler with a statue of a girl staring cross-eyed at a butterfly on her nose. Maggie read the hand-lettered plant signs: ShiShi Dwarf Camellia, Duchess of Cypress Azalea, Rose of Sharon, Tea Olive. The air was fragrant and rich, and for a moment, Maggie imagined curling up on the wicker sofa in the corner and closing her eyes for a long nap.

The phone in her front pocket began to vibrate as soon as she sat down.

"Where have you been? Don't you check voice mails?"

"Well, hello to you too, Lisa."

A loud sigh emanated from the tiny phone.

Sadie arrived with a tray. Maggie had known it wouldn't be just coffee. It was never just anything down here, she'd come to realize. She mouthed, "Thank you" to Sadie and while Lisa went on and on in her ear, Maggie munched crisp oatmeal and butterscotch cookies, dipped fresh strawberries into cold cream, and enjoyed mouthfuls of salty cheese grits slathered in butter, all washed down with a hot mug of sharp chicory coffee. She barely registered the details of Lisa's domestic disaster—a spare freezer suddenly defrosting and ruining a side of beef and enough crab legs to make Emeril cry in his roue.

Maggie couldn't stop thinking that Lisa had become a princess. Had she always been this whiney?

Maggie pushed the empty plates aside, then spread the photographs onto the table like she was laying out a card game. She snapped them over, making three long rows, scanning them, pulling the few that caught her eye for their composition, color, clarity. Then she went over the rows more slowly, pulling out the marina shots, quickly discarding the first three boats with the overly feminine touches. Another batch was rejected due to international hail ports.

She was left with one row of possible boats and one of touristy Savannah shots including the Waving Girl statue, the Cotton Exchange, the fountain in the square and Sonny. *Sonny.* Heat rose in her neck and cheeks. Her heart beat faster.

Nobody knows what I feel about Freddy I cannot make anyone understand I love him sub specie aet ernitaties I love him out of hand . . .

"Maggie, did you hear me?" Lisa said.

"Uh-huh."

"So? What should I do?"

Maggie picked up the photo of Sonny. He was in a classic David pose. Maggie squinted. Twenty years ago, even ten years ago, this could have been her husband, hand on hip, chest inflated, chin up and defiant.

"David," she whispered.

"What?" Lisa said. "Mags, are you okay? I wasn't talking about David. I was— wait a minute. You never said anything about the lawyer. What happened? Do you need me to come down there?"

"No," Maggie said.

"Because I could, I'll book a flight."

"Lisa. It was nothing," Maggie said. "David used the guy to look into some properties, a place to retire to someday. He wanted to pass on the information."

Maggie picked up another photo, one she'd shot from the end of the dock, back across the line of boats, toward the parking lot. She'd caught Sonny and the girl on the party boat, his face turned toward the camera as if he'd known Maggie was there, as if he'd been waiting for her. Her heart leapt.

"So, that was it?" Lisa asked.

Maggie set the picture down, picked up the one of the Waving Girl statue. "Don't sound so disappointed."

"I'm not. It's none of my business anyway."

"That's right."

Lisa was silent.

Maggie said, "I've got to go. I'll call you later." She hung up without waiting for a reply, gathered the photos and dishes then went to the kitchen.

Charles sat at the butcher block island, three cookbooks open in front of him. He held a stained, yellowed piece of paper. "Do you think this says butter or batter?"

Maggie put her dishes in the sink then reached for the paper. "Butter," she said. "Definitely. What is this?"

"Supper. What you got there?" Charles pointed to the stack of photos tucked under Maggie's arm.

"Just some shots from the other day."

Charles raised a brow.

Maggie hadn't told Charles why she wanted to go to the marina and he hadn't asked, just gave her his keys and directions. She shrugged then passed him the stack, watching as he skimmed the first third, chuckling at the boat names, taking a moment to synopsize the dwellings as she had. In the same way you can tell a great deal about someone from the contents of their medicine cabinet, boat decks were very revealing.

"I know some of these boats," he said as he flipped through the stack. "Not sure why you took the pictures. But this, I understand." He tapped the shot of the Victorian house. "Nice job capturing past and present, waiting for the lady with the dachshund to get to the end of the frame. I like the motion, the way you personified the building, making it more than brick and wood, more than a simple structure."

Maggie raised her brows. back at him.

Charles laughed. "I told you I know a little about a lot. My roommate was an architect, used to make me do historical walks every month."

"Roommate?" Maggie asked.

"That was a long time ago," he said. "Anyway, these are good." He lifted the stack Maggie had separated from the marina pictures. "The other shots look like something done for an assignment, not for the joy of it, but because you had to–but this, this is beautiful."

It was a picture of the Waving Girl Memorial with the Savannah River beyond. A long white barge entered the frame from the right, catching the glint of sunlight. It looked like the statue was floating on the barge, with Flora's cloth raised to the sky, the bronze hair of the dog at her feet almost billowed in the breeze.

"I'll bet the guy who does The Waving Girl tours would love this for his brochure."

"Who, Sonny?" Maggie said.

Charles looked at her. "How do you know Sonny Beaumont?"

"I don't," she said. "Not really. I met him at the statue and saw the postcards."

"You should go," Charles said. "You look like her, you know?"

"Who?"

"Flora Martus." He held up the photo. "But you're taller. Anyway," he said handing back the pictures, then tucking the grocery list in his pocket. "You should do the tour. It'll get you off dry land and out of my kitchen for a while. If you want, I can drop you at the dock on my way to the store."

CHAPTER 40

BOBBIE
1918

Bobbie thought at first, that going off to cover the war would be good for her.

That it would help her stop loving Sam so much. Stop needing him until it hurt. It was the destructive nature of their pairing. Bobbie and Sam together fueled a passion that sometimes took the shape of binge drinking, broken glass and bruises. Sam said in the heat of an argument, "I hate you so much that I love you right now." It made perfect sense to Bobbie.

Unlike war.

The Spanish flu passed through camp. The sick were shipped off, leaving a small unit waiting for reinforcements, waiting for orders, waiting, always waiting.

A small balding Private with a nervous twitch took over Jack's role. Bobbie called him Rabbit. She didn't want to know his real name, or anything else about him.

She was typing another letter home for the corporal who'd lost his fingers, when a soldier popped his head in the tent.

"Excuse me, ma'am?"

Rabbit looked up from his darning, started to rise. Bobbie waved him off swiveling on her cot to welcome the young man. "Come in."

He was young, like most of them, healthy enough but definitely too skinny for his frame. If they'd been home, she would have pegged him for a basketball player. Kid had the height and the hands for it. The buzz cut didn't do much for him and Bobbie could see where he'd tried to shave a beard that didn't need shaving.

She motioned to the cot across from hers.

The soldier took a step then said, "I've been to school. I can write okay, it's just that I don't have any paper and they said you were putting our stories together, like a book or something, so I thought, well, you know."

"Sit down," Bobbie said.

"Yes, Ma'am."

The kid sat, in the way that soldiers do so that they still look like they're standing, ready to attack or run or answer positively to the most ridiculous question.

"Knock off the ma'ams, kid. I'm not your mother." Bobbie softened her tone, "Listen, you can relax. Nobody's looking."

The boy darted his eyes around, seeing nothing in the tent besides a couple of cots, damp socks hanging from a makeshift laundry line and a black typewriter dented on one side. He slumped a bit but Bobbie could still feel the military sweating off him.

"Where you from?" she asked.

"New Hampshire, ma'am. I mean—New Hampshire. A small town. You wouldn't know it."

"Might be surprised. I've been lots of places."

"It don't matter," he said. "I ain't going back. Probably won't make it back. Not with all this—well, you know."

Bobbie did.

"Anyway, I just wanted to tell you about a girl I met. I think I love her and I wanted to put words down somewhere so that maybe some day she could read them."

"She doesn't know?" Bobbie said. "This girl?"

"What? That I love her?" The kid laughed, a smile brightening his face, letting Bobbie see a piece of who he must have been back home, back in a simple life where you did simple things like smile and laugh and had a life that wasn't dirt-caked or bloody or army green. Then the kid ran a hand across his mouth erasing his smile, smothering his laugh. When he looked back at Bobbie, he was serious and old in his eyes.

"She don't know," he said. "She don't even know my name. Arthur."

Bobbie looked up from the pad of paper. She thought she'd be writing to his girlfriend or fiancée.

"Hell, even at home they don't call me that. They call me Sky, because my momma used to say if I kept on growing my head would be in the sky."

He looked past Bobbie, toward the flap in the tent and the blue grey beyond.

He said, "I met her in Toulon Sector. We had no business being there, but a few miles back we lost our radioman and any contact we'd had with base. Captain thought we'd be better off heading south away from the shells and the blasts. We had to agree with him there. Not that we were scared or chicken or nothing. We was just tired and pretty beat up. Captain said it would be like showing up alive to our own funeral, and did we want to sing the hymns too? Anyway, we was marching through the town, taking things maybe a little easy, it was almost dark and we needed a place to bed down.

"This girl she's coming around the corner with a ratty, old loaf of bread in her hands, looked like she'd pulled it out of the mouth of a dog. I yelled, 'Hey!' to get her attention and also because she sort of startled me coming around the corner like that.

"When this girl looked at me, I could see the fear in her and I felt bad. Real bad. I was the one who should have been protecting her, but I saw myself like she did, a bad guy, the enemy."

The kid wiped his eyes and swallowed hard.

"She ran and I chased her. I don't know why. My buddies kept calling to me, like they thought I was in trouble or that something bad would happen but all I could see was this girl. Her blue eyes and black hair, her red lips. Her shoes were too big for her, must have found them somewhere. They slapped the stones of the streets tripping her, making it easy for me to catch her. Part of it might have been how she was weak and hungry, more tired than me. I don't know. Maybe she wanted me to catch her. Maybe I was supposed to all along. Like fate. Do you believe in fate?"

Sky looked at Bobbie then back outside. The day had grown lighter. The sun was rising somewhere else, giving them a peek of it, a taste of sunshine, something else they couldn't have. He ran his hands down his thighs, squeezed and released.

He said, "The girl, she sank down against the side of a building on this deserted street. I slipped on some rocks and cut my knee right open but didn't feel a thing till later. She was talking, saying stuff in French, too fast for me. I did learn some—in school and in camp—but not enough. She was talking behind her hands, trying to hide her face like she thought I would do her harm. I didn't say anything except no and it's okay, but maybe she didn't hear me, because she held out the loaf of bread. That lousy loaf of bread. Like that was what I wanted from her. What kind of man would do that? Steal someone's food. I didn't want anything from her—that was just it."

Sky went quiet, tears welled in his eyes. "It hit me then. The idea of destiny. Everything that had come before led me to that moment, that place, that girl, that stupid loaf of bread. Everything happened for a reason. And I could feel it like I feel the Holy Spirit in church on Sunday when Pastor Rick's wife sings. That girl was there for me. We're all supposed to save someone and this was my day, my task. This girl in France. A girl whose eyes could tell me things— that summer would never feel as warm, that wishing something wouldn't make it so, that an axe would never feel heavy on my shoulder again.

Sky cleared his throat and straightened up. "I must have found the right words, because she stopped looking scared. She turned her face to me and when I reached to touch her cheek she didn't resist. Her skin was cool, like the skin of a peach in the icebox. She was so pale, I could see blue veins pulsing at her temples."

Sky's lips turned up in a small smile that faded quickly. "I told her to do it. When they came with the dogs, yelling and pointing their guns, I told her to hit me with the rock, to smash it over my head. I even grabbed the loaf of bread and when her eyes went big and something dark moved behind them, she still wouldn't. I had to hit myself."

Sky touched a matted patch of hair over his ear. He pet the red stain then dropped his hand into his lap.

"She was gone when I woke up. They left me. Everyone left me. Took me two days to find my way back and the whole time I was seeing her—my French girl—around every corner. A girl with a loaf of bread and cornflower blue eyes. I didn't tell anyone.

"Some of the guys in my unit with kills on their belt, they went and talked to the Chaplain, said they felt better afterward, how he gave them solace. He said they were forgiven for what they'd done. But you can't forgive somebody for things they failed to do, can you?"

Bobbie sat with Sky in a drooping tent in the middle of a war that no one understood thinking about things they didn't do. They thought about places they hadn't been, things they hadn't seen and all the times they had pushed something away instead of walking right toward it with arms wide open.

By the time Bobbie was ordered to return home, she had collected two bulging satchels of letters and stories. They loaded them into the truck transport but left her typewriter behind with its tattered ribbon and the letter Q permanently depressed.

As everyone came out to send her and Rabbit off, she felt like she was leaving her family behind. They shouted their good-byes, Bobbie telling them to keep their heads down and watch their asses then reminding them to look her up in New York when they made it home.

As the truck pulled away, someone yelled and Bobbie looked back. Sky stood on the roof of the Red Cross ambulance. He wore nothing more than a small white towel, which he pulled off and waved with two long thin arms. He was saying something, but between the hoots from the other soldiers in the truck and the sound of the blasts in the hills, Sky's words were lost in the wind.

CHAPTER 41

FLORA
1940

I squint my eyes, measuring the distance, again. If there was a rowboat here, I might be able to do it. Then I wonder if the currents have changed, would they still pull me out to the oyster bed? How long would I have to float to reach my lighthouse?

I'm tired of thinking. I push my bare feet further into the wet sand, making a hole for the next wave to fill. Shells scooped from the sea bottom tick and clack against one another as they roll up and deposit themselves onto the beach near my toes. I reach into the swirling eddy of the receding wave, grabbing without looking. When I open my hand, I have to sift through wet sand, pebbles and crab parts to find my treasure, two tiny pink shells.

The next wave is stronger, reaching to my calves, threatening the edge of my skirt. As it pulls away, the sand is sucked from my foot hole. Something white bobs in the surf—a seagull skull—bone bleached white, eye socket tumbled smooth. I grab it before the sea can reclaim her booty, wipe it dry on my skirt and step out of the wash.

Up on the beach I drink from the whiskey bottle, try not to dribble down my chin. I lay with my seagull skull, the sand warm beneath me. Wind steals strands of my hair, dances them across my forehead, tickling me into wakefulness. After a while, I yawn and roll over. Small, clawed creatures scurry away. Cow Eyes stirs from her spot, pushes herself upright, belches loudly and laughs then crawls over to me, a goofy grin on her face.

I'm beginning to like her more and more.

She says, " Slu—blah, blah."

I don't know what she is saying. I pass her the bottle and watch her drink. She lies down again and I begin to talk. I rub my seagull skull and I tell her everything that happened with George and me. I am not afraid. I am not worried what she will think. She won't remember any of this.

"There." I point to the lighthouse on the oyster bed. "That's where it started."

George chased me up the round concrete steps with a stick dangling smelly seaweed. He knew all the things that frightened me, all the things I hated. Brothers have a way of taunting their sisters that no outsider could ever match.

It wasn't meant as anything more than a scare, but sometimes when your heart gets pounding, the fight and the thrill get confused. And in a round glass tower, there wasn't anywhere to hide.

I trusted my brother. He was my playmate, the only one on the island that I could relate to, the one who took me fishing, who swam with me when the current was swift, who caught me when I fell from trees no one should be climbing. I idolized him in the worst way and would have done anything for him. On the ride over in the boat, he had looked at me strangely and I felt things change. I sat where I always did, in the bow, dangling a hand in the water as he rowed. He looked at me the way Pa did in church when I wasn't sitting up straight enough, when my knee was jiggling.

And by the time the chase was on, him teasing, me running, the oyster bags long forgotten, I felt a certain power. The names he threw at me bounced off, the seaweed stick I grabbed from him and tossed over the balcony into the sea hardly smelled at all.

Alone on the island, we made our own time. Days of playing with blocks had become days of playing school, which became days of playing house. Even in our minds, when we were just being kids, we were really growing up. No matter how much we wanted to stall the future it was there. A knock at the door, a wind ripping branches from trees, a secret in the reeds. A hidden place in a barn at the bottom of a hill on an island no one visits.

I never stopped thinking about that day, how maybe I was the reason for the rest of it, all of it. Maybe it never was George.

I could say I was just a girl, an innocent girl who did her chores and read her books, the same as all the days before the lighthouse. I could claim that I planted and hoed and baked and cleaned—just like before, nothing had changed. But that would be a lie because under the surface of my skin, I was different. The new feeling was always there. Sometimes it felt dirty, ugly and wrong, but other days it felt like love.

I would walk through the marsh, lost in thought, my breath coming up short. There was something wrong with my body. I would get so hot and flushed and feel so damp down there. But, I had no one to ask. Instead, I listened to the voice that said touch here and you won't feel so sad or lonely or empty.

I'd lie under a cypress tree and run my fingers down my cheek, remembering the day in the barn. I could feel where the kitten's scratch had faded but the sting of the moment, the unexpected pain was still vivid in my mind.

I talk to the sleeping Cow Eyes for at least an hour, or three. By the time the boat pulls up, my voice is raspy and the sun is fuzzy around the edges.

"You all right, Ma'am?"

The men in the boat are sunburned and wind-whipped. The gray haired one in the front lets the younger guy do all the rowing, while he has the important job of talking.

"We was fishing out there," he says, waving his arm like he's stirring a big pot of sky. "And we thought maybe you needed some help, or something." He glances at Cow Eyes sprawled in the sand and the empty whiskey bottle, then he looks back at me drops his arm and shrugs.

"Mighty kind of you," I say, wondering for just a second if I should feel any sort of trepidation. After all, we are two women on a deserted beach and they are two men. Why in my day this would be cause for alarm—but it isn't *my day*, it hasn't been for a long, long time. I see it in their faces, even the gray-haired one. He sees his mother in me, the crazy lady from next door, a lost soul on the street. I'm a carbon copy of everyone's unavoidable mistake.

"There is something I need," I say, rising from the sand and tucking the sea gull skull under my arm. "I need to get into that lighthouse."

CHAPTER 42

MAGGIE
2011

There were three people waiting for the tour when Maggie arrived, an Asian couple who seemed unsure about everything and a large guy in thick glasses and a worn John Deere cap who might have been looking for a ride to the tractor pull.

Before Maggie could change her mind, Sonny bumped her arm with the cooler he was carrying. "Glad you could make it, " he said grinning.

She fell in line with the others and followed him to a sleek white and blue boat. It looked sturdy enough and had sides, better than those flat contraptions on metal tubes. The one time she'd been on a party barge, she'd drunk too much, forgot they were on the water and walked straight off it–much to the delight of David and their host, a jocular guy with a great memory.

Sonny helped them board, extending a hand. "Welcome to The Waving Girl Tour."

He explained safety procedures, pointing out their life preserver seat cushions, except for the Asian woman who had to be strapped into a puffy orange pillow vest when she said, "I no swim, need floaty."

Maggie chose a seat in the back of the boat, thinking she'd be out of the wind and would have a good view of the places they were leaving behind.

Sonny checked his watch. "We'll be on the water for about an hour and a half. You'll have plenty of time before high tide to explore the oyster beds or climb to the top of the lighthouse."

The Asian woman clapped her hands and smiled, then covered her mouth and lowered her eyes.

"What about the cottage?" The John Deere guy asked.

"Bad news, Jim. The cottage still isn't open for tours. You'll have to see it from the water, like the other sailors."

Sonny pulled in the lines, started the motor and puttered away from the dock. He stood at the wheel, pointed back to the town, beginning his tour shpiel. "Florence "Flora" Martus and her brother George came into Savannah every Sunday for mass at the Cathedral of St. John the Baptist on East Harris Street. It's the oldest Roman Catholic church in Georgia and recently underwent an eleven million dollar restoration."

The Asians shot a picture of the shrinking town, not a church in sight.

"Imagine rowing your way in," Sonny said as they entered the channel of choppy water. "Imagine riding in a small flat bottomed dory in rough weather with a just an oar, maybe a tiny engine—"

"And a prayer," Maggie said.

Sonny smiled. "They had that. She was a woman of faith, our Flora."

Maggie wondered about being called a woman of faith. How did that work? It made her a little sick—the whole unconditional love thing. She hadn't been to church in a long time, and certainly not the church she was raised in, the one that felt it was better to decorate a building than to feed the poor and cure the sick, though that's what they said they were doing. What was all the gold and the masterpieces and the wealth for? Everyone died anyway. She saw a bumper sticker on a new Aston Martin last week that said, "Don't let the car fool you. My riches are stored up in heaven."

If that was the case, David would be riding in a pimped-out limo in heaven. He never spent much on earth. Not that she knew of, anyway. What if Owl Man was wrong, that he hadn't really been on David's boat, only another one he'd borrowed?

Maggie gazed into the boat's wake. Swirls in the water formed letters, shapes, mountains and valleys. There was a small surge as the boat accelerated. Zipping across the water, bouncing on the wave crests, the spray and shoosh of the water was exhilarating. She pushed her hair out of her eyes, held it back with one hand and raised her face to the warm sun.

The heat of the day, combined with the thrum of the motor and the resounding vibrations through her seat was soothing, hypnotic even. She let go of the questions she couldn't answer and let her mind drift as she sunk back into the cushioned seat and closed her eyes. The dream came quick.

Maggie stood on a church altar. She wore a long white robe and held a bouquet of yellow roses. The church was empty of people and of furnishings, full of echoes. There was too much space to ever be filled, even with a very large God. She waited as time ticked away like a metronome in music class, her legs were too heavy to move though she wanted to leave. A man came down the aisle. He walked slow, in that fake half-march step of a bride. His approach was steady, sure, unstoppable.

David. It was his outline, his long legs and broad chest. But when the man raised his bowed head, it wasn't David at all. It was Sonny. He stepped onto the altar and reached for Maggie's hand with cold wet fingers. She turned to ask, "Are you okay?" But the question became a scream when Sonny became David, a rotting corpse with seaweed hair and a face of wriggling worms.

Maggie jerked awake, swallowing a yelp. The Asian couple admired the view off the port side while Jim, the John Deere guy, studied a map. Maggie stared at Sonny's back and when he turned around and smiled, it felt like a slice of the dream.

Once over a bottle of wine, Lisa had confided in Maggie about her imaginary affairs. She'd explained how it worked, that you took a simple situation and blew it up in your mind, like the childhood game of "What if" taken a step further.

The old Maggie, the married Maggie had never understood the desire Lisa could have to play such a game. The woman had everything already and God knows, could have affairs too if she wanted.

Lisa told Maggie how she'd drive away from a stop light believing the head nod from the handsome guy in the Jag meant a great deal more than it did, that the man would meet her at the next light and give her another signal, that they could play this game together for the rest of their lives and she would be a new person starting all over. The idea both excited and frightened her like riding a rollercoaster in the dark.

There were people who treated intimacy callously. People who had sex with strangers, who could drop everything, call the spouse and rush home for a quickie when they felt the urge. But most of the people Maggie knew waited. And planned. They convinced themselves there would be time later, after the dinner was cooked, served and eaten, after they'd washed and perfumed their bodies, brushed their teeth, checked their breath. And if asked, most of these people would admit they'd done all those things, then fallen asleep, the urgency of their need forgotten in the drudgery of daily activity.

Maggie's sex life with David had been like a chess game, one in which she'd figured out the moves ahead of time and knew her opponent so well there weren't any surprises. The game started the same way, ended the same way, even the cleanup and obligatory small talk that followed was predictable. Most days, it wasn't worth removing the game from its box.

Maggie wondered if she had done things differently in her relationships, if she had loved more freely, been able to embrace moments where the urgent need to be close had struck her—and if she had used those moments in one long extended period with David, would it have changed anything?

If she could have that time back, she'd string every moment together in a new order. She'd forget about needing the comfort and security of a spouse, filling the hierarchy of need, instead she'd go for the fireworks, for the thrill. The experience. And maybe not even with David. She'd be a different Maggie. One with wind in her hair.

Sonny slowed the boat. The lighthouse stood on a shallow oyster bed island, the edges of which seemed to undulate like a satin sheet on a waterbed.

She'd never been this close to a lighthouse, even when she was a kid and the family had gone to the Jersey Shore for a few weeks every summer. She hadn't been interested in climbing a narrow staircase or being stuffed into a concrete tube on a hot sunny day when there was swimming, clamming and boys in the bay.

"Wow. It's lovely, isn't it?" Maggie said.

"It beacon of hope," the Asian woman replied.

"I always thought of it as a big candle," Jim said. "You know how people used to leave a candle in their window so their loved ones could find their way home? Now, we light candles to celebrate birthdays, marriages, special life events." He tipped his chin toward to the lighthouse as the boat slid to a stop in the grassy shoreline. "She's like that, but with more meaning."

He looked at the tower with reverence.

And they came to a seashore where the great waves Threw their froth and foam beneath the lights . . . as it stands today, the Great Church of St. Foam and the Holy Child . . .

Sonny waded to shore and tied the boat to a steel rod.

"Here we are," he said, reaching for Maggie's hand, helping her and the others make the leap to land.

At the base of the lighthouse, their feet sunk in the soggy soil. Sonny picked up the tour. "Originally there were two simple beacons built between March of 1837 and November of 1839, one for the North Channel and this one in the South Channel. They were converted to lighthouses in 1849 to guide ships up the Savannah River past Tybee Island, around Elba and Cockspur Islands into Savannah. The North Channel light was destroyed during the Civil War and never rebuilt. This lighthouse became The Cockspur Light and was rebuilt after hurricane damage in 1857. The foundation is oyster shell, the rest of the construction is brick."

"How tall is she?" Jim asked.

"Forty-six feet to the tower," Sonny said.

They walked around the base to the built-in brick stairs. Maggie followed the group inside, noticing the newer bricks, fresh paint and clean windows. The woodwork shone. Someone loved this lighthouse.

"George and Flora kept the lamp lit in the worst weather, rowing over from Elba Island in the storm, climbing these stairs," Sonny said, starting the ascent. "It was their job to bring the light that might save someone's life."

Outside, a seagull cried, a shore bird squawked in reply. The smooth steps were worn in the center where thousands of visitors had walked before them. There was no railing, nothing to hold onto. Maggie pressed her hand to the cool brick wall and climbed to the service room to join the others. The round glass room was bright, hot and quiet. It felt like being inside a light bulb.

Sonny opened the door to the balcony. A salty breeze blew in, swirling around the room. "The 1849 lighthouse had five lamps with fourteen-inch reflectors. She would have been visible for nine miles. In 1857, they installed a Fresnel lens, fourth order, but when she was deactivated in 1909, all the optics were removed."

Jim sighed, disappointed. He bent to examine the empty housing.

"Why don't they use it anymore?" Maggie asked.

"No need," Sonny said. "She was deactivated in 1909 when the channel became too shallow for larger ships to navigate. She serves as a day mark now, which is why I have to keep up her white paint job."

"You do?"

"Yes. She's one of my projects," Sonny said stepping out to the balcony.

"I don't understand," Maggie said.

"I restore lighthouses," Sonny said. "I don't do the actual restoration, just the consulting. But this project was special to me."

"How many have you restored?" she asked.

"Sixty-seven. But I've visited almost two hundred."

Jim joined them at the rail. "Folks see a lighthouse and take it for granted. Some places, the Coast Guard is in charge of maintenance or the National Park Service, other places it's private money and donations. We're lucky to have men like Mr. Beaumont to step up and give their personal time and expertise to save such important historical landmarks."

"You know a lot about lighthouses," Maggie said, chuckling.

"I should," Jim said. "My great-great-grandfather was John Lightburn."

"A wonderful man," Sonny said clapping him on the back.

Maggie asked, "Who was Lightburn?"

"He was one of the first keepers here."

"*The* first," Jim said.

"And one of the lucky ones."

"Yep." Jim nodded.

"What do you mean?" Maggie asked.

Sonny leaned against the glass wall of the tower room. The wind pulled his hair from his scalp, spiking it up then laying it flat, an exclamation point to his words.

"Many light keepers died on the job. It was dangerous and demanding. No sick days and no one around to help for the most part. After Lightburn, The Cockspur Light was manned from 1851-1853 by keeper Cornelius Maher, who drowned when his boat capsized trying to save someone who'd fallen overboard near the tower. His wife took over the job for three years until she died of the consumption in 1856. Thomas Quinfiven followed, working until he died of yellow fever in the epidemic of 1860."

"Not exactly a way to draw newcomers to the job." Maggie said.

"Which is why it usually stayed in the family," Sonny replied.

"Like funeral directors?"

"Pretty much," Sonny said. "That was how it went with The Martuses. After the war in 1865, John's duties changed at Fort Pulaski." He pointed across the water to the fort. "Part of his job was to tend the light. The army moved the family into old engineer quarters on the North side of the island. When George turned sixteen in 1877, he became the Assistant Light Keeper, then took on the job of Keeper of the Light when his father got sick. Flora used to help him, though most folks remember her for greeting the ships, not tending the light."

Maggie said, "I guess if you do something every day and night for forty-four years, people are bound to take notice."

"She might never have stopped if the government hadn't made them leave," Sonny said.

"Could they do that?"

"Sure they could. They did. When George turned seventy in 1931, they gave him mandatory retirement and moved him and Flora into Savannah."

Jim said, "It was never their house, never their land. The channel was closed down and the light was self-sufficient by then. There was nothing for George or Flora to do."

They stood on the balcony staring across the water at the old fort, watching gulls and pelicans dive. Maggie thought of self-sufficiency, of relying on oneself, of living on a deserted island where your only job was wait for ships that never came and tend a lighthouse that no longer needed a keeper.

As they made their way down the spiral stairs, Sonny ran his finger over a black line on the tower wall. He asked Jim, "What do you know about the hurricane of 1881?"

"Only that there was some flooding in the tower, land damage on Cockspur, and The Martuses fled to the fort for protection."

"That's right," Sonny said. "This mark on the wall shows the water line. At twenty-three feet above sea level, the damage would have been tremendous."

Maggie put her face to the small rectangle window in the tower wall. She imagined being trapped in the tower, pushed to the surface like a floating bathtub toy. Part of the image excited her, the force of Mother Nature was fascinating, but the rest of the image was frightening, to think that something as ordinary as water could become something so horrifying, so evil, so deadly.

CHAPTER 43

FLORA
1940

You never know how much you miss something until it's no longer there, the touch of a man's hand on the small of your back, three blasts from a ship's horn, splintery boards on a dock, the thickness of fog.

I thought I missed my lighthouse that way, but as I step into her cavity, I am feeling only remorse. I start to second-guess my whole life with one lungful of air. It tastes like dust and lies.

Each rise on the curved concrete stairs takes me further away from today. I think for a moment that I am not at all who I think I am. I don't exist, nor Cow Eyes, the patch of heat behind me. We're just figurines placed on a table, the toys of a giant who blocks the light and drops ashes all around.

The men stay below. One claiming he has a bad hip, the other murmuring something about oysters and the boat. I can tell it's the lighthouse that spooks them. It's not Cow Eyes and her pale sweaty face or me with my ghosts. But they are good men and I won't hold it against them.

In the round glass room, I feel him. My George. Cow Eyes pushes past me and bursts out onto the balcony. Her color returns as she gulps the fresh air. I think this air would cure anything, least of all a drunken stupor. I welcome the breeze that wafts in, wrapping it around me like a cloak.

My fingers slide down the cool glass panels. They remind me of the length of a man's spine, remind me of things I've done here, and of the men who passed by. I try to not dwell on choices, on the what if's in a life that's almost over.

"I see it now," Cow Eyes says a few minutes later as we sit on the balcony, dangling our feet.

"What's that?" I ask.

"Why they call you The Waving Girl," she says, tipping her face to the sun.

"That was a long time ago," I say.

"No. They still do, like the men who brought us here." She turns to look at me. "It's not a bad thing. I think it's rather nice, actually. Something to be

146

proud of." She closes her eyes and drops her head back. "I love it out here, wish I'd grown up like you."

"No." The word escapes in one harsh huff ignited by anger, fueled by horror. "No," I say. "You're not like me. You won't be isolated. You'll be a movie star, people will know you for the joy you bring them, the wonderful things you do. You will be someone's hero."

Cow Eyes laughs, a simple "Ha!" Then she chortles, a low chuckle. "But then, I would be just like you."

She laughs harder, but I gasp as if someone has slugged me in the gut.

The wind on the balcony has unpinned my hair. Gossamer strands whip my face, my dress dances. I squint into the sky, turn toward the sun as if the whole world depends on me making my point. I am perfectly positioned as if I could only have one place to stand and I have chosen this very spot.

When Cow Eyes looks at me, I can read her face. She is sorry—for everything, and instead of saying anything at all, I put my arm around her and pull her inside.

"Miss Flora," she says. "I shouldn't have said that."

"Nonsense." I pat her back, soothing her like the baby I'd never had. "It started in 1915. They called me a hero, when George and I saved those men on the dredge. Or maybe it was before, but that was when I remember hearing it most, and that's when the letters and gifts started coming. From people who weren't even sailors, people who had never been to Savannah."

Cow Eyes leans into my hand. "Tell me.

CHAPTER 44

MAGGIE
2011

Outside the lighthouse, water had begun seeping through the oyster beds. Maggie slipped out of her flip-flops and stepped from the bottom stair into ankle deep water. As Jim led the way to the boat, she hung back with Sonny, lingering in the shadow of the white tower. It seemed less a symbol of hope and more one of loneliness, sadness and reclusion.

"You said George and Flora left Elba Island and moved into Savannah after he retired," Maggie said. "What about his wife and children, his family?"

"George never married," Sonny said. "And Flora didn't have a husband. They had a sister who lived in town but they weren't very close."

"Neither one of them married? Isn't that unusual? For the time?"

"Some people might find it unusual today."

Sonny was right. Maggie grew up with the mentality that there were mandatory pegs on the ladder of life. She figured it would be especially so in the south, where everywhere she looked she saw tradition.

"Well, that answers my next question about The Waving Girl."

"He never came back," Sonny said, then softer, "Some say he never left at all."

No one spoke on the short ride to Elba Island. Their words were quelled by the slap and splash of water against hull and the whine of the dual engines, as Sonny repeated the route of George and Flora all those years ago. The shore wasn't far, close enough to swim to if the tide was low, if the sea calm enough. Maggie pulled out the Hasselblad. With the telephoto lens she could see the Martus home. The once white cottage had burnished to a dull gray, paint had peeled and chipped, the porch sagged, some of the railings were missing and the screen door hung off its hinges, dangling askew. Sonny idled the motor, allowing the boat to drift in closer, past the broken planks and pilings of a rotted pier. On the shore through a weedy field, a section of a once red barn was visible, its roof caved in. A few carefully placed paths dotted the hillside, most overgrown with weeds and all inaccessible via the ratty, jagged shoreline tainted with fish guts and plastic bottles.

"Why don't they fix this place up, like the lighthouse?" Maggie asked framing her shot.

"Good question," Sonny said. "It's not as simple as it seems. Right now, we've got too many cooks in the kitchen, if you know what I mean, and they're all too busy to see the pot's boiling over."

"Damn shame," Jim said.

"It ain't over yet," Sonny said under his breath.

Maggie focused her camera on the wraparound porch imagining Flora waving a white cloth, or swinging a lantern at night. She shot the sky with a piece of tree, a section of railing, then adjusted and pulled in tight capturing a window in the upper story, the angle of the eaves. She swung right and clicked, capturing six shots of the remains of the pier, the shoreline, a nesting tern, a fire ring. The world around Maggie fell away. She saw the piece of earth Flora had inhabited. Her heart went soft for the lonely girl who gave up her freedom for strangers, gave up any chance at an ordinary life. Maggie wished she could ask her if it had it been worth it.

Once I cried Love me to the people, but they fled like a dream, and when I cried Love to my friend, she began to scream. Oh why do they leave me, the beautiful people, and only the rocks remain, to cry Love me, as I cry Love me, and Love me again.

Maggie asked if they could get out of the boat, but Sonny was adamant. No one was allowed on shore.

"Besides, we have to get back," he said. "But, there's one more thing I want to show you."

He turned the boat toward the south channel of the Savannah River. The water was low enough to see banks lined with red clay.

"In the early 1900's," Sonny said, "the government sent men to dredge this channel, just like they did on the north side, but no matter how often they came, or how long they worked, the sludge kept coming back. Savannah mud is as stubborn as the people who walk on it."

He explained the slow, dirty and dangerous work of a dredge boat crew, then told the story of how one night someone overfed the furnace of one of the brown-water workboats, causing it to burst, igniting the whole ship. The fire was visible for miles, but it was Flora who rescued them.

Newspapers caught hold of the story and reporters started calling her an Angel Of the Sea, when other rescues came to light. The Waving Girl was famous.

Maggie lifted her camera and turned around the catch the view of the receding island, the house on the hill. She said, "Tidewater meets Craftsman."

"What's that?" Sonny looked over the side of the boat into the water.

"No." She laughed, unaware she'd spoken her thoughts aloud. "The Martus House. I can't help thinking it's like an abbreviated Tidewater look combined with the influence of a Craftsman structure."

Sonny shrugged. "Don't know about any of that, but she was a good house on a decent piece of land for a long time. A place where a family grew up, a place Flora and George called home for more than forty years. If only those walls could talk."

Maggie raised her camera as Sonny turned back to the wheel, accelerating through the channel toward Savannah. She braced herself on the side of the boat and snapped shot after shot, trying to capture a moment, a piece of history, a slice of life from cottage to water to the lighthouse beyond.

Before she could focus on the lighthouse though, the boat turned, following the curving river and blocking the white tower from view. In its place rose an ugly brick and glass rectangle sitting awkwardly on a shaved slope, its concrete landscape screaming tourist haven.

Maggie cursed under her breath and lowered the camera.

CHAPTER 45

BOBBIE
1919

When they were first married, Bobbie had asked him about it, the dream. The one that curled his lip and made him chuckle, a sound she'd never heard before. She was jealous of it, of the person he was in his sleep, a man who seemed much different from her daytime Sam.

He told her that he could only remember the dream in pieces. He always saw the beginning; a meadow, a path, how the sun felt warm on his back before he saw it glinting off the lake. There was a rowboat, its splintered oars cocked at an angle. Sometimes a bird would alight on the bow then fly off, rippling the water with the motion of its wings, the weight of the bird releasing the boat into movement. The surface of the lake shattered out of stillness might then turn blue or bloody, depending on the night of the dream and the state of Sam the dreamer.

One morning, when Bobbie asked, Sam skipped the red water part, and went right to the woman waiting on the opposite shore.

"There's a woman," Sam said. "She's standing across the lake. She waves to me, and I—"

"Who is she?"

"I don't know. I can't see her face, but I have a feeling we've never met."

Bobbie wanted the woman to be her. She couldn't tell him that, because the way he looked so guilty she knew it wasn't.

"There's more to the dream before the water," Sam said, "Before the meadow, but it isn't always the same and it isn't ever as clear."

He started wandering a few nights later. He'd be gone for days and when Bobbie asked him where he'd been, Sam would flap his hand at the air and say, "Around. I've been around." He pretended to be callous and flippant, but she saw a tenderness in his eyes and felt him watching her when she wrote. Bobbie knew Sam. She knew how to move him off the cold, vague place, how to soften his edges. She knew that eventually they'd be right again as long as he stayed away from the dream.

Bobbie took him to places she hated to go: parties, galleries and social events. She bought him things he didn't need. She called in favors and tried to think of herself as kind and giving, tried to see herself as someone who gave a damn, but really she was only being selfish. She wanted Sam. She needed him as much as he needed her, maybe more. They weren't like some couples, the ones who compliment each other like a china teacup and matching saucer; both pieces distinctly different with unique uses on their own, but when combined become something beautiful and useful. No, Sam and Bobbie were like a cast iron frying pan and a tempered glass bowl. You could use them together, but it wasn't typical or even pretty and you never knew what the result would be.

New York had changed, or maybe it was just in Bobbie's eyes. She used to feel the pulse of the city as she walked the sidewalks, used to enjoy hearing music change from block to block. To her, faces on the street held secrets, doorways led to wonderful places, every corner offered a new possibility.

But after loss, after sorrow, death, defeat and war, Bobbie experienced a new city. She felt the anger of the poor, the hopelessness of the sick. Alleys were for skinny cats eating garbage. The crowded sidewalks made her claustrophobic, smothering her in the negativity of harried people. Windows and doorways were only portals to places she wasn't welcome, places where people mourned.

Sam had been missing for a week when Bobbie stepped off the ship into New York Harbor with all the other soldiers, people who had mothers and wives and children to greet them. Bobbie had nobody. She told herself that he would have been there if he'd known she was coming, that he must not have gotten her last letter, maybe none of them.

That week, she asked around for him at the bars, their regular hang-outs, but no one had seen Sam for a while.

There was a layer of dust on every flat surface at the apartment and the lady downstairs told Bobbie, "That Sam, he's a tricky one. Gave me the slip a time or two." She poured them a drink. "Here's to having you home. And to the end of this damn war."

Instead of thinking about Sam, Bobbie went to the newspaper offices with the satchels of soldier letters, dropped them on a new editor's desk and said, "I've got an idea."

The idea was that a team of staffers would put together a new middle section of the paper, an encouragement section. The letters of the soldiers would appear, as completely as possible, followed by a letter from the editor and a call-out for replies.

In the pitch to his bosses, the young editor said, "Imagine the reaction. It's like we're bringing their boys home early. Giving them hope. Everyone needs hope, don't they?"

If he'd asked Bobbie, the answer might have been different, because she knew hope in itself was never enough. Sam had hope—sometimes an inordinate amount of it and still, he was sick. Bobbie had held hope once, in the form of a baby—a child she was forced to give up when loving Sam got in the way, when he made her choose. And now, she had nothing but hope. Hope he'd come back to her.

He knocked on their door on the ninth day. "I can't seem to find my key."

Bobbie had a list of things to do, but when she saw Sam everything changed. When he dropped the bag he was carrying and reached for her she folded into him, burying her face into a neck that smelled of roasted chestnuts and pine. She pulled leaves out of his matted hair and later, ran her fingers over scratches on his legs and a nickel-sized bare patch on his scalp that would later grow in white. He was still Sam, even with the unexplained bruises and the clothes she'd never seen—high quality garments, things she'd never imagine him choosing for himself.

They fell into their old ways of loving and laughing, of drinking, fighting, talking, dancing and living the hell out of life. Bobbie made a vow she wouldn't bring up where Sam had been or what he'd been doing. She told herself no good could come from such a discussion. Nothing could change the way she loved him, or the fact that he loved her back.

She noticed new things about him, wondered where he'd learned them. An odd turn of phrase, the new way he held his cigarette, the way he crossed his legs and hung his arm over the chair back as if he was practicing the role of a regular guy. His new love of peanuts. The black coat he never seemed to take off.

Bobbie wanted to believe the changes were for her, that Sam was always for her. But she heard the late night calls, the whispered exchanges. She saw the way women eyed him as he worked the rooms at bars, restaurants, parties, She began to feel left out, like guest in her own life. She was re-living the war in their apartment, complete with secret plans, undecipherable codes and prisoners. And like war, there were wounds no one could see and stockpiles of ammunition that never seemed to be enough.

Time went on, stealing a bit of Sam and Bobbie every day and leaving reminders behind, things they never asked for. Bobbie looked across the table at Sam one morning and saw a craggy-faced man with a patch of white in his receding hair. She pushed up her reading glasses, cleared her throat and turned the page of her book.

He said, "What is it? What's wrong?"

What was she going to say? That her whole life was wrong? That she'd made a mistake? That she felt like she was drowning?

CHAPTER 46

FLORA
1940

Somehow, she convinced me. So, I'm telling my drowsing Cow Eyes how Ma had been dead for six years, how it was just me and George on Elba Island in 1915.

❧ ❧

Things had changed. We moved slower and forgot more. But, I wrote in my journal every day and greeted the ships. People knew me. Heck, after twenty-eight years of waving, they expected me.

I may have become complacent. Or maybe it was just the onset of a fugue. Autumn could do that to me. Whatever the reason, the night the party barge passed, I didn't wave.

I had come out to the porch, to call in Dan, our young collie. We'd lost Cornbread and Tallulah over the years. Two stakes in the garden marked their resting place. I missed the dogs, but this pup kept me on my toes, needing something all the time.

He ran to me across the grass then up the porch steps, his white mane flying. He pranced in place as I patted his head, scratched his ears, lost my fingers in his ruff.

"Good boy," I said, wrapping my shawl around me and turning to go back into the warm house.

Suddenly, his ears popped straight up and swiveled, like a hare. He pulled away, went to the railing overlooking the water and stuck his head through the bars.

"What is it, boy?"

Dusk slipped into dark, making quick the trip from gloaming to night. I glanced at the lantern I hadn't lit. Dan barked. I heard a throaty motor ricocheting off the river banks and closed my eyes trying to guess where it would appear, trying to guess what sort of boat it would be, where it was going and why. I felt my white handkerchief folded neatly in my pocket.

The mockingbird broke into song in the garden. His stolen tune drowned out by a shout then the laughter of a woman on the boat. I opened my eyes to

155

see a low-slung vessel come into view. Colorful lanterns hung across its bow. People shimmered in white and silver party clothes. They sang and danced as a small band played. Small lights flickered like question marks punctuated by the red glow of cigarettes. Someone threw a bottle overboard. I saw the arc of its flight in the moonlight, heard the splash. A deep man's voice boomed, "Shark!" Women squealed, one caught the joke and chimed in to more laughter, "You'd better jump in and catch us some breakfast, Freddy!"

I thought about calling out, as so many others had done to me. Instead, I stood there with my hand in my pocket until the laughter faded, until I heard silence instead of music.

By the time I went inside, George had gone up to bed. The house was dead quiet, save the cricket in the pantry, a hardy little critter that knew the sound of my footsteps.

Alone in my bed, I hummed the song I'd heard them singing on the party boat. "I had a dog named Fido, that I loved very much." I became the girl on the boat, the one who made the men laugh and cheer. I was the reason for the party. They were celebrating me.

Sleep took me deeper and I felt it all slip away.

When I looked down, I was standing in mud. There was no boat, no party, no shimmering dresses. I was surrounded by mud and sinking fast.

I woke to my dog Dan's teeth tugging off my bedcovers. I jerked awake, swatting at the collie, but he backed up, barked at me then paced in front of the window, glancing back at me.

"All right. I'll let you out," I said, throwing on some work clothes—woolen britches and an old shirt of George's. Downstairs, I could smell something like fire. I checked the kitchen. Nothing. I opened the back door.

Smoke hung in the air, made me cough. Burning oil. I followed Dan to the cliff. Out on the water, men were shouting. I couldn't see anything until the wind blew across the water cutting a path.

The government dredge was on fire. There were people aboard.

156

CHAPTER 47

MAGGIE
2011

Her plate was untouched. Gravy ran off the buttered biscuit, dripped onto the tabletop as the mound of sliced turkey cooled. The other plate, filled with desserts, all of Maggie's favorites, was partially hidden under the lacy curtain that had blown out of place when she'd cracked open the window.

She sat cross-legged on the rag rug in her room, palms on her knees, rocking. Photographs of Flora's cottage, Savannah houses and buildings, boats at the marina were spread everywhere. "Where are you?" she murmured.

There was a knock on the door.

"Come in," Maggie said without looking up.

Charles poked his head in. "Hey." He opened the door wider, looked around. "Everything okay?"

Maggie reached for the shot taken at the marina of Sonny on the boat with the girl, then picked up one of him at the helm during The Waving Girl tour. She looked at Charles, then turned around a picture of the Elba Island cottage. "I saw it. And the lighthouse."

Charles scanned the photos on the floor. "I don't see a lighthouse."

"Yeah, I didn't get any pictures. I was thinking I might need to go back. Saw your fort, though."

"That right?"

"Quite impressive. I can see how you'd be drawn to it."

"That's something," Charles said with a laugh. " Coming from you."

"What do you mean, coming from me? You're the fort expert around here."

Charles knelt beside Maggie, rearranging the pictures. "But you're the one who knows buildings—intimately. Like you're one of them."

"What?" Maggie said. "You're crazy."

"No. I mean it."

"Charles, I am not a *building*."

"Sure you are, darlin'."

Maggie glared at him, pursed her lips.

He smiled. "I don't mean that in a bad way." He showed her the photo in his hand. The Baldwin House on East Hall Street, built in the Romanesque style, all curves and arches and inlays. "Maybe you're like this house. It's beautiful. Sturdy. Strong walls. But what's behind that? Shoddy insulation? Leaking pipes? You put up a good front, Miss Maggie. But I know there's something else, maybe a secret hiding place, or a few cracks in your foundation from the weight of the brick wall you work so hard to maintain."

Maggie wanted to disagree. She wanted to argue, but mostly she wanted to ask him how he knew her so well when he hardly knew her at all.

Charles said, "Have you ever been to someone's house and think you know exactly what you'll find when they open the door?"

"I guess," she said.

"I'd bet that if you took me to three different houses in your city, I could pick yours."

Maggie thought of her renovated saltbox. Would Charles see *her* in the sparse clean lines of the home she'd stripped bare?

There had been a time when the rooms were filled with antiques and oddities she and David had collected in their travels. A time when the mantle had been a holding place for artwork until an open space became available. This had been their way, a comfortable manner of living. It was part clutter, part art, mostly laziness and familiarity, as that was how they had grown up, in homes where more was better and style ran second.

A few years ago when David refused to go to couples therapy, Maggie turned spring cleaning into a spring clear out that became a new uncluttered way to live. At first David asked where all their stuff was—their things—as if they were who they were because of the stuff surrounding them.

Maggie told him she was adopting a minimalist lifestyle, that her therapist had suggested she should try living less encumbered, not as a slave to things. She took David to modern galleries, to houses that were warm without carpets or drapes or chunky furniture.

One week he was away, she painted all the walls white, packed up all the knick knacks and non-essentials and hauled it to a storage place on the other side of the city. Still not sure she was ready to give it all up, she paid the bill each month, and at Christmas, offered the address and key to David, so that he could choose.

They became used to the open space, the breathability. A leather couch, a soft chair and an old ottoman draped in a serape changed places in the living room. Moving furniture became redecorating. Books became furnishings. Less was more, as elements of their work became décor: fancy ink pens, thick leather journals, stacks of photographs.

How can Something envision Nothing?. . . Where's your philosophy gone?

Only the outside of the rustic saltbox spoke of "before." The front lawn, enclosed by a peeling white picket fence, was dotted with wildflowers that Maggie planted from free seed packets. The walkway from the creaking gate to the wide plank porch had been carefully constructed of bricks they'd rescued from a downtown Philly building demo. The white wicker swing she won on Ebay hung under a brace of well-watered ferns and ivy, suggesting an owner with a green thumb, when in reality, Maggie lived by the survival of the fittest mentality and figured five bucks for a new fern was worth all the watering, fertilizing and pruning she'd avoided.

She wondered what Charles would make of that—how the exterior she and David chose to show the world was nothing at all like what they were behind closed doors.

CHAPTER 48

BOBBIE
1930

It shouldn't have been that simple. There should have been something that tied them to the place. Maybe not the apartment itself, but the neighborhood, the area, the people, the life they had become accustomed to. A life they had once thought ideal.

But the world had changed and Bobbie had become the woman in the corner tapping her foot waiting for something she couldn't name, ready to escape a past she couldn't reclaim.

When they pulled the car away from the curb and out into the traffic of New York City, Bobbie reached across the seat and laid her hand on Sam's thigh. "Where should we go first?"

Sam covered her hand with his, then lifted it to his lips and kissed it.

"South," he said. "Let's head south."

"New Jersey?" Bobbie made a face.

"Well, yes. New Jersey, and then some. I was thinking—"

"Let's just take it state by state, cowboy," she said knocking him on the shoulder then pulling on a pair of tinted glasses and tying a bright yellow scarf over her hair.

Sam hummed as he drove, broke out into song a few times too, startling Bobbie at first, but she never thought to ask him to stop. She began to think this trip was going to be better than the one she'd imagined years ago, before the war. *On The Road With Sam. Adventures and Real Stories. Life Across The Country. Real Folks Living Real Lives.* The headlines wouldn't stop coming.

They were going to drive the donated 1929 Chrysler Imperial until it died, logging history one story at a time. Bobbie had signed agreements from four newspapers to run a weekly column. Despite the uncertainty many people faced, Sam and Bobbie had maps, money and contacts. Their trunk was filled with clothes, food, water and paper. Lots of paper.

It was June and the weather was perfect. With the number of people strolling the beach communities, Bobbie figured they weren't the only ones to think the Jersey Shore was a good idea. Instead of crossing onto the long narrow chain of islands off the coast, they kept driving, skirting the shoreline until they stopped for the night in Tuckerton.

People were very friendly and for a while it seemed the crush of the world had left them all. Sam was in one of his happy moods, the kind that drew people to him. They sat in a little Mom and Pop joint on the water eating fried clams and hushpuppies washed down with near beer enhanced by an order of "imported coffee," the code for rum. They shared a picnic table with a local couple and their friends from Ohio. Bobbie had her story before dark, an exciting tale of a bootlegging boat hi-jacked by a pilot who apparently had no knowledge of hidden sandbars. The Ohio couple had been sufficiently spooked when the story progressed from the theft of the boat to a deadly explosion that lit up the sky for a mile in all directions, leaving pieces of hull embedded in the rooftops of three houses.

After dinner and a visit to Mom and Pop's kitchen, Sam and Bobbi stood on the sand behind the restaurant staring at the wide expanse of beach.

"Go for a walk?" Sam said pulling back his jacket to reveal a shiny silver flask in the breast pocket.

"But of course," Bobbie said in a put-on English accent hooking her arm through his.

They walked barefoot in the hard-packed sand. The tide pulled away exposing shells and debris. Sand crabs skittered across the surface, too close to Bobbie's feet. She jumped, squealing and Sam caught her in his arms then led her up the beach away from the slapping waves. He found a small alcove sheltered on both sides by sharp sea grasses where they could sit shoulder to shoulder, sipping from the silver flask, sharing a cigarette and watching the ocean, daring it to change.

Bobbie could have ruined the moment by talking about her plans, or the story she was already writing in her head. But she didn't.

"Look," Sam said.

The clouds had cleared and the sun was readying her descent, a huge fireball, sending a stripe of orange and red across the shimmering surface of blue.

"It's beautiful," Bobbie said.

"Absolutely beautiful," Sam said looking at her.

Some days the stories found them. People knew who Bobbie was and why she was there. They followed them to coffee shops and diners with heirlooms, photographs and letters, eager to reveal family secrets, to tell truths that might only be their version of reality. It was up to Bobbie to filter through it all. On the days the town ran dry or the weather kept people away, the stories had to be sought out, leaving Bobbie to follow a trail that might lead to something deeper, or end suddenly in a place no one wanted to go.

If she had to draw a map from story to story, like the map from town to town, she'd call the rivers disappointment and the mountains obstacles. She'd call new roads opportunity and flower-filled valleys love. For every main street there would be a woman who pined for someone she could never have. For every town square's old oak or elm or maple there would be a man with dreams larger than his surroundings, a man forced to stand still because he'd been born in the wrong time, lived in the wrong place, married the wrong woman.

The stories became the way she remembered the towns. Sometimes she'd see the landscape in the same way, matching bustling, booming towns with tales of inventions and progress and families that strived to better their world. She pitted these places against quiet backwoods towns and forgotten shore villages with desolate coastlines and barren fields and their sad stories of loss.

Sam and Bobbie slept among the townspeople in borrowed beds and barns. When they tired of talk and social niceties, they slept under the stars or in the backseat of the car, the sound of Sam's tortured breathing the only noise around.

Bobbie lay next to him, willing herself into his dreams, whispering in his ear, "You love me. You can't live without me. You need me."

In the morning she stared at him across a café table, looking for signs of the dream, for signs that she was losing him.

"How did you sleep?" she asked.

"Fine. A little tightness in the chest this morning," he said, rubbing a fist over his heart. His breathing was shallow and the dark circles under his eyes betrayed the word, fine.

"We should see a doctor in the next town."

"No."

"Are you taking your pills?"

"Sure."

"Sam?"

"Do you want more coffee?" He asked flagging over the waitress, ending the conversation.

They'd gone from the shore in South Jersey across the bay into Delaware on a ferry and now were making their way to a town Bobbie had picked called Little Heaven.

"I need to be able to say truthfully," she said, "that I have seen a little heaven."

"I know I have," Sam said reaching over and sliding his hand up between her legs.

"Hey!" Bobbie squealed, squeezing her thighs, trapping his hand then removing it and placing it back on the steering wheel. "Eyes on the road, hands on the wheel, buster."

"Now what fun would that be?"

She waggled a finger at him in mock anger, but there was happiness under the teasing. It shone in her eyes.

The town of Little Heaven was far from Nirvana, at least the part they drove into. It reminded Bobbie of Tarrabelle.

"Let's go for a swim," she said, sliding across the seat and tucking herself into Sam's side.

Sam turned onto an oyster shell road that was still being used by horse drawn carts from the look of the ruts and fresh droppings. They took the car as far as they dared and when salty air overtook the scent of horse manure they knew they were close to the ocean.

Bobbie jumped out and ran through the low brush over the dunes, unruly copper hair flying everywhere, her light skirt drawn taut outlining long, thin legs.

Sam was panting, gripping his chest, when he caught up to her.

"You shouldn't run," Bobbie said. "You know what the doctor said."

"Fuck. The. Doctor," he wheezed dropping into the sand, then propping himself up on his elbows, following Bobbie's gaze.

The view was spectacular, a barren beach with sand as white as sugar. Breakers crashed far enough out to suggest a long shallow sandbar. The sky was cloudless, clear and blue, a western sky.

"I'm going in. Come on." Bobbie stood and stripped off her shoes, skirt, blouse, and undergarments.

She let Sam look at her, let him choose.

"Get started without me," he said with a grin. "I'm going to get a few things from the car."

"All right," she said, bending to kiss him. "But, no more running."

She looked back as she made her way down the beach to the water. Sam was still sitting in the sand, a pained expression on his face, one Bobbie had a hard time reading.

Floating on her back, she was a dot from the shoreline, a human crucifix, arms splayed, feet together, she bobbed in the waves, letting the current carry her.

She thought about the story she was going to tell, of the baby tossed overboard as a ship sank off the coast of Maine. They must have known they weren't going to make it. But somehow they had faith that a tiny body sandwiched between two featherbeds could float to shore and live on.

They called her Seaborn, the Whyte family that found her and raised her as their own. She was a fair-skinned, gentle blond in a family of tall, dark, stern-faced people. Bobbie questioned the story's basic elements, not the authenticity. She'd seen the girl herself and been intrigued wondering if Seaborn was so kind and gentle because of the nature of her genes or if she was that way because the Whytes had raised her as a blessing.

Bobbie swam to shore, dried herself with her skirt then sat on the blanket next to her sleeping husband. She smoothed his shirtfront, pushed an errant hair out of his face, then reached for the bottle of whiskey. Sam was good to her. He'd brought her notebook and pencil down too. She cracked open a new page and began to write.

"If someone knew nothing of their past, couldn't they create the best one possible? And if someone was raised in a family that thought them special, extraordinary, a blessing, would they not become that type of person?"

She couldn't help thinking of Florence, the baby she had given up to have a life with Sam. A child who was being raised in London as Stevie, as the daughter of Sadie Smith, her ex-housekeeper.

Bobbie wrote until her hand cramped, then took a long drink, wiped her nose and lay down, curling her naked body into Sam, dragging his arm over her, tucking it underneath. And when he rolled toward her, she spooned in closer, trying to melt into him.

CHAPTER 49

MAGGIE
2011

Maggie woke to the sound of chirping birds. She rolled over expecting to find a soft pillow within an arm's reach but felt only floor. The last time she'd crashed on the carpet in a pile of papers she'd been studying for a calculus exam.

She was tired, sore and a little hungry, but when she reached for her camera the needs left her. A few minutes later, she was walking down a tree-lined street cursing her dietary choices as she felt her waist jiggle like a cream-filled Southern pastry. Her thighs burned with the effort and the camera slung across her chest smacked her ribs like a penance.

As she turned the corner to another gorgeous block of historic homes, Maggie tried to see them from an uneducated point of view, though it was hard to unlearn things. The yellow trim of the first house caught her eye, a brazen choice for the pink-hued brick. The second had bicycles piled in the small yard, the way they had fallen reminded her of modern art like a sculpture of excess or a yearning for one's childhood. She smiled. You could take the architecture out of the photographer but you couldn't take away the artist's eye. She reached for her camera, already framing the shot.

As she captured the image, a curtain moved in the second story window. A woman with a blue scarf around her head appeared. Her eyes moved down the sidewalk, stopping on Maggie. Without thinking, Maggie shot a frame before the woman could drop the curtain. The image that appeared on the camera's display was stunning. Instead of her typical building shots—the ones some critics called cold, calculated and dispassionate, the mere addition of a human being plus the blue of her scarf, the grip of her hand on the curtain, all served to give the photograph depth. It made the picture a story.

Maggie unzipped her backpack, found a notebook and wrote down the picture number, the date and street address. She added a caption, the first thing she'd thought when she saw the woman's worried expression change to despair. "It's not him."

Her brain whizzed, sending messages like ricocheting pinballs. She shot picture after picture, blending old and new. On a street of stone and iron-faced historic homes she captured a spiky-haired boy whizzing past on a bright red scooter. She caught joggers in headsets passing a horse-drawn carriage transporting a bride and groom. She shot antique storefronts with clerks dressing mannequins in hip-hop gear and latte-sipping customers sharing a newspaper at the café across the street. She found a lady shaking out an old quilt behind a fine example of a brick carriage house on Bay Street, then made her way downtown where poor black kids played with hoses and buckets in front of ramshackle apartments. A few streets over, she stumbled on a lavish birthday party in full swing on the manicured lawn of a modern plantation home.

By the time Maggie hit the waterfront, she had to swap out memory cards. She swung her backpack around, smacking her hand with the dangling keychain of The Waving Girl. She rubbed her thumb over the figurine and grabbed the edge of the silver cloth. "I see you," she whispered.

Another block and Maggie had to take a break. Her hands were cramped. She needed to pee. She stopped at the first place she came to, pulled open the heavy door and stepped into Frank's Bar. The woman behind the bar looked up as Maggie entered, nodded then went back to stocking bottled beer.

Maggie grabbed a bar napkin, wiped the sweat from her forehead and pointed to the beers. "Can I get one of those and a water?"

"Sure," the barmaid said, snapping off the cap and sliding the beer across the bar.

Maggie reached for the cold bottle then hesitated. "Um, where's the restroom?"

"Straight back. On the left."

Maggie made her way through the dark-paneled space. Her feet stuck to the floor in places and the air was as stale as the interior of a smoker's car. She pushed open the door with the gold reclining woman on it.

Unlike the bar she'd entered, this room was a creamy pastel sweet smelling retreat, like a mouthful of sorbet between meals, which struck her as funny seeing as it was a bathroom. There was a single toilet complete with an oversized gold flush handle, a furry pink toilet seat cover, matching throw rug and an ornate toilet paper holder that looked like a well-groomed white poodle. Maggie giggled.

She used the toilet then washed her hands with tiny pink poodle soaps and dried them on a pom-pommed Eiffel Tower hand towel. Before she left, she shot a picture for posterity. A French boudoir in the middle of Savannah, minus the obligatory bidet.

There was music playing when she returned to the bar, a soulful bluesy rendition of a Motown classic. Maggie put her backpack on one stool and sat in another. She nodded to the barmaid, pushed the glass of water out of the way and downed the beer before the song ended. She had to refrain from sighing out loud, but when she looked around the deserted bar she figured it wouldn't have mattered if she had.

The door opened, a beam of light illuminating the stained and worn wood floor. Two men with hotel nametags came in, chattering and laughing in the carefree way of youth and particularly, youth who are done with work for the day.

"Hey, Belle," the first guy said, echoed by the other. "Could you bring us two drafts and some cheese fries?"

"You got it." Belle finished wiping the bar top then tucked the cloth into her apron.

Maggie watched her fill their beers and pass an order slip through the service window to the kitchen. A large black hand swooped down, snatched up the order then disappeared.

The guys sank into a rear booth, simultaneously firing up cell phones.

Maggie thought about David and his opinion on cell phone use in public–the man had had his issues she remembered, chuckling.

"Another?" Belle asked.

"Sure. Thanks."

Two beers later and another visit to the boudoir, Maggie returned to find the hotel workers perched on stools near hers. They leaned over the bar, reading a section of Belle's paper.

"See? I told you," she said.

"Yeah, okay," the taller guy said. "I guess you can get arrested for that. But what if you—"

"Forget it, man," the other one said. "She's right. It wouldn't be worth it."

"Everything's got a price," Maggie said, climbing onto her stool, almost missing the first time, then catching herself and readjusting. She pushed her empty glass toward Belle and nodded.

"You got that right," said the tall guy, raising his beer in her direction and giving her the thumbs up.

"Yep. You wanna play you gotta pay."

"Amen to that," Belle said folding up the newspaper and popping the cap off a beer for herself.

They all drank quietly for a moment. Maggie picked at the label on her beer bottle. "Can I ask you something?" she said. "If you died and were cremated, where would you want your ashes scattered?"

"Dude, that's cold," the smaller guy said.

"Yeah, kinda morbid," the other guy said. "What got you thinking about that? You're not gonna die or anything are you?"

"Hey, if it was me?" Belle said, "I'd want my ashes blown all over this bar. Have a big bash in here one night, live music, food, booze, and bring in one of those air machines, you know? The kind that shoot t-shirts at concerts? I'd have someone shoot my ashes out of that."

"Get outta here," the tall guy said. "You'd end up on everyone's clothes and shit. They'd just wash you down their drains the next day."

Belle smiled. "Yeah, but think of that night. I'd get to go home with everyone."

She looked wistful as she leaned against glass shelves of booze. Then she burst out laughing. "Christ! You didn't think I was serious, did you?"

The smaller, dumber guy, as Maggie saw him, said, "Nah. Course not.

Right, Jimmy?"

Maggie drew her backpack onto her lap and unzipped it. She reached in, then set David's urn on the bar.

Belle crossed herself. Jimmy laughed. "Good One. Fuckin' A." He put his hand on Maggie's shoulder but when she looked at him, her eyes were wet and he cursed under his breath. "Aw, shit."

Maggie sniffled, drew a finger under her nose. "It's okay. That's my husband, David. Well, not really. They never found the body. It's mostly his stuff, and a book."

"His stuff?" Jimmy's co-worker said. "You got his stuff in there?" The kid winced and covered his crotch with his hands.

Jimmy smacked him in the chest. "Shut up, man."

Maggie said, "David told me I'd know where he wanted his ashes to be scattered when the time came. But I don't know. The more I think about it, I don't know anything. I don't think I even knew him at all." She tapped the lid of the urn. "Why couldn't he just tell me?"

Belle said, "Would be too easy. Too final. Best thing he could do is leave it up to you, up to someone who loved him. That's what I'd do." She laid her hands over Maggie's, removed them from the urn. "Don't worry. You'll do the right thing."

"Besides," Jimmy said, "It's not like he'll know, right? I mean the guy's dead, ain't he?"

Belle shot him a look and his buddy elbowed him, but Maggie just raised her glass. "To David."

Why do I think of Death as a friend? It is because he is a scatterer. He scatters the human frame The nerviness and the great pain, Throws it on the fresh, fresh air And now it is nowhere.

CHAPTER 50

FLORA
1940

I want to stop telling her the story. I want to stop remembering, but there is a certain love in the memory. Parts of my past might even be deemed honorable. So I tell Cow Eyes that it was me that woke up George that night.

❧ ❧

I was panting when I barged into George's room.

"Get up!" I said, shaking him. "There's a fire. At the mouth of the river. The dredge!"

George pushed himself up, blinking. "What?"

"Come on, George." I threw pants and shirt in his direction. "We have to help them. I'll grab some blankets and meet you at the boat. Hurry!"

I had ropes, floats and blankets loaded in the dory when George arrived. I started the motor, praying under my breath the whole time and as soon as his feet touched hull, I gunned it.

The river water was black and still. Mother Nature's perfect backdrop to a man-made horror. I usually preferred the rushing water of the channel to the slapping unpredictability of the sea, but that night, I would have rather had noise and spray to distract me from the scene across the water.

I aimed the dory toward the burning dredge. It had never been a pretty ship and now with its boiler bent over and flames licking at either end, she looked like the slapdash project of an eight-year-old. Fire engulfed the bow of the dredge, where at least five workers were trying to staunch the flames.

George cupped his hands around his mouth and shouted, "Get out of there!"

The men in the water echoed his command until that was all you could hear over the crackle and snap of the fire. Men jumped from the port side and splashed toward the dory. Instead of dwindling, the fire grew.

George turned to me, "We'll have to bring them ashore in shifts, take the weakest ones first."

I nodded and dropped anchor.

George tossed a float on a rope to a huddle of survivors. "Swim to us if you can! Or grab the float and I'll pull you in!"

The men swam. I could see their white teeth gleaming above the black water. George hauled two of them in. The current was strong and the water cold. No one would last very long.

I held the boat steady as three more climbed in. They were sooty black, wheezing, shaking and all talking at once, offering up a prayerful blend of thanks and praise.

By the time the ninth guy was pulled in by his buddies, six men were treading water an arm's length away. George counted heads. Our boat was already low in the water. We couldn't take on any more weight. I hated leaving anyone, but everyone understood the physics. They said they'd wait for us to come back with an empty boat, knowing their choice was freezing water or a floating firebox.

We raced back to the pier at Elba Island, men huddled in the bottom of the boat, wrapped in damp blankets, shivering, weeping, cursing.

We paused long enough for the men to leap off, George shouted orders as we turned the dory around. "There's water, whiskey and dry blankets in the barn. Make a fire on the shore and get out of those wet clothes."

The rescued workers bumped into each other on the pier, shocked and confused, until one of them took charge. As George and I pulled away, we saw the men formicate to the barn, stripping off their wet shirts along the way.

The dredge was still burning when we returned. We pulled more smoky, singed men into the boat, each one looking worse than the guy before, blue-lipped and shivering, but they were alive.

"Damnit," George cursed as water seeped into the boat. "We'll need to make one more trip."

I looked at the men clinging to the side of the dory, their faces illuminated by the fire that still raged on the dredge.

"I'm sorry," I yelled over the sound of the fire, over the moans of the injured men in the boat. "We can't take any more."

They let go when I promised we'd return. I told them to hold onto each other, to keep their arms and legs moving. I couldn't look back as George gunned the motor and the dory jerked forward then pushed its way home.

The men from the first trip were gathered around a small fire on the shore. They passed bottles of whiskey and fed the flames with small branches. They might have been overgrown boys spending the night camping if not for the bloody few in bandages fashioned from torn clothing and the burned ones wailing in the dark.

We dropped off the second load and headed right back out.

Pulling up to the dredge site, George told me to count the remaining heads in the water. "We can take all the rest," I said. I'd make them fit.

We started hauling. As soon as one flopped in, he would turn to help the next one, like a conveyer belt of aid. My arms were weak, my lips puckered from the salt water. I felt my bones.

George looked across at the dredge, now a third submerged in the murky water. He asked, "How many?"

"Thirty-one," a big, bearded guy said. "Including the captain." The man tipped his head toward the dredge.

I followed his gaze. "Sweet Jesus."

Someone appeared through a cloud of black smoke. He made his way toward the crooked boiler. Something was wrapped around his hand, a cloth, perhaps his shirt. The man was large and dark. I couldn't tell if it was smoke or God that made him that color, until he stood in front of the flames and it was apparent that he was black all over, a shade that wouldn't wash off. The man leaned into the smoke, then impossibly into the flame itself.

The dredge workers understood what he meant to do. Two men dove from the dory and surfaced near the dredge, yelling and waving their arms trying to erase the man's actions. But when they realized it was too late, they dug their arms in making frantic, splashing strokes away from the dredge boat, away from their crewmate.

The sound the boiler made when it exploded is what annihilation would sound like if every word had a voice.

Time was reduced to fragments. The heat on my face was baby's breath, if the baby was the spawn of Satan. The man burned like a tall orange candle. He spun, screaming, a faulty Chinese firework that never left the ground. There was a sizzle when he hit the river. The men in the water swam his body to the dory, pulling him by clothes that fell apart under their touch. We used a blanket as a sling and hauled up their captain like we'd netted a precious fish.

I could barely discern the man from the wet wool. I told myself it was because it was too dark and I was too tired, not wanting to think of the other reasons, that the man's skin was no longer skin and might as well be wool.

George steered through burning debris and aimed the dory home. Behind us, the river workboat gurgled once then sank.

On the shore of Elba Island, the rescued men stared out at the sea or into the crackling fire and sometimes in the direction of the beached dory. They were safe and alive, all thirty-one. For now.

David Jackson, the captain of the government dredge lay in the bottom of George's dory writhing in pain. His head was cradled by the big bearded guy; Chet, who grimaced as he poured a shot of whiskey into David's mouth. Though I wouldn't have called it a mouth, maybe more of a hole in the man's face, and using the word face may not have been quite right either.

❧ ❧

I wished I had Ma's morphine. I wished there was someone else to lay the wet cloths on his seared flesh, and I wished more than anything that Chet would quit pouring the hooch in the gaping maw and instead hit David's skull with the bottle. Then for a while anyway, the man would have peace.

Someone on the beach started to sing. It was the kind of song hummed while walking home from a day in the fields, the kind of song heard coming from the Baptist church windows on a Sunday morning in May, the kind of song that was thankful and mournful at the same time.

The voice was smooth and rich and when the other men began to sing I could still hear it. Chet chimed in, singing the female part in a keen falsetto and David lay still for the first time.

The sun was coming up when I placed the last strip of cotton on the captain's chest. I sat back, exhaling loudly and when George appeared behind me, I leaned into him.

George said, "He gonna be all right?"

I stretched my arms, shoulders and back. "He's gonna be fine," I said. "Aren't you, David?"

But I saw in George's face the memory of flesh peeling from the man's bones when we tried to move him. If I had not seen the captain upright and walking before the explosion, I might have believed the mass of charred skin and skull in the bottom of our dory was an animal that had been forked over a roasting pit and seasoned for eating. I could have called him David all I wanted, but what was left wasn't a man anymore.

CHAPTER 51

MAGGIE
2011

She didn't know when it had started raining again, and now that she was cold and wet, she was sobering up quickly. Her mouth felt thick and cottony, and she had to pee again, but she kept rowing.

Maggie looked back at the shore, squinting through the water draining off her forehead, through the haze off the river. She figured she was still on the right track because she could see the shape of the fort on the point. The wind picked up, stripping her of any warmth she might have reserved. This time when she glanced over her shoulder she saw the lighthouse.

The aluminum rowboat was heavier than it looked. She leaned back, hauling the boat onto the squishy shore, didn't remember the land feeling this soft when they were here on the tour. Actually, the whole place seemed smaller. She tied up to the same pole Sonny had used but not knowing any fancy knots, she made a substantial lump out of the rope and looped it around.

"There," she said, then tripped and landed face first in a pile of slimy oyster shells and seaweed.

"Great, just great." She wiped her mouth on her t-shirt, then turned her face up to the rain, though closing her eyes made her sway a bit. It felt good and what did she care that she looked like shit and probably stunk now too. She started toward the lighthouse steps, singing, "Row, row, row your boat, gently down the stream . . ."

The door was unlocked which was good, because the last thing Maggie needed to add to her rap sheet under theft of rowboat, trespassing and public drunkenness was breaking and entering. She shrugged off the soggy backpack then pulled her camera out of its case. The rain made a dull hammering sound on the glass tower, but there was still light, a nice natural light, with the shadows, gray hues and dull tones that came with it on a day like this. There was something spooky, something . . . she shivered, then settled on the word "cinematic" about the place, in a sad, hopeless way.

She shot the space from left to right then eased herself onto the cool block floor and snapped a dozen shots that way. When her foot knocked over the backpack the clunking sound reminded her of the other reason she'd come.

Maggie carried David's urn up the spiral stairwell and set it in a narrow window outcropping. With the dark sky and white clouds beyond, the blue and gold Raku urn was the only piece of color against the whitewashed brick.

"Is this what you wanted, David?" she whispered as she captured the image. There was a responding flash of light, a roll of far off thunder. Maggie tucked the urn under her arm and trudged up the rest of the stairs to the glass dome where the wind whistled and the smattering of rain seemed crueler, alternating between slapping hands and the scritching of rat feet. Maggie dropped the camera and backpack, then leaned into the heavy exterior door, easing it back against the glass. She grabbed the railing and started to walk around the tower.

Rain pelted her from all directions, smacking her chest, threatening to topple her with the force of the wind behind the water. She swept her soggy hair off her face, spit and squinted. There was a boat out there.

"Hey," she called, waving the one arm she'd been grabbing the rail with. "Hey!"

Poor son of a bitch, Maggie thought, then she looked closer.

"Shit! Shitshitshitshitshit!"

She was the poor son of a bitch. That was her rowboat out there.

Maggie ran around the rest of the tower and looked. Sure enough, the boat she'd borrowed was having no problem at all making its way back to Savannah.

"Goddamn it!" Maggie yelled.

She was screwed on all sides. The water was higher than the steps and the sky was getting darker and more evil-looking every minute. Maggie went inside, slamming the door behind her. She paced the tiny room alternating between anger and laughter. After she got dizzy pacing in circles she sunk to the floor and reached for the backpack, thinking a picture of her shitty situation might one day be funny. Instead of her camera, her fingers found something else, something she needed more at the moment, a half-full bottle of bourbon.

"Thank you, Jesus."

The guys at the bar must have stashed it when she told them she was going to row to the lighthouse. Maybe things weren't so bad after all. And hell, it wasn't like no one knew where she was, right? Rain can't last forever, come low tide, she could swim back to shore. Maggie opened the bottle and looked around. It wasn't so bad in here, except for the fishy smell.

She raised the bottle in a silent toast then drank, gasping as the bourbon went down like fire. The second swig was easier. Maggie went to the window and stared out. She took another drink. "If you're listening, Waving Girl? Hello? I could use a little rescuing."

❧　❧

Later, sitting cross-legged under the glass dome in her underwear and a dirty t-shirt she'd found in a rusty toolbox downstairs, Maggie drummed her fingers against the empty bourbon bottle–an impromptu jam session accompanied by the "donk" of water dripping from the wet clothes she'd hung around the room, the whoosh of a gentle wind, cries of night birds, the buzz and thump of insects as they flew into the glass walls. But something was missing in her concert. Rain.

Maggie got up, swaying and giggling. "Woah. Steady girl." She stumbled to the tower wall, hitting something with her bare foot, feeling it a second later.

She might have been more wary, but she had bourbon brain, so she simply reached down and grabbed the round, white thing she'd kicked. Holding it up to the moonlight at the window, she saw it was some kind of bird skull.

"Boo," she said pointing a finger at it. "Boo. Bird." She snorted. "Oh man, it's a boo bird." She broke out in belly laughs. "I crack me up."

 . . . *Dust to dust . . . the grave yawned wide and took the tears and the rain, and the poor dead man was at last free from all his pain, Pee wee sang the little bird upon the tree again and again . . .*

Maggie braced herself against the cool glass. A full moon was reflected over the black water. She closed one eye, saw the perfect shot, but when she looked over her shoulder, the backpack with the camera seemed too far away.

"Screw it. Come on, Maggie. Finish what you started."

She set the skull on the window ledge, then snatched up the urn and stepped out into the night. This high up, with so much wind, she figured some ashes might make it to land. "And *that* is pretty fucking ironic." She choked back a sob, gained her balance then pried the lid off the urn and upended it.

For a second it seemed as though the ashes were stuck in mid-air, defying gravity and reality, hanging as a mass of dark floating debris like the troubled cloud over Eeyore, a chunk of badness in the form of ash and despair. But Maggie blinked and the cloud dispersed, the ashes blowing in a million directions, then they were gone.

"Good-bye, sweetheart."

She tossed the urn as far as she could into the darkest part of the ocean.

CHAPTER 52

BOBBIE
1930

They woke on the beach, chilled, sandy and salt encrusted.

Bobbie kissed Sam. "Morning."

"Yes, it is," he said, squinting at her then looking around at the gray morning. "Sorry ass excuse for a day too."

They lay there until their stomachs grumbled, then they drove into town, ate some breakfast and found a room at a small boarding house.

After checking out the size of the tub and the stack of towels, Bobbie announced she was going to wash up.

"And I'm going to watch," Sam said dragging a chair into the bathroom and sitting down.

Bobbie laughed.

She kissed him as the tub filled. The sound of water became the ocean they had just left. She lost herself in sensation—the heat of Sam's skin through his shirt, the pressure of his lips and his sharp teeth behind them, the way his wide smooth fingers followed the bumps on her spine. She let him undress her, let him choose the order of her nakedness, then straddled his lap wearing only her shoes.

Her skin turned red under his touch, a blush grew on her neck, as the heat inside bubbled to the surface.

She was fire and he was water.

Sam pulled off her shoes and set her into the tub then undressed himself in two quick movements. The water lapped over the edges of the tub sloshing onto the floor as he lowered himself into her arms.

Bobbie climbed out first, bringing Sam a cigarette and a drink, talking to him from the other room as she dressed. "I have to send some columns out. Do you want to go into town with me?"

"No," he said. "You should go on without me."

Bobbie hesitated, then hobbled around the corner, one shoe in her hand. " What did you say?"

Sam coughed. "I said, you go on." He coughed again, this time wincing and gripping his chest.

"Sam? Are you all right? Do you want me to stay? I can stay."

He waved her off and after the coughing fit passed he said, "I'll be fine. Just come here and give me a kiss before you go."

Sam's smile could melt Bobbie. No matter how angry she was with him if he turned on that grin, that little sideways smile, it was over. She couldn't resist him. She loved the helplessness of her adoration. It was its own entity and she gave in to it whenever possible.

He kissed her, pulling her to him in the tub, threatening to slide her into the water then at the last second releasing his grip and allowing her to pull away, to stand up, to smooth her skirt and push her hair out of her eyes, composing something that should have been left untamed.

They never said the words I love you, instead they said, "You are my heart." They were never complete without the other, as a significant amount of their soul was missing.

When Bobbie leaned over to say goodbye, Sam gave her a kiss that said more than goodbye, it said stay and sorry and help and go. It was a forever kiss, a piece of him tinged with love, regret, happiness and disappointment and she almost didn't leave because this wasn't the same guy who had woken up a few hours ago on the beach.

But leaving was something Bobbie did well.

On her way back from town, she thought about what Sam had said earlier, how he felt they were on a quest. Not a knight in shining armor quest, but a search of sorts. Bobbie had laughed, but now, if she thought about what he was saying and about the people they'd met so far, she could see he had a point, how they all needed something, how they were all searching in some way or another. Even her. It was worth thinking about, worth writing about.

"Sam?" she called unlocking the door. "I was thinking about that quest idea. I think you may be right."

The door to the bathroom was closed. Bobbie paused, one hand on the knob. "Sam?" When there was no answer she pushed it open.

In the dim light she saw him, head fallen back, pale arm dangling over the side, empty pill bottle in his hand.

CHAPTER 53

MAGGIE
2011

Maggie woke on the cold, hard floor clutching the flashlight. It was still dark, but she could feel the dawn. Her arm ached, crushed beneath her. Her mouth was dry, lips caked, teeth furry. She tried to spit, wished for a glass of cold water, then grew nauseated at the thought of swallowing anything. She tried to remember why she had thought this was a good idea.

Better that she kept her thoughts on a chain, For now she's alone again and all in pain; She sighs for the man that went and the thoughts that stay To trouble her dreams by night and her dreams by day.

She struggled upright, jamming the flashlight into a wall crack and found her jeans. She had one leg in and was hopping around muttering expletives when Sonny appeared on the curving stairs, catching her in the beam of his flashlight.

Maggie yipped, stumbled and fell into the wall. She slid to the ground, more embarrassed than hurt.

"I'm sorry," he said shining the light away. "Belle called me. She thought you might be out here, something about ashes?" He started toward her. "Do you need some help?"

"No. I'm okay." Maggie waved him off. "Could you turn around. Please?" When he did, she slid the rest of the way flat and wriggled into the damp denim.

Sonny watched her reflected in the glass, a shadow in the dying ray of the flashlight beam. He said, "This is going to sound stupid. But I could feel you. I mean, I knew that you—"

"Needed rescuing?" Maggie said as she stood, zipping her jeans then snatching up her wet bra and socks that hung around the room. She stuffed everything into her sneakers.

Maggie groaned. Bending over wasn't such a great idea.

"You okay?" Sonny reached for her, helping her to her feet. When Maggie felt his warm hand on her back, then felt it move up to her neck all she wanted to do was sink into that hand, let it catch her when she fell, applaud for her when she succeeded, touch her in all the right places late at night under a down-filled duvet.

"Here," he said, positioning himself behind her. He began to massage the knots from her neck and shoulders, her pleasure urging him on. She leaned into the window, her fingers splayed against the cold glass.

Cool and plain, Cool and plain, was the message of love on the window pane. Soft and quiet, soft and quiet, it vanished away in the fogs of night.

When Sonny kissed her, Maggie didn't object, instead she let out a sigh. A small sound like *ahhh*. A small sound like yes.

❧ ❧

There was no sign of the lost rowboat, though Maggie couldn't see much from her position, lying flat in Sonny's boat.

"I'm sure it ended up in Anderson's cove. That's where the current would take it," Sonny said looking down at Maggie. "Are you warm enough?"

"I'm fine. I feel stupid, but I'm fine." She was wrapped in three blankets and had a shot of whiskey in her belly. "Just to take the edge off," Sonny had told her. He was right. She felt better. Though it might be partly because of the sex. The amazing sex.

Dear Darling, lie beside me, it is too cold to stand speaking, He lies down beside me, his face is like the sand, He is in a sleep of love, my heart is singing.

Maggie refused to feel guilty, seeing the moment instead like a photograph she'd label and frame: Woman Comes To Life. Opportunity is a Lighthouse. That One Time She Didn't Stop Herself.

Maggie had read an article once about a lady in Vermont who grew her hair and grew her hair, then one day, shaved it all off, dyed it black, spun it into wool and knit herself a suit.

She knew there were people in the world who approached love like the lady prepping the hair suit. They wait. They prepare. They plan for a future moment, a perfect moment, a chance that may never come, a day that may never turn out right, a suit that was never meant to be.

David was like that. He apologized for moments that fell short of his imagination, as if Maggie could see inside his head. She tried to tell him once about the theory of client transparency—something she used in her work. No one knew what was missing unless you told them and no one needed to know everything.

But what a person chooses when the day comes to cut off the hair, to cuff the bad guy, to accelerate down a runway—that's what makes the difference in two people.

There's a split second where you may second guess your intention, your desire may wane and for some that's enough to stop, put an end to a dream, delay the action and go back to waiting.

That's how beards are born. How cancer happens. How cars crash. How people drown.

CHAPTER 54

FLORA
1940

I still think about those boys on the dredge. I tell Cow Eyes how the men we saved that night went on to father children, to start and run businesses that bettered Savannah. They traveled and explored, they taught and passed on secrets. They fought for their country. They loved and lost. They were allowed second chances and took them. They reveled in the love of God and were more grateful than ever for their lives because they had been saved, because they had seen death and walked away from it. They had been working a job seemingly without purpose and now, after this significant event, they knew they were necessary. There was a reason they were alive.

"I like that story," she says like a three year old. I pat her head.

The men call from below, "Miss Flora, Ma'am? It's getting late, we really ought to be heading back now."

Cow Eyes looks at me. I tell the men, "We'll be right there. Thank you."

She gets up first, stretching and twisting, her body moving in the wind like a leaf caught in a gale. "Ready?" she says. Cow Eyes is framed perfectly in the tower room door. In the expanse of glass behind her, the sun is setting, sending a warm orange glow across the water, bleeding it into the edges of the world.

"Ready," I say. I rise, every bone arguing, then follow her through the tower room. The seagull skull in my hand. I'd almost forgotten.

"Go on." I nod toward the narrow stone steps. "I'll be right there." Cow Eyes hesitates, then turns to leave. I hear her footsteps, the cautious drag of her hand as she skims the wall. There is no railing to catch you if you fall.

I trace the skull with my fingers, weigh it in my hands, then lean over the hole in the center of the tower where the powerful lens used to be. The skull fits perfectly in the dusty old fitting.

Its empty eyes follow me as I back away, whispering, "For you, George. For all the things we couldn't see."

⊷ ⊷

Back at the shore the men help us off the small boat. I think for a moment that the man at the motor is my father in the flat dory going to check his traps, going to bring us some dinner. Then the man lifts his face and I see that his smile is too broad, his eyes too kind, his hurt negligible.

We wave as they putter away. Cow Eyes turns slow circles yawning. "Where's the car, Miss Flora?" Her voice is a soft sleepy sound, muffled by the back of her hand. It's my wool blanket, something to cover me, something to pull over my head and keep out the cold.

I think for a minute that I'll walk the long way to the car; maybe I'll walk forever, stopping only to eat, forgoing sleep, as it is rarely a pleasant experience after sixty. I think that I will steal this girl and her ideas, her youth, her potential. That if I steal her, she'll have a chance. She won't be like me. She won't die alone. She won't make choices she'll regret. She won't live a lie.

Cow Eyes says in her dreamy way, "I could stay out here forever."

"I almost did," I say under my breath. "But that would have been the easy way."

I run my fingers through her hair, wishing I had a brush and wondering if this is what having a daughter would have felt like. I think about the walk to the car, about the return trip to the funeral home—to her job, to my cold brother—to what is left of my life.

I rouse Cow Eyes. "Let's go." This time I am the strong one and she is as helpless as a baby bird.

My nephew is waiting when we return to Clark's Funeral Home. I feel his presence before I see him. People act differently around a man who talks to God for a living. Not me. I changed this man's baby diapers. I know he is no different than any of us. More pitiful maybe.

"Monsignor Brennan!" The man who rushes out of the office trailing my nephew looks like my Cow Eyes. He says, "I know what this must look like."

Thomas Brennan shushes the man with the simple raising of his hand then approaches me.

"Tommy," I say, leaning in for a kiss. "How are you boy?"

"Aunt Flora? Have you been drinking?"

I smile and pat his arm. He places his hand over mine and steers me toward the door, glancing over his shoulder at Cow Eyes and her father huddled in the corner. They look like they're seriously discussing her future at the funeral home. I wiggle my fingers in her direction. She hides a grin behind her hand.

"Aunt Flora?" The Monsignor hates being ignored.

"Did you see him?" I ask.

He starts to say, "Who?" when he understands. He takes a step back. "No. I will see him tomorrow, at the viewing. We should go now. We need to talk about the funeral. What Uncle George's wishes were."

"Let's ask him, then," I say, mixing my stubborn old lady ploy with a bit of crazy.

Tommy sighs. He's become a sigher in his old age. Where is the boy I knew? Where is the fun little Tommy who swore he'd never be like his father then grew up to be more like his mother?

I call across the room, "I'd like to see my brother." Then add, for Tommy's benefit. "Please."

Tommy purses his lips and nods. "Mr. Clark?"

The sweaty little man hurries over after offering one last waggling finger in Cow Eyes' direction.

"Of course," he says. "This way."

They have been busy with my brother. George looks better dead than he did last week. Why do they do that to corpses? It only makes it harder to let go, when the last image you have of a loved one is that of a healthy, serene, composed body on a soft bed of velvet. Perhaps I am only being morbid, but wouldn't it be easier to say goodbye to the dead if they looked like they were in pain, tired of living, or wasted away?

Mr. Clark seems to have collected himself on our walk to the viewing room. He stands near the door, arms behind him, suit jacket buttoned, hair plastered to his head, concerned yet competent, eager to help, ready to empathize.

I am quiet. The room is quiet. The world is quiet when Tommy says, "I'll miss him."

He says, "There are times when I think about who I might have been. That is to say, things were different then, weren't they? The choices we made were not always the right ones."

"But there were so little choices," I say.

My nephew paces in front of me, lost in his role of politician or thespian, or what he really is, a lecturing Monsignor.

He says, "It wasn't enough that we survived a flu pandemic, mob lynches, political upheaval and a World War. What was our country's gift to us? Prohibition. But like all things foisted upon a society, even this brought opportunity to a wise man."

I squelch the desire to add an "Amen, brother."

Tommy runs his hand down the smooth wood of the coffin and continues his soliloquy. "I know my father was just as guilty as Uncle George. I didn't see it that way then. He always said a man had to do whatever he had to do to feed his family, to survive. These days, they would have been treated like common criminals, but I remember folks revering Uncle George, saying he had a good thing, living out there on the island."

He needs no encouragement, and certainly, my nephew will bide no interruptions, so I let him speak. Let him tell his version of the events.

Me, I remembered what it was like to look the other way when strangers tied off at the dock and followed George into the barn. I made sure to sweep away their footprints and keep the entrance to the clearing well hidden by boughs. I stopped going to the cliffs after dark and learned the difference in the sound of a bootlegging speedboat and a ship I wanted to greet.

George would come home smelling of fire and rum and sweat. He'd slip into my bed drunk and sloppy, his words thick and strangely peppered with Spanish. I'd kick and fight but in the end, I gave in.

"Things were different then," Tommy says and sighs. He makes the sign of the cross, bows his head over the coffin and offers some murmured prayer absolving George of all his sins. He looks for a minute like the strong young man he used to be in Savannah.

⊰ ⊱

My sister Mary invited George and me to spend the evening with her family on the square. The older Brennan children, Vivian and Tommy, sang and played the mandolin, while the younger children chased balls and hoops. They ran in and out of the banana trees and elephant ears, hiding behind grand moss-draped oaks.

Most nights when we visited, we'd eat fried chicken, corn and buttery biscuits with pie for dessert, then retire to the piazza to sip cocktails and enjoy the cool breezes wafting through the open doors. For a few quiet moments, we could pretend there was no seepage of war in our lives. We'd focus instead on what we could touch—each other and ice cubes melting under mint leaves.

This particular evening, Mary had outdone herself. The meal had been highlighted by a juicy cut of beef and bowls of fresh vegetables, followed by platters of imported cheeses and thick loaves of bread. Thomas uncorked wines with foreign labels and poured them freely.

I wondered how my sister and her lumberyard husband could afford any of it; a grand house, nice clothes, this extravagant meal, on what he earned.

We were almost done eating when the men knocked at the back door. They didn't say anything to the women, just nodded in our direction, their gazes lingering longer on me, then followed George and Thomas into the study. I tried to not let it bother me, the stares I got from townies, the whispers on the street, the taunting from their children. Being called crazy wasn't so bad when you'd been called worse.

I never thought it was a bad life I led, that I was doing anything different or wrong. But I suppose, to the people of Savannah, to anyone that had happened past my island, I was as odd to them as a three footed duck. But, it was all I knew. It was the life I'd been given, if one believes in such rigamarole.

With my sister, it was easy to see where I stood. I saw myself in her eyes every time I visited. Her pity smelled like rotting lilac blossoms. It was inescapable.

I would never be the woman she wanted me to be, I would never be someone she wanted to sit next to in church. I couldn't talk about children with her. I had none. I couldn't talk about husbands, all the problems or joy that came with them. I could barely talk about the world, as mine was small and surrounded by water. What could I talk about with her that would be interesting?

Why Mary of course. She was always the focal point. I never resented her for that. After all, she was my beard.

She was the best of the Martuses, even with her secrets and her husband's indiscretions. She was the kind of woman others emulated in church, the sort ladies would bow their heads for in prayer meetings. She went on mission trips. She saved orphaned children. She was the kind of person who became all the good things anyone wanted to be if you were raised right.

I had lost my appetite and had to pretend to eat, stuffing meat in my napkin and smashing peas into the underside of the table, a midnight snack for the dog.

Vivian took the opportunity to excuse herself, saying she was going to a friend's house and Tommy slipped into the study with the men. I helped Mary collect the younger children. We sent them upstairs with the nanny and the baby.

Through the open door of the study, I watched George argue with one of the men. Things looked to be heating up until Little Tommy stepped in, patting their chests, leading them back to their corners, offering his easy smile.

Mary cleared her throat, stepped between me and the door, closing it quietly while brushing imaginary crumbs from her bodice and saying something about boys being boys.

Her uneasiness was foreign to me. Mary always seemed to have the answers.

"Is everything all right?" I asked.

Mary took my hand in hers and rubbed her thumbs over my weathered skin. "Yes. No."

"What is it?" I asked.

"It's nothing," she said. "Really. Oh, look at you. Bless your heart." Mary embraced me. "Everything is fine. Just fine."

As she pulled away, she attempted a smile. "Come on. You can help me tuck the children in."

Following Mary up the stairs I paused at the landing to peer out the window into the moonlit yard. Tommy was loading the back of his father's pickup with crates marked "Black Pekoe Tea." George snapped a cover over the crates, tucked it around then tossed Tommy the keys and climbed into the truck before they drove away.

CHAPTER 55

BOBBIE
1932

The South was nothing like Bobbie remembered. She was not as pretty or innocent as she used to be. Not as kind or welcoming. She was more like a bitter old woman, hardened and rough, her sweet parts gone. Bobbie had driven through the small towns looking for familiar faces then realized how silly that was, given the number of years she'd been gone.

By the time she pulled up in front of the low brick building she'd given up any chance of reclaiming the place of her memory. A hospital was never the friendliest place.

She followed the directions to the room. A doctor stood at Sam's bedside, examining a chart. The body in the bed seemed small and pale.

Bobbie cleared her throat and when the doctor looked over she tilted her head toward the hallway.

"I'll be right back," the doctor said hanging up the chart then patting Sam's leg beneath the sheet, as if they were good pals and one would miss the other if something happened.

"I'll still be right here." Sam raised a shackled arm a few inches off the cot then let it fall jangling.

In the corridor Bobbie threw worried glances over the doctor's shoulder as he repeated his concerns, his warnings, his ideas and the options he'd carefully considered, the same things he'd said in the letters he sent to New York. Nothing had changed. The mental health folks were having a heyday with her husband.

She nodded, feigning agreement. "Well, that sounds fine. Let me talk to Sam. I'm sure I can convince him." She leaned in, lowering her voice, angling the doctor away from the door. "You know how he can be. Why don't you give us some time alone in there and I'll see what I can do."

"Good luck," the doctor said and turned to leave, but not before Bobbie pulled him close in an awkward hug, saying, "Thank you, Doctor."

He murmured something about it being his job, that was what he was there for, then made a little bow and backed down the hall, as Bobbie slipped into Sam's room, locked the door behind her then sauntered over to the bed dangling a stolen ring of keys.

Sam's eyes snapped open, going from dull and sleepy to bright, animated pools in seconds. He grinned. "Hot damn. It's about time."

A dozen colored pills spilled to the floor as Sam swung off the cot.

"They can put them in your mouth, but they can't make you swallow," he said.

"Good boy." Bobbie kissed him. "I missed you."

"You can tell me all about it later. Hand me some clothes, darlin'."

They were half a mile down the road before the nurses realized the pillow in the bed wasn't Sam Winter.

A few hours later, Sam pulled the car off the road into a grassy area near a copse of hardwoods. Bobbie didn't know trees well, having spent most of her life in a city, but these trees seemed important. As big as they were they must be old, and the way they had grown, twining into each other, made her think someone had planted them that way, like a message left by strangers in the past.

"What are we doing here?" she asked.

"Bring the map." Sam lit a cigarette, took a slug from a flask then passed both to Bobbie. He unfolded the map and flattened it on the ground with the help of a few stones.

"Stand there," he said pointing to the other edges. Bobbie kicked off her shoes then stood on two corners in her bare feet, the east coast between her legs. Sam came around behind her, unpinned her hat and handed it to her.

"Hey!"

"Here," he said, handing her the long hat pin. "Close your eyes and drop it. Let's put our future in the hands of fate."

"Are you sure?" she asked.

"What do we have to lose?"

Bobbie dropped the pin over the map. It didn't stick into the paper, instead bounced and rolled into her toe. "Ow!"

Sam laughed.

"Not funny," she said giving him a hard look—hard from the lips and chin only—her eyes teased him.

"Try again."

She retrieved the pin then leaned over a little and closed her eyes. The pin jabbed into the map, quivering.

Sam kneeled and read, "Bensonville?"

Bobbie bent down, squinting. "That's what it says beneath those brown ridges and under the blue splotches, surrounded by a whole lot of green. Bensonville, Virginia."

"Bensonville, it is. But first, we have some other business to attend to." Sam swiped Bobbie's legs out from under her and tackled her to the ground, rolling off the map onto the grass, as she squealed with delight.

Bobbie wasn't as young as she wished but there are a few things you never forget and under a canopy of leaves with Sam in her arms, she thought maybe she'd been wishing for the wrong thing for too many years.

They found Bensonville the next day and took a room at a small inn near the town center. Sam joked that they should give their names as Mary and Joseph, because the town was that quaint, but Bobbie could tell he liked it. They made their way around town, stopping at the post office.

"You here to visit kin?" the postmaster asked.

"No. Just stopping here for a while. Need a bit of a rest from things," Bobbie said gesturing toward the envelopes in his hand, the air in the room, the world outside, and nothing at all.

The man nodded as if he understood. Maybe he did. Everyone tired of something, didn't they?

CHAPTER 56

FLORA
1940

Tommy returns to the chairs and sits beside me. He reaches for my hand. "Aunt Flora, Do you remember the night I went with Uncle George to Red's place?" He smiles, then chuckles. "Mother was so angry."

Red McClaren had come over from Ireland hungry and determined, making promises to do better in this country than he had in his own. He was introduced to peaches, corn and warm saltwater swims and spent two years scrambling around doing all he could for his boss, an obese pig-eyed man named Maxwell Channing. Red did things he wouldn't have done for his own Da'. And finally, it paid off. A little encouragement and, according to Uncle George, "The lazy old shit ate himself to death," leaving the pub to Red.

Max Channing was buried in a custom-sized coffin that took eight pallbearers to heft. Halfway to the burial site they had to lower the massive container and take a break before heaving to and completing the task. There was quite a bit of speculation about the number of worms it would take to do old Max in, bets no one planned on collecting.

Timing, never being Red's strong suit, acted against him again. Within a month of slapping a fresh coat of paint on the interior and hanging a new sign, "McClaren's," Prohibition made its way to the south. Red hung on as long as he could legally, figuring it would take the law months to hit every establishment in Savannah. He secretly moved most of his stock before they shut him down, digging holes in the woods for barrels of beer, filling the basements of widows with bourbon and rye and the attics of pious churchgoers with trunks of gin and cases of wine. He even had suitcases and pianos outfitted with false bottoms, to hold quart bottles of whiskey.

Red took a new approach to keeping an establishment in town and opened Issy's Tea Emporium, courtesy of his second wife. The lace and doily décor of the street-side shop was feminine enough that tough guy inspectors were in and out quickly, never staying long enough to find the hidden door in the back or the stairs that led to the basement. Issy's potent teas, herbs and floral soaps

188

drew in the richest customers in town and masked any alcohol odor that might have escaped.

The tea shop was an excellent front for the new McClaren's, a basement speakeasy with live entertainment three nights a week.

Red's clientele arrived after dark like spooks and vampires. It was a closed, select membership. If had to ask where the hooch was, you wouldn't be told.

⸘ ⸙

As Tommy drove the pickup, George told him where to go, doling out the directions like he was feeding a bird. "There," George said, pointing to a narrow alley entrance. "Pull up then back in slow."

Tommy rolled the truck to a stop near a wall of gardenias. George opened the door, glanced at Tommy. "Wait here."

"But, Uncle George, I thought I could come."

"What?"

"I thought I was, you know, going in."

"For what?"

"Never mind."

George watched the kid squirm. "You want to go in there?" He jerked his thumb over his shoulder.

Tommy nodded.

"All right. But when I say go, we go."

"Yes, sir."

Tommy followed George down concrete steps to a cellar door. There was a sweet smell in the air from the overgrown gardenia bushes and something else, like vomit or sour milk. He wrinkled his nose, looked around, playing cool.

"Just relax," George said. "Try not to look so green. You'll be fine."

Tommy exhaled then nodded, puffing his chest out a bit.

George rapped out a pattern on the door. A few seconds later, it opened a crack, just enough for a guy to stick his head out.

"Nice night," the guy said.

Tommy looked at the cloudy sky, felt a few drops of rain.

"Always nice when I'm with you," George replied.

The man smiled and opened the door surprising Tommy who'd figured a wise-ass remark like George's would have earned him a bop in the nose or at least an equally snide reply.

"This is Tommy," George said grabbing him by the jacket and pulling him forward.

"Good to meet ya," the guy said.

Tommy strained against George's grip, twisted his neck around. "Good to meet you too, sir."

George shoved him. "C'mon."

The guy locked the door behind them, ramming a heavy metal bar into place.

Tommy followed George down a narrow hall. They could have been in the basement of any Savannah building, until they turned the corner and slipped through a thick curtain.

The walls of the speakeasy were covered in scraps and swatches of faded newspaper. A section by a long bench was a masterpiece in progress. Someone had drawn moustaches on the models, added hats and hair to the politicians and given an advertisement for Sears, Roebuck & Company a whole new twist by putting a bottle of booze in the homemaker's hand.

The room was warm and quiet, sound muffled by thick rugs underfoot. At least twenty people sat in mismatched chairs at round tables. Their faces illuminated by small candles appeared as yellow ovals in the smoky dim.

At the bar, two lamps reflected light from a tin ceiling someone had thought to paint red, giving off a womblike effect as if the strangers at the tables were much more intimate than simple drinking partners.

A man in a rumpled suit lay stretched out over three chairs with his arms crossed on his chest. His eyes were closed. He held a limp yellow flower in his teeth. His chest rose and fell. A sudden dribble of piss onto the floor assured anyone who cared that the man was alive. Blotto, but living.

George headed straight to the bar—an old door shellacked to a high sheen resting on two oak barrels. He nodded at the barkeep who handed him two coffee cups. Tommy recognized the guy from the lumberyard, a Northerner who always got the shit jobs from the Foreman and usually kept to himself.

George said, "Hey Buddy. Where's Red?"

Buddy kept pouring hooch from a ceramic jug into a line of cups. He bobbed his head at the corner table. George finished his drink, gave the guy back the cup then walked over to the table. Tommy tried to throw the drink back like George but gagged on the last swallow. In a vain attempt to cover his shuddering, he shot a grin to the barkeep, as he wiped his tearing eyes.

"That's mighty potent. Better watch out, boy."

"I can handle it," Tommy said.

"Yeah?" Buddy reached for Tommy's cup. There was a bit of a struggle until he said, "Then have another," and gave him a refill. "George is good for it."

Tommy looked over at the table. George was talking to a white-haired man with a bushy beard. A redhead had her arms wrapped around George's neck like she was his scarf. Tommy took the cup, prepared not to make the same mistake this time of smelling the stuff. He eyed the barkeep as he sipped a little off the top.

"Ain't tea, mamma's boy," Buddy said. "Ya ain't got to sip it."

Tommy met his eyes and tossed back the hooch. "Tastes like tea to me. Sweet tea." He tipped an invisible hat and bowed.

It was only five paces to the table, but for Tommy it was like walking in a tunnel on a boat during a storm. He sat down, hard, next to the redhead, wishing she'd wrap herself around him, or at least look his way. He stared at his hands on the table, flexing his fingers and giggling. George glanced at Tommy, then at the barkeep, who shrugged.

"You all right, Tommy?" George asked.

"I am fi-ine." He held up his hands and moved them in the air, pushing around light and smoke. "Just fine and dandy."

"All right then. You just sit here with Miss Evie, and I'll be right back. Okay?"

Tommy tried to nod, but that sent the room into a spin, so instead he made the o.k. sign and smiled.

When George and Red went through the wall, Tommy rubbed his eyes. "Hey!"

"What's that, sugar?" The redhead melted into him. Her breath was warm on his cheek. He tried to focus on her face.

"You are so beautiful," he said, the words coming out like Swedish.

He ran his finger down her arm then leaned in almost smashing into her forehead and inhaled. He told her she smelled like tangerines. Vanilla frosted tangerines and sunshine.

She giggled. "That is the sweetest thing I've ever heard. Now why don't you buy Evie a drink and maybe I'll give you some sunshine."

Tommy pushed his chair back, tipping it over as he stood. A man at the next table pointed and his pals laughed. Tommy made his way to the bar. "I'll take two more!"

"Easy there," Buddy said. "No need to shout. Hell, the music ain't even started yet."

"Why not?" Tommy turned to face the room. "Would y'all like to hear some music?"

The barkeep clapped a beefy hand on his back. "They'll be here soon," he assured the crowd, then softer, told Tommy to sit down and stop being such a pain in his ass. "Go on. You got someone waiting on you."

Tommy grabbed their drinks and returned to the table where Evie was powdering her nose. He lifted an arm in the general direction of the bar and said, "And don't you forget it, pal," then fell into his chair, sloshing the hooch onto the table.

Evie patted his arm and reached for her drink. She kissed the air between them. "Thanks, Sugar."

Tommy watched her lips on the cup's rim, full, red and wet. Her eyes were as twinkly as fireflies on a hot August night. Her blonde hair puffed out around her heart-shaped face and looked as soft as the down of his favorite pillow at home and her pale breasts peeking over the edge of her dress were the most wonderful thing that God had ever divined. Tommy was in love.

❧ ❧

A short while later when Tommy was wiggling his toes, wondering why he only had four and thinking he should have seven, he heard the angel.

191

He closed his eyes as the angel sang. She took him under her wing, flew over trees, skimmed the tips of waves, then ran through a field and stopped at a cliff's edge. The voice pulled Tommy back, rocking him, soothing him with a ballad of love and loss that made him cry.

A clarinet played as the angel's voice faded, brass horns picked up the melody so Tommy had a hard time telling the difference. The sounds flowed into each another infusing them, enrapturing him, as they swelled and strained.

CHAPTER 57

BOBBIE
1933

The people that visited Bensonville came for the water. If it could be sipped, dipped, dunked or drunk, it might be a cure. Bobbie hadn't thought much of the blue patches on the map, indicating the water in and around Bensonville. She'd thought it was a lake town, a riverside village. She soon learned the place held magic. It was a town of healing waters fed from natural hot springs, where secret sulfurous mineral pools were marked on maps and deep dank wells were dug by the hands of people who believed in miracles.

Visitors weren't regular tourists. They were folks on a mission. People that came to Bensonville believed nothing easily acquired was worthwhile. You didn't deserve it unless you worked for it. It wasn't any good unless it was almost unobtainable. The people who could, would hike into the woods hoping to scout the newest spring that had bubbled up overnight. They might fashion their own medical marvel in the form of a cool, still, ionized pool with a salve-like mud bottom. Within days, directions would be carved into trees, notes left under doors at The Inn and soon, the crippled and sick would be carted in to the new places by the seekers, followed by the believers and the tellers.

"To find your purpose in life you need to know which of the four you are," Sam said repeating something The Cherokee had told him.

"What four?" Bobbie asked. It might have been a play on words if Sam hadn't been so quick to answer.

"The four jobs given at birth," he told her. "You are either a teller, a seeker, a builder or a believer."

"That sounds pretty simple," she said knowing the trouble associated with simplifying humanity.

"What's wrong with that?"

Bobbie didn't have an answer for this Sam, the introspective sober guy who hung around herb-drying Indians and mapped trails for rich women seeking eternal youth.

❧ ❧

As the days grew into weeks, Bobbie wrote her columns and sketched the people she met in Bensonville, while Sam spent hours walking trails at the base of the mountains and dipping into the mystical hot springs. He'd come back to her soaking wet and exuberant, hope dripping from him leaving puddles of faith on the worn rag rug.

They had both been there when the doctors said there was no cure for Sam's lungs, but they never said anything about his soul. They had been there when the pin dropped on the map choosing Bensonville, a town where people could change and things unspoken could happen and they had both been there when the wind blew through the oak tree raining leaves on their naked bodies as Bobbie pledged to never leave him, to be with him always.

Neither one of them had planned anything, but if there was a place that called more to Sam's fragile soul and Bobbie's yearning, they didn't know where it could be.

In Bensonville, the damaged were so numerous they were invisible. They shared a camaraderie in hope. A common cause. We are here. We need healing. Water is our cure.

Bobbie had never thought of herself as religious, or faithful even, in that sense of the word, but she was spiritual. It was hard to deny the existence of God in this town. Dying people got better. Lame children walked.

The people who came to Bensonville changed it a little more each day. They flooded themselves with healing water, washing out the bad, bringing in the good. Believers filled themselves with cold, clear liquid life, combining the power of the water with the power of the mind.

Bobbie sat by a spring fed pool. A sign, "Drink to Health" was propped on a ledge of rock above the bubbling spring, and a tin cup was chained to a root outcropping. Birds called in the trees above. Insects buzzed. She smelled jasmine. Her reflection in the surface was the face of someone she thought she should know but didn't recognize. She reached for the cup and dipped it into the water. It was colder than she expected. She closed her eyes and drank then waited—as if the effect would be instantaneous, as if she could fix whatever was broken in her with a tin cup of spring water.

Time was both enemy and hope in Bensonville. One more drink at the spring. Three more sessions at the mineral pool. Two more hikes back to the caves. One more week.

But disease and misery and depression were on their own schedule, they took more every day, worked faster every week and sometimes no matter how hard you prayed and how much water you displaced, a body couldn't be saved.

Bobbie began to believe the miracles that did happen came from hope that washed off every body that stepped into the waters, and that the level in the pools was maintained not by underground springs but by the tears of those who cried while they prayed, while they floated, while they died.

Bobbie watched Sam measure herbs into a cheesecloth, count sprigs of something green. She said, "It's time we left Bensonville. We could try the mountains or the desert."

"I'm not ready," he said.

"Sure you are. You said you felt great, that being here helped."

"I can't leave."

She reached for him but he slipped away, and instead she wrapped her arms around herself. "What is it?" she said.

"I'm working on something. I need to stay."

"What? Those bags of bark and herbs? Let your Indian pal do that," Bobbie said.

Sam set the cheesecloth bag on the counter and went to her. "Listen, Bobbie. For the first time in a long time, I feel like I'm doing good. Like I'm helping people."

"But we had a plan," Bobbie reminded him. "We have a commitment."

"I know." Sam drew his head close to hers and kissed her forehead. He said, "I release you."

Outside an owl hooted, branches scratched the clapboards of the house, bugs smacked the glass panes, the moon swelled and waned, as Bobbie's heart split in half.

CHAPTER 58

FLORA
1940

When Tommy swipes the back of his hand across his eyes, I notice he's been crying. I notice my foot has fallen asleep and I notice we're still here in the funeral parlor, in the dark quiet room with the box that holds my brother.

Tommy sighs again. I nudge him. He needs to tell the end of his story, the rest of his night at the speakeasy and I am a good listener.

"You all right, honey?" Evie asked flattening her palm against Tommy's chest, red nails like exclamation points against his white shirt. He felt her heat as she leaned into him. Behind them the music dwindled to a single sad clarinet. The singing angel stepped out of the shadows to close the tune and everyone turned as she came into the light.

Tommy stared. He saw what everyone else did, a fine brunette with big blue eyes and curves in all the right places, a real looker. But when he looked closer he saw that woman just a girl, a kid playing dress-up in a borrowed gown that looked familiar and shoes too big for her feet.

"What the hell?" Tommy jumped up, knocking over the table. Cups shattered, the candle blew out. Evie screamed. The girl burst into tears and raced from the room.

"Vivian!" Tommy yelled. "Wait!" He lunged after her, slipping through the secret door in the wall before it closed. Tommy grabbed his siter's arm, ripping the sleeve of her dress.

"Look what you've done!" she cried. "You've ruined it. You've ruined everything." Vivian wiped her eyes then twisted away from him. "Leave me alone!"

Tommy tried to catch her, but ended up with a fistful of hair. The wig came off, freeing her soft red curls. She spun around. Without the wig and all the makeup, she was nothing, just his little sister, his best friend.

Her lip trembled. "Don't tell," she whispered. "Please."

"I won't," he said, handing her the wig. Tommy stepped closer. "You were good out there."

She shrugged, staring at the floor.

"You were real good," he said, swaying a bit.

Vivian lifted her face, wiped her nose with the back of her hand. "You think so?"

"I do. You were like another Mildred Bailey or something."

Viv scoffed. "Nah."

"Yeah, you were." Tommy tipped her chin up, ran his thumb across her lip. "But next to you, Mildred Bailey looks like a horse."

She gazed up at Tommy. Little Vivian Brennan, too skinny to ever amount to anything until she opened her mouth and sang. He held her face in his hands and saw all the things another woman would never be and before his brain could tell him it was wrong or he should stop, he kissed his sister.

Her lips were soft, full, still quivering and salty from her tears. She pressed into him and Tommy felt a rush from his heels to his neck, like an electric jolt. Everything around them faded. There was only this—this soft, warm place where he fit perfectly, where he was safe and understood and needed. All he wanted to do was stay there forever—blocking out the world, drowning in contentment.

A door at the end of the hall opened. Tommy heard George say, "Pleasure doing business with you, Red."

He came up behind them quickly, humming a ditty and drinking straight from the bottle. He slapped Tommy on the back, then took a slug. "C'mon. Bank's closed. Tell the lady you'll see her later."

Vivian ducked her head too late. George pulled Tommy by his ear. Vivian fell back into the wall, her lipstick smeared from lip to cheek, her black ringed eyes going from lust to fear as she pushed past George and ran into the speakeasy, tugging the brunette wig over her red hair.

George moved his grip from ear to shirt, yanking Tommy back when he tried to follow her.

"C'mon, boy. Let's get you some coffee. Real coffee."

George left Tommy at the table with Evie, told her to keep an eye on him, get him talking and keep him away from the booze.

Evie slid her chair close and ran her finger down Tommy's arm. "Talk to me, Sugar."

Tommy smiled and leaned forward to tell her something, his lips brushing her ear before he keeled over crashing to the floor, his nose breaking his fall.

~ ~

He woke sweaty and naked in a day that was too bright with the worst headache of his life and the sounds of his mother and uncle arguing in the kitchen. They sat at the table, Mother spinning the gold band on her finger, Vivian scratching at the edge of the table, a slumped mess of red hair and shame and George, tipped back in his chair unlit cigarette dangling from his lip.

"I don't believe this," Mother said. She didn't believe that her son was drinking, that George had brought him to such a place, that her daughter had lied about where she was going and what she'd be doing when she got there.

"Who else knows about this?" Mother asked.

"No one," George said. "No one that you'd have to worry about running into at church, anyway."

Tommy stifled a laugh as pain striped his vision.

Mother cleared her throat, then laid her hands firmly on the table and pressed herself upright. "That's the last I want to hear of this. Any of this. Do you understand?" She looked at each of them, then left the room.

"I'll talk to her," Tommy said moving slowly, trying not to vomit.

"I wouldn't do that," George said. "Give her some time, now. This will all blow over in a few days." He patted his pockets, found some matches then stepped out to the back porch.

As the door slapped shut, Vivian finished etching the heart shape into the wood and reached across the table for Tommy's hand, splinters under her fingernail.

I touch my nephew's hand. He tries hard not to flinch. We all have our secrets.

I tell him, "You were just a boy, Tommy."

He nods, then leans back in the stiff funeral home chair and wipes the tears from his face.

"It was me," I tell him.

"You what, Aunt Flora?"

I chuckle. "I suppose George suspected, but I never told anyone. Until now. It wasn't rum runners that ruined your uncle's business. It was me. I sank his still."

"You did what?" Tommy asks.

It's nice to see I can still surprise them.

CHAPTER 59

BOBBIE
1935

Bobbie drove down the long street in the center of town. It was early in the morning, but as always, people were awake in Bensonville. She waved to the clerk at the general store, and nodded to the nurse with her charge on the bench in the square. A family posed for a photograph in front of the fountain. The mother with the sunken eyes and headscarf stood in the middle attempting to look brave as her children thrust their hands into the spray.

She paused at the crossroads—west to the mountains, east toward civilization—then glanced in the side mirror of the big Chrysler. A series of images flashed: a dying woman being lowered into the pool, a mustachioed man behind a red table hawking bottles of healing potions, someone on a wide white porch waving goodbye.

It took Bobbie almost a week to reach New York and when she pulled the car up in front of the offices of The Times she made the rounds, shaking hands, kissing cheeks, avoiding any specifics, trying to sound mysterious instead of miserable.

After all the quiet driving days with only the wind and whirr of the road and her thoughts to occupy her, plus a few singing drunks in Pennsylvania, verbal barrage hit Bobbie full force. She only wanted to go home. She wanted to take a long bath, sleep in her own soft bed and read long books with happy endings.

She dropped a week's worth of copy on an assistant editor's desk and was down the hall and through the fire exit door when someone shouted, "Bobbie! Wait! There's something you should know."

She heard them, but kept walking.

⊱ ⊰

Bobbie wondered why there was a hole where their building should be. She checked the sign for Brunswick Street. The trees were in the same places, the market was on the same corner, the crack in the sidewalk might be larger but the rest of the street was just as she'd remembered it, except for the amount of sunshine. It was much brighter without the brownstone, as if the building had been hiding the sun the whole time. She should have been devastated; she should have been angry, sad or surprised. But instead, Bobbie felt relief. She was the farmer who woke to find the pig she'd meant to slaughter had died peacefully in its sleep.

She walked three blocks north and seven blocks east, and knocked on Harry Riggs' door.

"Aw, hell," Harry said opening the door. "No one told you?"

"No one told me," she said.

"Come on in."

Harry was still running the show down at the paper even if he didn't go in every day. Things were different now that he had to share the helm with one of the owner's sons, a wiry little squirrel named Nelson.

"Guy wants everything free whenever he goes somewhere. Like it's owed to him or something. I swear, you got people out of work, whole families begging on the streets in some places and this guy wants his drinks free, wants tickets to Minsky's every week. Ke-rist." Harry poured Bobbie a drink then refilled his own glass.

"You been there lately?" Bobbie asked.

"Where?"

"The burlesque show."

"Yeah. Why? You wanna go?"

Bobbie spun her empty glass, shrugged. "I don't know. Maybe."

Harry grabbed the spinning glass, filled it with another shot of whiskey and handed it back. "Tell you what, you're staying with me for a while."

"No. I shouldn't. "

"I wasn't asking you."

They drank in silence until Bobbie whispered, "Thanks Harry." Then, "Shit, it's good to be home."

Bobbie moved in and they eased into a routine with Harry not asking about Sam and Bobbie not asking about Harry's friends, men of a dubious nature who wore loud suits and red ties, men who bleached their hair, plucked their eyebrows and broke out into song more often than Sam ever had and sounded better too.

Harry took Bobbie to odd museums they accessed through hidden doors and barely advertised theater events that had Bobbie wishing for a hidden door—to escape. They had dinner with actors and directors and when Harry got a bit part on a movie being filmed in Central Park, Bobbie called Sam.

"Did they pay him?" he asked.

"Sure," she said. "They have to."

"Did you get to meet Katherine Hepburn?"

"She wasn't in this movie. Nobody you'd know, darling."

Bobbie heard him rustling around. They were in the same time zone but she swore every time she called he was either in bed or just getting out of it.

"You sure everything's okay down there? I could come back for a while."

"No. Things are swell," he said. "Really."

"I'll see you next month. You're going to send the train information, right?"

There was a pause, the sound of a match being struck and the deep breathy inhale as Sam lit a cigarette. "Yes," he exhaled drawing out the word then coughing. "I'll do that." More coughing. "I have to go now."

Bobbie hung up without any mention of anyone's heart, without a hint of love, without a single good-bye.

⁖ ⁖

In her new life without Sam, a life where she didn't leave the state, slept in the same bed every night and sometimes went a whole day without getting drunk, her columns centered on the entertainment industry—Broadway and beyond. She wrote about movies, music, art, burlesque shows and despite the rumblings at the Times, she knew she was on the right path. People wanted to escape their dreary lives and instead of Bobbie showing them the world she showed her readers their city—places their wallets couldn't take them and their modesty wouldn't.

When Sam stopped calling every month and took longer and longer to answer her letters, Bobbie began keeping company with one of the female singers at Minsky's, a tall, limber redhead named Cricket. They went on weekend trips with Harry and Connie, the sister of his good friend Bert. Sometimes, Connie would leave mid-trip to be replaced by Bert and sometimes Bert would already be there when they arrived, like the time they rented a place on Martha's Vineyard and spent a week playing croquet and drinking martinis.

Some days Bobbie was able to trick herself into believing this had always been her life, that the things she'd seen and heard and wrote about in the past all belonged to someone else. Until she got the telegram from Bensonville.

CHAPTER 60

MAGGIE
2011

Maggie sat up, tossing off the blankets and tucking her hair behind her ears. "Hey."

Sonny took his eyes off the horizon and looked at her.

She smiled. "Thank you."

"My pleasure," Sonny said, grinning. "And I mean that."

Maggie laughed.

"You have a beautiful smile," he said. "My mother used to say, 'Happiness is contagious.' Do you believe that?"

"Sure. As contagious as pessimism," Maggie said.

"Well, that's optimistic."

Maggie tried not to laugh, but he was much too adorable. "Clever, aren't you?"

"Most definitely," he said. "You'll see."

"I will?"

"Just wait till I get you back to My Tara," he said, slowing the boat as they approached the marina.

"Your what?" Maggie asked.

"My houseboat."

❧ ❧

After a long, warm shower, Maggie pulled a chair up to the breakfast bar. The eating area was decorated like the rest of the boat, an expected nautical theme of blues and creams and grays with a smattering of seashells and fishes. She still had to remind herself that she was on the water, not in a cottage or a landlubber's apartment, as there was every modern convenience, from double ovens in the gourmet kitchen to a large flat screen TV in the sunken living room.

She rummaged in her backpack for her camera, wanting to take a picture of Sonny at the stove. Her fingers found the bird skull. She'd forgotten it completely. She ran her hands over the smooth bone, down the beaklike protrusion. She set it on the counter, then reached over to the fruit bowl, and tugged two grapes off their cluster. When Sonny turned around the skull had green eyes.

"Larus attricilla," he said.

"Pleased to meet you," Maggie said.

Sonny smiled. "May I?"

Maggie nodded.

His hands turned the skull over tenderly, as if it was a rare gem and he had been granted permission to hold it, but only for a moment. Maggie began to believe the skull was something more, and felt guilty about the way she had tossed the bleached out bone into her backpack.

It shall never grow dull or grow less . . . Father, mother, we have been blessed by a sea-child, Who gave me this for a token.

"Larus attricilla," Sonny repeated. "Nice specimen. They call this the laughing gull. Does that mean anything to you?

"No. Why?" she asked.

"No reason. It's just that, sometimes things find us for a reason."

Maggie blinked. That was exactly what David had believed.

CHAPTER 61

BOBBIE
1937

The Cherokee met Bobbie at the train. Still ruggedly pretty from afar, lush and green, the town of Bensonville had changed. Quaint herbal medicine shops and healing centers had been replaced by tacky restaurants and overpriced souvenir shops.

The big Indian led her through a town she hardly recognized, apologizing in his soft staccato voice, "They used to come for the water, for the promises. For salvation."

Bobbie remembered the common eyes of the visitors; a shallow tenuous hope hooded by heavy lids.

He continued, like a poet tour guide, saying, "They used to come by horse and cart, lifting their crippled from beds of hay, the same bedding they'd feed to the horse when they understood the return trip would be lighter.

"Some of the hopeful would gather on this lawn for picnics," he said as they passed the park and the gazebo. "There would be parties on Saturdays, celebrations on Wednesdays. The church never closed its doors, the streets were always swept."

He was quiet for a moment and when he spoke again, his voice was tinged with anger. "They used to come for the water. Now they come for the story, the experience. To say they tried it all, saw it all. They come from cities I can't pronounce on trains that move too fast and make noises that scare my dog. They come in fancy cars, waving walking sticks and parasols, throwing coins to the deaf boy who carries the luggage to their suite."

Bobbie wondered how many visitors were surprised that the baths were only shallow fountains and ordinary swimming pools, that the life-changing walk through the woods was merely five hundred feet long, ending in a puddle the size of a kitchen sink where they, like thousands before them would bow to drink from cupped hands whispering the words etched on the stone: " You will not die." And under their breath, they would add their own words: You will walk again. You will see. Your heart will be restored.

Believing, yet not.

And as time wore on they would know doubt. They would feel hope fade.

The Cherokee said, "We have all changed. Look at us. We throw our garbage out the back door, let dust build up in the kitchen. We've stopped greeting strangers. We draw our shades on cloudy days and we sit in a quiet place that is neither good nor kind. They used to come for the water. Now they come for bones."

They walked on in silence, taking a trail through the woods where the markers on the trees were faded and worn. A bird screeched.

"Sam, did he…" Bobbie couldn't say it.

The Cherokee shook his head.

The house was a tidy cottage on the edge of a field of sunflowers. The Cherokee opened the door and held it for Bobbie to enter. She ran her hand over the back of a chair, swore she could feel Sam.

The telegram she'd received in New York had said only that Sam had passed on and it was time for Bobbie to return to the valley. Having been spared any decisions regarding Sam for so long, Bobbie was grateful for any reprieve regarding the husband she felt she'd abandoned.

"He left you this." The Cherokee handed her a note.

"I'm sorry," she said. "I don't know your real name. Sam always called you The—"

"Crip," he finished with a smile. He lifted his pant leg to show a complicated metal and leather brace.

"You can call me Sequoyah," he said.

"Sequoyah. Thank you."

He left Bobbie alone with the note. It was written on the back of a page torn from a Spanish book. She recognized some of the words and wondered when Sam had learned to read another language.

She ran her finger over his words.

"Bobbie, I'm sorry. The fire inside consumes me. Not enough water in the world. I will always love you, Sam."

Bobbie sank to the floor, draining herself of everything, of her love for Sam, of her indecision, of her confusion, of her guilt, of her need, of her understanding of life. The light went out of the room and still she lay there mourning the loss of her heart.

When she felt she could, she rose and found Sequoyah.

He fed her food she couldn't taste. He gave her hot tea and whiskey. He showed her to her room and told her that in the morning they'd take Sam's ashes and scatter them from the foothills.

Bobbie lay awake in the strange bed searching her soul for Sam. She'd always been able to feel him, no matter how far apart they were. When did that change?

Outside a mockingbird sang, its song almost drowning out the small voice telling her to let go. Sam had completed his own circle and was finally at peace. It was time to release him.

❦ ❦

They stood on the porch at dawn. Sequoyah checked the wind then pointed north. They climbed high into the foothills until they overlooked the town below. Bobbie upended the basket of ashes and watched as pieces of Sam rode the wind and floated over Bensonville to coat the surfaces of pools, streams and ponds of healing water.

CHAPTER 62

FLORA
1940

I'm enjoying this day of telling. A day of coming clean. And with Tommy, The Monsignor sitting beside me, holding my hand, it feels like my last confession.

❧❦

October 29, 1929. I stood on the porch of the white house on the hill as Hal Berk's pride and joy, a big white and blue cruiser motored past, but Hal wasn't at the wheel and there was a cloth covering the name he'd emblazoned across her stern: Sea's My Mistress. That could mean only one thing.

I logged the vessel in my journal, then went to the barn to find George. The big door rolled open smoothly. It was warm and quiet. Too quiet for a barn, though there weren't many animals left. Most had grown too troublesome to care for. We didn't need the goats and cows anymore and when some friends from Savannah offered to find homes for the birds and exotic animals that the sailors had sent me, George jumped on it before I could change my mind.

I heard coughing, a hack and spit, then the buzz of a poorly-tuned radio.

I followed the noise to the stalls in back of the barn. George had christened the last one his "Still Stall." The name was a tongue twister after a few hooch samples.

I started talking before I turned the corner. "What do you know about Berk? I just saw his boat."

"Shhh." George was lying on a pile of hay. He held two tin cups and took turns sipping from one and spitting into the other. Since I forbade him to smoke in the barn after the last haybale fire, he'd taken up chewing tobacco. It was more disgusting than cigarettes, but safer.

I tried again. "His boat just went by."

"Shhh!" He turned to me, finger to his lips, eyes half-lidded from the hooch.

The radio crackled, "It is a Black Tuesday on Wall Street. Stock prices plummet to mark the worst drop in history. Speculators cease to be optimistic as billions of shares become worthless. The latest word from Washington is—"

George leaned forward and twisted a dial. "That's a crying shame, ain't it Flora?"

Scratchy music hissed from the speaker as a woman sang the same words over and over. "Love, love, love..."

"Isn't it, George," I said, tired of correcting him.

"Yes, it is," he said. "All them money bags gonna be living a different life. Gonna be a new day 'round here." He tipped his cup to take a drink, upended it when he saw it was empty.

I stepped between George and the still as he struggled to his feet. I said, "Looks like some of those changes have already hit home. I just saw Hal Berk's cruiser go by with someone else at the wheel."

George made it to his knees. "Expect the speakeasies will be full tonight."

"What does that mean?"

George shrugged. "Just what it sounds like."

"George."

"I ain't going nowhere, I'm just saying that they might be needing some stock, that's all."

"Look at you! Getting rich off someone else's misery. You should be ashamed of yourself, pushing that drink at them."

"I'm not rich!" George said. "And I am not pushing anything. Folks make up their own damn minds. Besides, ain't you ever heard of supply and demand?" He found a half full bottle in the hay and took a swig. He looked at me, then wiped the back of his hand across his lips and laughed. "I know you know what I'm talking about. Supply and demand." He laughed, his face reddening. "That's us, ain't it? I demand and you supply." He grabbed my arm. "I demand and you supply."

I slapped the word out of his mouth. A spray of tobacco juice escaped his loose jowls and splattered the hay, black drool leaked down his chin. He stood there, swaying, uncomprehending, then raised a hand to his face, patting at it like you would a dog's.

I was more shocked than him. I backed up, stepping gingerly over the hay-strewn floor, making my escape, but he came at me. He was strong for his age, and the booze only seemed to fortify him. He lunged at my thighs, knocked me into the wall. My head made a crunching sound as it dented the planks. I fought, pounding his back, arms flailing, connecting again, this time my nails drew blood.

"Damn you, woman!" George shoved me onto the thin mattress of hay then fell on me, pinning my outstretched arms to the scratchy pile.

"George Martus! Get off me!" I writhed beneath him trying to free myself, but his grip tightened. I screamed as he twisted my wrist. "Stop! Right this instant!"

Something snapped. George was too far gone, and through the pain and tears I saw all that I had trusted in, all that I had believed to be real and good, vanish.

The next morning, I wanted to blame it on the hooch or George's increasing senility, so much like Ma he'd always been. But the vicious nature and the suddenness of the attack, I couldn't forgive. I avoided him that day, taking the long way around the island, staying away from the pier and barn, and when night fell with no sign of him, I took it upon myself to light the lamp.

I rowed the flat dory to the lighthouse, thinking about what I needed to do and how I was going to do it. Approaching the oyster bed island, I let the boat sluice in, coasting over sea grasses, scraping the shelled shore. As I tied off the boat, it felt like someone was watching me, and I wondered if this was George's hiding spot. A place he might have swum to when the tide was low.

But he wasn't there. It was just me in the shadow of the white tower, surrounded by water and the sounds of boats in the distance trying to get home.

CHAPTER 63

BOBBIE
1938

They went to a Broadway show, then dinner and drinks, which led to more drinks and a card game in a back room somewhere. Bobbie vaguely recalled red walls and soft leather chairs. She still didn't know whose idea it had been to drive to the end of the island. She only knew she was drunk when she agreed and still was, thanks to the case of bourbon in the trunk. Cricket slept beside her, the girl's warm breath sweet against her neck. Bobbie tapped Harry's shoulder with the bourbon bottle, then passed it forward.

"Thanks," Harry said taking a swig.

The sun rose over the hood of the Ford reflecting a pinkish hue onto this flat scrubby piece of Long Island.

"Looks more like Arizona than New York doesn't it?" Bobbie said.

Harry grunted.

Connie stirred in the front seat, the springs squeaking beneath her as she yawned then sat up. "I've never been to Arizona, but I'm telling you once you get to the tip out there you're going to think you're on the west coast, like Oregon or Washington or Northern California."

Harry lit two cigarettes, passed one to Connie then glanced in the rearview mirror at Bobbie. "She used to date a professor of geography. Got bored at night and read all his books."

"That good in the sack, huh?" Bobbie said.

"Ha-ha," Connie said exhaling smoke out her open window.

The morning air was cool. It felt thick and salty in Bobbie's nostrils, each inhale weighing her down. Harry turned on the radio and twisted the dial until a saxophone solo filled the car.

By the time the song ended the landscape had changed. Instead of desolate, arid land, it was lush and green with trees lining the road. They passed small farms with checkerboard fields and yellow farm houses that reminded Bobbie of another time, a better place.

Cricket woke yawning and stretching. "Are we there?"

"Almost," Harry said.

"Morning, lover," Cricket whispered to Bobbie before she kissed her.

Bobbie kissed her back, taking her face into her hands. She was beautiful, all boozy-breathed and mussed. Cricket had been a surprise, coming into Bobbie's life as a voice behind a curtain, a girl on stage telling the secrets of Bobbie's life in her songs without knowing it. She wanted to tell Cricket everything—about Sam, about her life before, about living in Tarrabelle, about the way a woman loves a man, about the girl she used to be, about the scars on her wrist and heart.

Connie smacked the dashboard. "Stop!"

"What? What?" Harry downshifted, slammed on the brakes. The Ford jerked to a stop, throwing Cricket into Bobbie's lap.

"Look." Connie pointed to a moving field of white.

They climbed out and stood beside the car.

"What is it?" Cricket said shading her eyes against the rising sun.

"Long Island ducks," Bobbie said.

Harry took up a pitching stance. "Batter up." He lobbed the empty bourbon bottle into the thick of the flock. Some of the ducks squawked when they saw it coming, others took flight when it landed. The sky turned white as they rose up flapping, quacking, fluttering. They smelled muddy and fishy, the breeze from their wings a single buffeting as they flew overhead calling to each other.

The land they'd vacated was trampled and sodden with their feces, the grass plucked and nibbled. Thick scum on the pond was bright green and fragrant, home to any number of small organisms.

"Woah. Let's go, kids," Harry said plugging his nose and backpedaling.

They watched the flock of ducks circle the field twice more as they pulled back onto the road. In front of them, the changing morning burned blue and violet. Farmland gave way to sand dunes and spiky, sparse grasses. The sky grew. They ran out of road.

"End of the line," Harry said, stopping the car.

Connie and Cricket ran to the edge of the cliff laughing. Their hair blew around their faces like brown and red halos. They grabbed for their skirts, then gave up and let them whip as the surf boomed and crashed below. When the spray cleared they saw a lighthouse on the farthest reaches of the point. Banded red and white and topped with a black dome, it looked like a giant's saltshaker resting precariously on the rocky coast.

Harry said, "That reminds me of your Waving Girl and her brother. I saw something about her in the paper yesterday, said the whole town of Savannah is throwing her a 70th birthday party at some fort. Supposed to be a big deal. You should go."

❦   ❦

Bobbie wasn't sure why she was going to Savannah. Mostly because she'd run out of reasons why she shouldn't. The packing hadn't taken long and now that Cricket was mad at her, the good-byes had been even shorter.

She tried to explain how the woman was someone she hadn't seen in a long time, that she didn't know why she still even remembered her and her brother, it seemed like it had all happened in a dream. But sometimes the people who change you the most are the ones you can forget, and sometimes the ones you barely knew remain important forever.

Bobbie arrived the morning of the birthday celebration, in the heat of a Georgia summer. It was easy to fall back into the old rhythm, talking press language and connecting with the newspaper guys. It was easier still to find out where Flora lived. Bobbie promised the reporters an exclusive interview if she could borrow a car.

She wasn't surprised to hear that both Martuses were alive and well, even less surprised that neither of them had married. She drove out to the salt flats. There was only one white cottage on the edge of nowhere. She parked the Chrysler on the scrubby lawn.

It was nice. Quiet, stark, and interesting in a half-decorated room sort of way. It was the kind of place someone might say has potential. Bobbie opened the gate of the low picket fence and stepped through, latching it behind her as the distant sound of trombones, trumpets and a bass drum broke the silence. They would be here soon, the reporters and the band on the flatbed truck.

Bobbie followed the rows of carefully planted peonies to the front porch. She knocked and waited, trying to ignore the smell of dog shit. The dog came to the door first, scratching and snuffling at the gap underneath. A man's voice called him away, then the door opened and Florence Martus, an older, softer version of the Flora that Bobbie had met years ago was standing there.

Bobbie extended her hand. "Miss Martus? Bobbie Denton. We met once at The DeSoto Hotel. I'm not sure you remember me but I wrote a few articles about you and I'm here to do a follow up for the papers in New York. We all wanted to wish you a Happy Birthday."

"Of course I remember you, Miss Denton. George and I did enjoy reading those stories. Please come in."

Bobbie followed Flora into the cottage. The front room was a mixture of white and blue. White floors, walls, curtains and lamps. Blue chairs, a settee, and a blue and white rug. Blue flowering potted plants lined the space below the windows and a vase of fresh flowers were visible through the doorway to the kitchen. It smelled like cookies, like what she'd always imagined a real home should smell like.

George sat in one of the chairs, a graying collie at his feet. He started to get up, but Bobbie hurried over. "Mr. Martus? Bobbie Denton with The New York Times. Please don't get up on my account. I came to town when I heard of the birthday celebration. Quite a thing, isn't it?"

"Yep," George said reaching to pet the dog.

"Miss Denton, could I get you some sweet tea?" Flora said.

"That would be nice and please, call me Bobbie."

"We used to live in Savannah," George said in a trembly voice. His bright eyes held Bobbie's gaze. "Flora said the city was drowning her, too noisy and dirty with all those cars and people. And the dogs didn't like being cooped up.

We had two of them then. So we got this place. It's not much but it's better to be out here where you got space and water, air to breathe."

Bobbie knew what he meant, how a place could never fill you with what you needed. It only took. That was why she always had to leave, move on, even if someone thought it was about them, about love, and maybe a little of it was.

Flora returned with a cold pitcher of sweet tea and a plate of shortbread cookies. She placed it on the low table by the settee then sat smoothing her perfectly ironed dress over her legs.

"It may not be Elba Island," she said in her soft voice, the Southern accent making simple words sound pretty. "But it's close." Flora smiled. "Sometimes at night, I sit on that little front porch and hear the clapper rails calling to each other across the marsh. I can smell Muscadine grapes in the arbor, the bouquet of sweetbay. And I think I could be in our old white house on the hill, if I believed a dim light from town was the cloud-hidden moon and the stray cat yowling was a raccoon in the sugarberry tree. If I believed that."

By the time Bobbie finished her cookies and tea, the cars of reporters and photographers had arrived, their tires kicking up oyster shells, horns blaring and not far behind, the flatbed band playing a feisty rendition of "Dixie."

"Guess we ought to get you out there," she told Flora.

At the door, the old woman paused to pull on a pair of white gloves and pin a wide brimmed hat on her head.

Stepping onto the porch, the sunlight blinded them, reflecting off the shiny cars and the shell-littered sandy soil. Bobbie stood beside Flora blinking into all that brightness, squinting more than smiling. George hung behind in the shadows of the cool blue and white room.

A snappy little reporter in a brown suit yelled, "Miss Martus! Our readers want to know. Who was the man you were waving to all those years? Did he ever come back?"

The photographers snapped away as Flora's smile disappeared. She looked past the men and their cars, past the road and the flat scabby land toward the sea. Bobbie felt Flora shrink beside her and become less.

Another reporter said, "That's not what they want to know. What they want to know is: Was he your lover?"

"Hey," Bobbie said, "I thought this was a birthday party, not an inquisition."

One of the guys in the flatbed band called, "Yeah. Happy Birthday, Waving Girl!"

He blew the opening notes of *The Birthday Song* on his trombone and others joined in. By the time the police escort showed up, the unanswered questions were forgotten.

They made their way out of the salt flats and across the water to Fort Pulaski, where three thousand people were waiting. It was a motley parade, rumbling black police cruisers followed by dusty, overloaded cars of reporters with sweaty photographers hanging out the windows.

Bobbie brought up the rear in the borrowed sedan. She drove slowly behind the band on the flatbed, its banner swinging in time to the beat, announcing "Happy Birthday to The Waving Girl."

CHAPTER 64

FLORA
1940

We are sitting in the funeral home, staring at my brother's casket, waiting for something that may never happen, when I tell Tommy how I ruined his uncle's business. How it took under an hour to dismantle George's damned still and sink it forevermore.

❦ ❦

Finding the hidden stash of hooch took longer and by the time the sun came up I was sore all over, my arms and neck scratched and bloody from the brambles, but I rowed out as far as I could and dumped everything over the side.

I practiced how I'd tell George what had happened. I practiced how I'd look worried and sorrowful when I told him. The only thing I didn't practice the whole time he was away, was how he'd look hearing that his still and his hooch were gone and the miscreants who'd taken it had threatened his life and that of his sister if he ever went into business again.

❦ ❦

George returned two weeks later wearing new clothes, sporting a haircut and shave. The rest of the country was going broke, banks locking their doors left and right. Children were starving, houses were cold, people were fighting for any sort of work and here was my brother looking like a million bucks and smiling like nothing had ever happened.

He said, "I saw the picture show—one of them new talkies up in Charleston. You ought to come with me sometime. I think you'd like it."

I looked at him, trying to figure out his game. I was disgusted with myself for noticing how handsome he looked, how young and strong.

After I told him about the still and the trouble, I told him I was planning on leaving. I didn't tell him I was planning to get a new start, that I had ideas. Because those ideas were born when I was alone and now George was back and I liked seeing him.

215

We walked together up to the house. He said, "If you was planning on leaving, where would you go?"

I shrugged.

He opened his long arms, turned a slow circle. "This is your life, Flora. This is who you are. This is where you belong. This is where we belong."

And in the end, that was my comfort.

Later, in our warm kitchen, I could see my plans for what they were, dreams. And not even good ones at that. They were the dreams of a woman people called crazy.

I watched George hang his coat on an empty hook, take a coffee cup from the shelf above the sink, then shoo a fly from the chicken potpie cooling on the counter. I figured everyone has a dashed dream or two and if this was all my life had been intended to be then I'd finish it. And maybe I'd be remembered for some of the joy I had brought to others, that it would never be about what I didn't do or where I didn't go or what I didn't have, but about the things I gave, when all I had to give was myself.

"I'm sorry, Miss Flora. Monsignor," says Mr. Clark appearing in the doorway. "I have to close up now. There are things the night staff needs to do."

"We understand," Tommy says. He pats my arm then runs his hands through his hair, adjusts his tie and jacket. We make our way down the aisle of chairs to the exit where Mr. Clark waits.

Tommy says in a quiet voice most unlike him, "Aunt Flora? Would you tell me something?"

I yawn into my hand. "Sure, Tommy."

"Did he ever come back, the man you were waving to all those years?"

I look back into the room at the shiny wood coffin. "He never left."

My brother is in the ground and I am still here. The dog won't get up today and the birds seem to have forgotten how to sing joyfully. There are no words for loss. It is a hole, therefore it is full of nothing and nothing has no word. I move as a person waiting for their turn at nothingness. I am pathetic, I know. My strength is gone. More than my strength. I have led a full life but now time dwindles and I have no desire to postpone my fate.

There are those who fight the inevitable. I have seen them in hospital waiting rooms with their files and their arguments and their dreams. I have seen them on their knees in churches. They would be better served to simply enjoy their last days, if only they saw them that way, instead of battling life, a life that becomes more and more tenuous daily with the final outcome always the same.

People still come to visit me in the house on the salt flats. They bring me food and gifts, take photographs and tell stories, calling me, The Waving Girl. I want to tell them, "You don't understand. I wasn't waving. I was drowning."

But how do you admit that to someone who says you were their hope when they went out to sea? That you were the last thing they saw as their ship pulled out and the first thing they laid eyes on upon their return. How could they not love someone who did that for them?

How could I not love them in return?

CHAPTER 65

BOBBIE
1938

Colorful flags snapped and fluttered above the walls of the pentagon-shaped fort. Bystanders cheered for swimmers in the cool, dark moat. Once designed to keep out the enemy, on this day the water welcomed the bobbing heads of competitors making their way to the finish line—a taut yellow ribbon strung across the hundred-year-old drawbridge of Fort Pulaski.

Inside the walls through the sally port, the two-acre parade ground bustled with activity. Paunchy, red-faced men yelled pumping fistfuls of money as they clambered around a makeshift boxing ring. The boxers, tired, hot and bruised, shuffle-bounced to the center where one of the panting, bloody-nosed men was declared the winner.

Children ran and chased playground balls on the grass where soldiers used to line up for war. And on a stage decorated in flowers and ribbons, burly Edward Dutton, the chairman of the event, stepped out of the shade and into the heat of the day.

He said, "Welcome to Fort Pulaski. Please make your way to the parade grounds so that we might welcome our guest of honor, Miss Florence Martus."

The drum major for The Parris Island Marine Band raised his mace as the men of The Savannah Police Band joined in a drum, trumpet, trombone and French horn welcome. The crowd cheered as Flora crossed the parade grounds. Cameras clicked and flashed. Red, white and blue balloons were released into the cloudless sky as she climbed the steps onto the stage.

Flora faced the audience and pulled a handkerchief from her skirt pocket. She raised it to the wind. The crowd roared for their waving girl. She smiled then took her seat next to the birthday cake, a perfect replica of the Elba Island house on the hill, complete with seventy candles and a figurine of Flora waving the famous white cloth, a collie lying at her feet.

From her place in the front row with the other reporters, Bobbie jotted notes on her pad, but mostly watched George and Flora. When the Coast Guard Cutter, *The Tallapoosa*, gave a three-blast salute from its dock at the old quarantine pier, startled children covered their ears but Flora seemed to revel in the moment, her face crinkling with delight.

Chairman Dutton introduced Congressman Peterson who introduced the mayor, a fluffy man with a pretentious moustache who looked miffed that his round of applause was faint compared to the love the crowd had shown Flora.

With gesticulating arms and a booming voice, Congressman Peterson said, "Miss Martus is a unique figure in the civilization we now enjoy. She is typical of the spirit of America, the spirit of service, and the spirit of Christianity. Although she lived a lonesome life on the wind-swept sand dunes of Elba Island, a life many might consider hopeless and useless."

Bobbie scratched out the congressman's last words, wrote "unremarkable" while mumbling, "Pompous ass."

The congressman continued, "She made herself a benefactor to mankind with her wave of cheer."

The ladies of the reception committee seated behind Flora applauded and dabbed their eyes. But it seemed the applause was too loud, too close, too much for Flora. Bobbie saw the panic rising in her eyes and when photographers jostling for position bumped the platform, shaking it, it unsettled Flora more.

Bobbie saw Florence Martus for the first time as she might have been on the island—a young girl, lonely, scared and unsure—a girl who waved hello then kept waving, her arms saying all the things her mouth couldn't.

She waved for everyone who ever needed to be saved or seen or heard.

The whole day was wrong, this thing that Bobbie had a hand in years ago when she wrote about a fairytale life, about a tower, an island, a beautiful woman. When she pointed the finger of the press at Savannah and helped create a heroine, a maritime legend.

The people had needed Flora then and maybe Bobbie thought she could give them what they yearned for—a love story, a romantic tale of unrequited love. Because wasn't that better, in the way the idea of good is enough to drown evil, the way a tale can be embellished and passed down for centuries until no one remembers that in the original fable the wolf wins, the children die and the lost never return.

Bobbie knew pretending always failed. The unsaid parts of a lie would eat at your soul and never being known for who you really were was the worst tragedy of all.

But this truth, this story? It wasn't hers to tell.

At the podium, the Congressman was saying, "By a mere wave she has placed small bits of sunshine in the hearts of the men who have passed her door. Florence Martus is the sweetheart of mankind."

Flora wrote something on the back of her program, passed the note to Chairman Dutton who read it then whispered something to her.

Flora nodded, teary and flushed. She tried to smile.

Dutton rose to the podium, cleared his throat and scanned the crowd. "Miss Martus has asked me to read something for her."

"'I am proud to be a Georgian. To have been born right here at Fort Pulaski.'"

The crowd cheered. Flora raised her bowed head and caught Bobbie's eye as Dutton read, "'I'd like to thank all of those people who made this day possible. This is the grandest day of my life.'"

❧ ❧

Bobbie drove Flora and George back to their cottage in the borrowed car. She took her time leaving the fort grounds, thinking Flora would say something, would share something. She was trying to think of how to ask her the things she wanted to know, how to ask her anything with George seated beside her.

She pulled off the main road following a path that was almost too narrow for the Chrysler. Branches scraped the sides of the car, the tires bounced over ruts and holes.

"Where are we going?" George asked.

"I wanted you to see something," Bobbie said. The trees grew sparse until finally they could see through them. Across the water stood the old Cockspur Lighthouse.

"Oh, George, look," Flora said. "There she is."

"Didn't think I missed her," George said leaning over the backseat and peering through the windshield. "But hell, she sure is a sight for sore eyes."

Bobbie pulled as close to the water as she could and they sat watching the waves break, listening to the shore birds call until Flora said, "He's asleep," then "Thank you, Bobbie."

They drove slowly back to the salt flats, Bobbie glancing at Flora in the rear view mirror. She said, "I saw you once, I mean after that time at The DeSoto. It was late at night, and our boat was coming back from a day of fishing. You were on your porch and waved a lantern."

Flora's face didn't change.

Bobbie said, "I heard you never missed a boat in the forty years you were there. Is that right? Not even when you were sick?"

Flora stared out the window. "I was never too sick to get up. I don't think I missed anyone, did I George?"

George snored on the seat beside her.

Flora, in a perfect impression of her gruff brother said, "Not one ship in forty-four years."

Bobbie laughed. She watched Flora's face as she asked, "Any truth to the rumor you kept journals all those years?"

It was Flora's turn to laugh. "Don't have those anymore."

"What happened to them?" Bobbie asked.

Flora turned away from the window and met Bobbie's eyes in the rear view mirror.

"I burned them. When we left Elba Island, I burned all of them. I figured no

220

one would want to read that old stuff."

Bobbie stared at her so long she nearly ran them off the road. "Tell me you're kidding. Do you realize that by burning those journals you destroyed what would have been the most complete maritime accounts the world had ever known? If I knew you better, I'd give you a big kick!"

Flora said, "Well, I guess you ought to." Then she lay her head on her brother's shoulder and closed her red-rimmed eyes.

When Bobbie left that evening her clothes smelled like the Martus's cottage, a combination of fire, fish stew and cherry tobacco. She rolled down the car window, letting in a breeze that was invigorating and refreshing, yet had an urgency to it, as if its high-pitched tune was trying to tell her something.

She accelerated down the oyster shell road, the damp, salty voice of the wind slapping at her cheeks, pulling at her blouse, filling the car interior too quickly. She reached over to roll down the passenger window, as if another opening would allow the gusty harbinger free passage, an escape. In reply, the wind whipped open her notebook, fluttering the pages to the place where Bobbie had tucked the embroidered handkerchief Flora gave her, the one she'd pressed into Bobbie's hand when they parted, when she said, "Remember me."

Bobbie had run her fingers over the design on the handkerchief, a blue hand like a wave in the sea, the red words inscribed below: *Love can drown us.*

She wanted to tell Flora that she understood. That she knew we might wade out too deep or get pulled from the shore, still most of us believed that someone, somewhere would see us, hear us calling for help. But words can get lost in the wind and waving arms can't tread water.

Bobbie turned the bend in the road and the wind rushed in flaring the handkerchief wide skimming it along the page dancing across the words, "I was just a girl," before it was snatched out the window, swept across the windshield and drawn like a breath toward the sea.

CHAPTER 66

MAGGIE
2011

Sonny set the skull on the bar, angling it just so, then went back to working on breakfast.

Maggie saw the dreamy expression on his face before he turned away. She picked up the skull, held it the way Sonny had. Nothing. She looked at it closer wondering how a stupid sea gull skull makes a guy look like that.

"Aren't you going to ask me?" he said, his back to her.

"Okay," Maggie said, "I'll ask. What are you putting in those potatoes?"

Sonny laughed. "Not that. Aren't you going to ask me about the skull?"

"No. Unless you want to talk about dead birds."

"It was hers," he said.

"Whose?" Maggie asked.

"Flora Martus, The Waving Girl. She found that skull in 1940 and brought it to the lighthouse. She claimed it was a talisman, a charm for her dead brother."

"Wait a minute, " Maggie said. "Is this another story like her pining for a long lost beau?"

The word "beau" stuck in her throat when Sonny looked at her and grinned. She swore his eyes twinkled.

To cry Love me, as I cry Love me, and love me again...And I fear that his eyes will open and confound me with a mirthless word, That the rocks will harp on for ever, and my Love me never be heard.

Sonny opened the cabinet and took down two plates, then put a mug of coffee and a serving of potatoes in front of Maggie.

She said, "I don't understand."

Sonny pointed. "That's coffee and those are potatoes."

"Not that." Maggie laughed. "The Waving Girl. She was a crazy recluse, wasn't she? Living alone on that island with her brother, waving to all those people?"

Sonny sat across from her. "I think she was more than that. From everything I've read, she became a symbol of hope and faith. Men returned safely from days, even weeks at sea because of her. Sometimes, the idea of a person is better than the actual person. More important, more lasting."

222

Maggie didn't know what she was supposed to say. This guy was too much. He was the missing parts of her, a guy who said the things she was thinking before she thought them.

She picked up her fork and began to eat. "This is terrific."

"Don't look so surprised. That's just one of my specialties. It's a Greek family recipe."

"Beaumont doesn't sound Greek," Maggie said.

"My great grandparents changed it when they came here, said they were tired of everyone mispronouncing their name." He tipped his head toward a framed photograph on the wall in the living area. My mom, Scarlet, grew up more Southern than Greek, but kept her roots."

Maggie took another forkful of potatoes then approached the picture. She gently lifted the frame from the nail, angling the sun off it. The woman in the deck chair looked like a young Jackie O, with Sophia Loren's sensuality. There were children's toys at her feet, sand buckets and a metal Tonka truck. A hand-painted sign hung crooked behind her: Welcome to My Tara.

"What's she like?" Maggie said, talking about his mother, but thinking of Flora, too, wondering how she'd ever compete with a Greek goddess and a maritime legend.

"Mom's great," Sonny said. "Very strong. Independent, you know? I mean that in a good way. My father called her The Queen. I used to think it was because she was so bossy, but then later I realized it was because he loved her so much. She made him feel like a king."

"And your father, what's he like?"

"I don't know. I never really knew him. He traveled a lot, was always on his way to some place else. Eventually he stopped coming back at all."

"I'm sorry," Maggie said.

"Nothing to be sorry for. Mom was a great single parent. And, hey, I turned out okay."

Maggie looked closer at the photograph. It sat crooked in the frame, as if someone had dropped it and never fixed it properly. She unhinged the rear and pulled the photo out. It had been folded to fit, rather than cut to size. She smoothed it flat.

It was still this houseboat, still Sonny's mother in the deck chair, a drink in one hand, waving off the photographer, laughing. But she was no longer in the center of the photo. On the right side of the frame, behind the fold, a man filled the archway to the salon, his arms braced against the trim in the familiar fashion of her late husband, David P. Morris of Philadelphia.

But who is this beautiful You? We all of us long for so much is he not our friend and our brother, Our father and such?

Maggie gasped as Sonny came up behind her, placing his hands warm and heavy on her hips. He leaned in and tipped his chin at the picture. "He made me promise to never take his picture, hated the way he looked in photos. That one slipped by him. Now it's all I have."

He took the picture from Maggie, put it back in the frame. "Mom's happy.

She got over him, finally." He hung the picture back on the wall and returned to the kitchen. "That's what you have to do, right? Move on?"

Maggie nodded.

Oh, no no no, it was too cold always (Still the dead one lay moaning) I was much too far out all my life and not waving but drowning.

Sonny turned back to the stove and the frying pan, broke two eggs into it. He said, "She told me there's someone else, a guy from Philadelphia and it's pretty serious. They're in Crete right now looking for a place to buy." He chuckled. "It's funny. I've never met him but I heard him on the phone the other day. He calls her The Queen too."

"Over easy?" he said glancing at Maggie.

She swallowed hard. "Yes, please," she said, then watched her lover snap the pan upward and deftly flip their eggs.

224

ABOUT THE AUTHOR

Linda is a writer, novelist, editor and blogger agented by Josh Getzler of HSG. She's a rabble-rousing Atlanta area mom who takes girls night out seriously—every time. She's a travel junkie on a time budget. She's just a girl standing in front of a reader asking you to love her.

Her award-winning short stories and essays can be found in Skirt! Magazine, Atlanta Journal-Constitution, The Gwinnett Daily Post, Dana Literary Society, The Duck & Herring Company Pocket Field Guide, , Divine Caroline, NPR's I Believe, Europe From a Backpack, Golden Short Stories, O'Georgia! A Collection of Georgia's Newest and Most Promising Writers, Big Water, Moronic Ox, and Weird Year, among others.

※ ※

This is her first novel, but surely not her last, with two in the queue and a series on the way.

Follow her online at linda-sands.com, on Twitter @lindasands or on Facebook, facebook.com/TheLindaSands.

She'd love to hear from you.